FIRST CONTACT:
MANKIND AND MARTIANS

It was actually no one more important than a junior geologist of the Smithsonian Institution, J. Chase Huebner, speaking through his helmet's radio to his colleagues Weston Reese and Marisa Louie. "It's time for lunch," were the immortal words of Dr. Huebner. "Let's head back to the aircar and put on the old nose bag."

The Oneness joyfully echoed the exact sounds, peculiar as they were, back into the minds of the three Earthlings. It was the first telepathic communication between different species. Unfortunately for Huebner, Reese, and Louie, however, the volume and intensity used by the Oneness in its excitement was the same as that employed to communicate to its own several billion widely scattered attributes.

The three geologists were found later by a search party, wandering at random across the Martian desert. For the rest of their lives none of the geologists were able to say anything beyond repeating over and over: "It's time for lunch. Let's head back to the aircar and put on the old nose bag."

BEN BOVA
Presents
Phylum Monsters

Hayford Peirce

A TOM DOHERTY ASSOCIATES BOOK
NEW YORK

PHYLUM MONSTERS

Copyright © 1989 by Hayford Peirce Living Trust

A TOR Book
Published by Tom Doherty Associates, Inc.
49 West 24 Street
New York, NY 10010

Cover art by Bruce Jensen

ISBN: 0-812-54894-9   Can. ISBN: 0-812-54895-7

First edition: October 1989

Printed in the United States of America

0 9 8 7 6 5 4 3 2 1

to POLLY

belated but heartfelt tribute to a remarkable woman—
and mother—whose most remarkable quality
all these years has been putting up with her son

1

"I am *not* a bodybuilder," I corrected the legalist for the plaintiffs with both firmness and asperity. "I am a life-stylist."

"A life-stylist, eh? You don't think that in this particular case the term *death*-stylist might be rather more appropri——"

"Objection!" cried a dozen voices from all sides of the courtroom. Or it might have been two dozen. The defendants were being sued for $660 billion; they were in consequence extraordinarily well represented by the legal profession.

"But it *is* true, is it not," pursued the plaintiffs' shyster, "that in this particular case *death* was the inevitable result of the malicious, incompetent—"

"The demise of a number of nonsentient grapevines," I elucidated. "If that's what you mean by death, then—"

"Objection!" This time it was a dozen legalists from the plaintiffs' side of the courtroom who raised their voices in shrill indignation.

"The witness will refrain from personal observations," directed Judge Flanders, a sour-faced woman with very little of the lofty dignity I normally associate with a Gravitas Maxima.

"Yes, Your Honor," I murmured, but my words were lost in the babble of several dozen legalists noisily attempting to justify their outlandish retainers. While they gathered to haggle in front of the judge's bench, I let my gaze travel wearily around the paneled courtroom of the Sixth Federal Court of

San Francisco. Except for the outsized American flags hanging on either side of the bench there wasn't much to catch the eye: seven apathetic jurors in a small enclosure to my left; a number of holoscan lenses nesting unobtrusively against the ceiling; a scattering of spectators; fifty or sixty assorted legalists, each with his own small black comscreen.

Most of the shysters had now crowded before the bench, arguing vehemently. In spite of their miserable profession they were a highly distinguished-looking group of men and women, most of them obviously upper-line models from the Big Seven. I have never taken the trouble to learn much about legalist models, but even so I thought I recognized two John Marshalls and a Learned Hand, a Gravitas Ultra as well as the more standard Gravitas Maximas, two Apple-Boeing Stalwarts, and three of the relatively new IBM Dauntless Arbiters. Scattered among these standard, if costly, American models were a number of more exotic legalists representing the plaintiffs from such European crèches as Siemens-Peugeot and Svoboda-Benz.

I stifled a yawn while the shysters haggled, asking myself why, against all my lifelong instincts, I had ever let the government dragoon me into representing it as a expert witness.

Boredom? Curiosity? A seriously misplaced sense of my own importance in the scheme of things? Free publicity?

Nonsense! I barely kept myself from snorting aloud at the preposterousness of the latter notion. I, Robert Clayborn, founder and president of Robert Clayborn Design, hardly needed to bolster my worldwide professional standing by going to court to defend the United States Government in a seedy lawsuit!

"—disqualify yourself!" The words snapped my wandering attention back to the crowd of legalists gathered in front of the judge's bench. One of the legalists, an obvious European model with a high, broad forehead and a shaggy mane of fluffy brown hair (a Nestlé Garibaldi, perhaps?) was now haranguing the basilisk-faced federal judge with a rare passion. The gist of his argument, as I understood it, was that the learned judge herself was a conceivably tainted product of those very life-design processes now being contested by the plaintiffs; in logical consequence, therefore—

Judge Flanders banged her gavel indignantly, interrupting the shyster's smooth flow of words. "You are asking me to disqualify myself because I happen to be *alive?*" she asked incredulously.

"Your Honor willfully misrepresents my—"

"Motion denied!" The judge impatiently waved the crowd of legalists back to their tables and comscreens.

I settled back in my hard wooden chair with a tiny smile of wry satisfaction. Basilisk-faced she might be, but if the learned judge had disqualified herself from the proceedings merely because she was a product of a crèche, then where would *any* of us be?

For the next two hours I did my rather competent best to defend what was, after all, an impregnably defendable position. In a sense, of course, in spite of the stupendous legal batteries brought to bear by the plaintiffs, my testimony was child's play. The plaintiffs (and their shysters) before the Sixth Federal Court were numerous enough, and weighty enough— that was impossible to deny. It was the totally frivolous nature of their complaint that rendered their eminent legalists' task so difficult.

The facts in the case, of course, were simple enough to be beyond dispute. Once they had been well known to the entire world—but nearly five decades earlier. Now, as the longest recorded case of litigation known to the American Bar Association dragged its way relentlessly through one court after another, the original events had long since been forgotten by the general population. But while the public yawned and turned its attention to more diverting matters, two generations of shysters had waxed fat and sleek on the pickings from *l'affaire* Boyderkowski—and another generation of legalists impatiently awaited its turn in the wings.

For those of you gestated since the turn of the century, herewith a brief recapitulation:

For the better part of a decade—that of the 2290s—Charles Boyderkowski, a moderately esteemed vintner in the Napa Valley an hour's drive to the northeast of San Francisco, had gloomily watched his company's once-lucrative share of the highly competitive cabernet sauvignon market dwindle in the face of increasingly fierce competition.

Boyderkowski (a Danville Dasher from Diversified Life) chose to overlook the inconvenient fact that his wines were no longer winning medals, or even honorable mentions, in the hundreds of annual fairs and wine tastings held in the state of California. Instead, he focused his ire upon what he deemed the unfair trade practices of his French competitors in Bordeaux. The day after Yountford Vineyards was at last forced into bankruptcy in March of 2296, Boyderkowski began to plot his revenge.

Like most modern vintners, Boyderkowski held advanced degrees in several fields of biochemistry. For two long years he labored in the deepest secrecy, experimenting with the winemaker's deadliest enemy, the phylloxera plant louse. These tiny beasts will, if left unchecked, invest the roots of the grapevine, leading to rot and the plant's inevitable death. Once they had been the scourge of wine producers the world over. But for three centuries now, ever since the last great devastation in nineteenth-century France, these predatory lice had been kept under firm control, thanks primarily to the development of resistant strains of vines.

At the end of two years of feverish research the bankrupt vintner emerged triumphant from his clandestine laboratory in the Oregon rain forest and booked passage on a hyperjet to France. Concealed about his person were several hundred thousand specimens of mutated phylloxera. A few days later he exacted an exquisitely satisfying revenge by covertly introducing them into the world-famous vineyards of those six noble châteaux in the Bordeaux region that were rated Premier Grand Cru: Château Margaux, Château Haut-Brion, Château Mouton-Rothschild, Château Darr-Michel, Château Latour, and Château Lafite-Rothschild.

The man-made plague spread quickly into the neighboring vineyards of St. Emilion; from there to the Loire Valley; thence to the Rhône, the great vineyards of Beaujolais and Burgundy, and all the other wine-producing regions of France. Within a year that nation's wine industry had been destroyed, causing hundreds of billions of dollars of damage and the fall of the Seventh Republic.

Marginally appeased by the incalculable devastation he had wrought, the addled California vintner returned to the Napa Valley; here he disposed of himself in grotesque fashion by plunging headlong into a ten-thousand-gallon vat of fermenting cabernet sauvignon in the sheds of the beloved vineyard that had once been his.

The billions of ravening plant lice that had nearly destroyed a sovereign state were eventually eradicated by the genius of France, though not without agonizing sacrifice. Scientists at the Pasteur Institute isolated an amino acid unique to that unlovely ascomycetous fungus known to gourmets throughout the world as the truffle. First concentrated a thousandfold, then gasified, the resultant aerosol mist nullified an enzyme in the phylloxera's tiny gut essential to its digestive functions. Once deprived of this enzyme, the pests rapidly starved to death.

The entire French truffle harvest of 2304, all fifty-six tons, was confiscated from outraged farmers by heavily armed troops; three weeks later the Pasteur Institute's distillation of 3.7 gallons was dispersed across the skies of western Europe as a pale green cloud. Two weeks after that the last of the phylloxera had shriveled and died.

The following year, as newly planted grapevines were taking root all over France, an unexpected side effect made itself known to horrified gourmets: the world's entire truffle crop had been irretrievably destroyed by the antiphylloxeral compound: not a single one of the succulent edible fungi was uprooted by the most determined searches in France, Italy, or Spain. The prime minister of the Eighth Republic undertook a fact-finding mission to the devastated city of Cahors; there he was savaged by a trained pig set upon him by a disgruntled truffle searcher from Périgord whose livelihood—as well as that of the pig—had been destroyed. On the Paris Bourse, futures in truffled foie gras plummeted from 287 francs to 42 centimes. There was open talk of a Ninth Republic.

Somewhere, Charles Boyderkowski smiled.

2

As I said earlier, the instrument of all this senseless destruction was a sixty-three-year-old Danville Dasher from the Oakland crèche of Diversified Life. This is one of the oldest crèches in the United States, and one of the largest and most reputable. Its production in the previous year of 2344 had been impressive: 267,000 children gestated in 312 basic models for the domestic market; 564,000 more for overseas military sales—models that were, of course, somewhat more Spartan in nature.

The Diversified Life Danville Dasher is a model designed nearly 120 years ago by the legendary life-stylist Oleg Wilcox. Its lines are rather old-fashioned by today's more sensual tastes—the nose is definitely too thin, the mouth too broad and narrow—but it remains a classic of its kind. Its unrivaled cachet over the years derives from its most noteworthy—and totally unanticipated—trait: the almost irresistible attraction it exerts upon those myriads of beautiful girls from the IBM Whispersilk line. For a century now, Danville Dashers have been considered the stuff of great lovers—not of industrious and meticulous winemakers.

But whatever cunning arrangement of genes is contrived by the master life-stylist and is eventually given bodily form in the crèches of the Big Seven, nothing about the consequent flesh-and-blood human being is ever irrevocably programmed into his activities, no more than the lives of our primitive bloodbirthing ancestors were predestined to be lived out following some rigidly fixed heavenly plan. Indeed, with the exception of a few primitive thals deep in the Arkansas woods, certainly no one in present-day America ponders the problem of Free Will—or even knows what the term means, so thoroughly has it vanished from our social and intellectual consciousness.

But now—here in the year 2345!—the hundreds of legalists representing the Winegrower's Association of Bordeaux, the Collectivity of Provençal Wines, the Friends of the Noble Truffle, 3,289 individual French vintners and truffle merchants, and the French Government itself were, for want of a better case, attempting to turn two hundred years of secular common sense upon its head.

Charles Boyderkowski was, if you will, *predestined*, by reason of purposeful design that was both faulty and malicious, to commit the unspeakable criminal acts that had nearly destroyed a sovereign state.

Amazing! *This*, from the most highly paid and most sophisticated legalists in the world—an argument you might expect to hear on the lips of the Old Pope in Carthage or from some other befuddled religionist!

Unfortunately for the plaintiffs' case, Charles Boyderkowski had long since departed the living. According to their legalists, therefore, the whole ghastly responsibility for his deeds—civil, criminal, and financial—must now fall upon his heirs, his estate, his life-stylist, and his crèche.

Mercifully, perhaps, both his heirs and his estate were destitute; and even mighty Diversified Life was far from being worth the $660 billion that the plaintiffs were demanding in reparations.

So now, eleven years earlier in 2334, an even more startling legal notion had been advanced: that the United States Government itself, in particular the Department of Human Services, was ultimately responsible for having knowingly and recklessly certified the design, gestation, and sale of a criminal psychopath bent on the destruction of France.

For nine years the Government scoffed at the absurdity of such a notion—until the Nine Old Women of the Supreme

Court in the fullness of their wisdom upheld the plaintiffs'
right to name the Department of Human Services in their
lawsuit.

The criminal proceedings had long since been divorced
from the civil; it was the civil suits that had been sent to the
federal courts in San Francisco. And it was here in the old
Federal Building on Pier 37 that I—along with a score of
other equally prominent expert witnesses, I hasten to add—
was expected to prove to the federal jury of seven good men
and women and true that the Diversified Life Danville Dasher
Charles Boyderkowski was no more defective within the ex-
cruciatingly stringent standards delineated and certified by
the United States Government than any other of the 187 million living Americans gestated in the crèches of Diversified
Life and the rest of the Big Seven.

"—and thus it is the so-called life-stylists such as yourself who determine the genetic characteristics of the children propagated, gestated, and then brought to term in
factories such as that of Diversified Life?" demanded the
plaintiffs' legalist in the most disparaging manner at his
command.

"That is correct," I said, "except that the Diversified Life
crèche in Oakland should no more be considered a factory
than your own fine home should be considered a garage for
a mindless piece of nonsentient protoplasm. Although, of
course, I am always willing to grant the occasional exception. . . ."

This earned a sharp rebuke from the Gravitas Maxima on
the bench, of course, but the satisfaction I got from seeing
the Stalwart shyster flush an angry red was more than worth
it. For the rest of the afternoon I tediously went over ground
that a dozen previous witnesses had already covered in excruciating detail.

I began by explaining what everyone in the civilized world
knew from the time they could talk: that prospective parents
wanting a child had only to visit a local outlet of one of the
nationwide dealerships run by the Big Seven, such as Apple-
Boeing, Diversified Life, or Earthly Integument, taking with

them, of course, their parenting license from the state board of equalization.

At the dealership they would choose the physical model and potential—I say *potential!*—personality they wanted, and the order would be placed with the crèche. Ten months later their infant would be delivered directly to their door by the friendly blue-and-pink Storkbubble, the child's body and mind fully warranted for six full years against any and all defects in manufacture.

In the United States, of course, the only crèches where infants are actually gestated are those of the Big Seven. But parents wanting something a little more special in the way of their child can also place an order through the specialty boutiques of the more elegant department stores such as Macy's and Neiman-Reagan.

Or, of course, they are free to use a licensed life-styling service—such as my own Robert Clayborn Design. We do cost a trifle more, that is true. But what we offer in terms of quality is a *great* deal more. Most of us, after all, are the same life-stylists who anonymously design the more pedestrian models marketed by the Big Seven and the high-class department stores. Here in our own shop we are able to give full expression to our artistic abilities and imagination.

If the parents insist, for instance, we can even do an individualized editing of their own personal DNA to enhance whatever traits they particularly desire in their children. The decisive encounter of sperm and ova takes place later in the Big Seven crèche, of course, but all of the essential work has been carried out by the life-stylist beforehand. Surprisingly few parents are willing to bear the negligible added expense for 100 percent individualized children, but for those who do the rewards are great: their progeny can be found at the ultimate levels of the arts and industries.

I had just begun to explain to the court the intricate process by which a potential personality specified by the parents and designed by a life-stylist such as myself was actually wedded to the tabula rasa of the newly gestated infant's receptive mind when Judge Flanders suddenly startled the court by uttering a decisive yawn. She blinked twice at the courtroom and adjourned for the weekend.

That was Friday, July 17th, 2345, the day everything began to fall apart.

3

The sun was dazzling in a deep blue sky as I stepped out of the Federal Building on Pier 37 and into the clear, brisk air of mid-afternoon San Francisco. From somewhere the breeze brought the mouth-watering tang of freshly baked sourdough bread. The ancient fortress of Alcatraz stood sentinel in the middle of the sparkling Bay waters, while the white sails of a flotilla of small sailboats darted past in the foreground. On the far side of the Bay the sun-dappled hills of Marin County were sharply outlined against the sky—but just to the west the tops of the Golden Gate's mighty twin towers had already vanished into the dense gray bank of fog sweeping in from the Pacific Ocean, cold, ominous, disquieting.

I shivered slightly and wondered again why San Francisco's purported summers were so much colder and foggier than its winters. I knew there was undoubtedly some simple meteorological reason, but still it seemed perverse—like the notion of Christmas in Australia coming in the middle of summer. But I also knew that the infamous Underwood-Gonzalez administration of the 2070s that had actually canopied a weather bubble over San Francisco for one memorable summer had immediately been recalled from office by an indignant local populace and removed to jail on a number of remarkably unconvincing charges. So summer fogs would just have to be put up with for the forty-three years and some odd months that remained of my life.

I glanced again at the oncoming fog, then asked Angus the

time. No reply. I scowled, and slapped at my rock-pocket: empty—I must have left Angus at home. I squinted down at my wristcom, which to me was only a wristcom. Some people, I know, have programmed their wristcoms to tell them exactly how many days and hours remain until their final sleep, but this has always struck me as being obsessively overprecise. I mean, what's the sense in carrying on a seventy- or eighty-year countdown? We're all going to get there in the end, aren't we?

In any case, it was now 3:47. Too late to drop in on my downtown office on Washington Square, too early for my daily squash game in the forty-through-seventy ladder at the San Francisco Tennis Club. Definitely too early for a drink.

So what was wrong with actually going home early for a change? I belatedly asked myself.

A question that only a Puritan Ideator could be troubled by. I spoke softly into my wristcom. Seconds later a Yellow Bubble slipped out of the passing Embarcadero traffic and glided to a halt. I stepped into its cramped confines and was borne away in silence to our home in Presidio Heights. Sylvina will be surprised to see me so early, I thought with a sudden tingle of pleasurable anticipation. Friday afternoons were spent at her tantric sex class in Noe Valley; this was slightly raffish activity for a Presidio Heights matron, but she always returned in such wonderfully high spirits that I could never bring myself to object. And she generally had something new and amusing to demonstrate. At least to Sylvina at twenty-three it was always new and amusing; to me at fifty-seven it was at least generally amusing.

The transparent bubble ran smoothly up the steep slopes of Divisadero Street to the top of Pacific Heights, then turned right on Broadway. Our home was a short distance to the west, a 350-year-old marble-and-granite town house with a stupendous view of the Bay and Marin County. As the bubble drew to a halt the first whirling wisps of fog came gusting out of the dark forests of Presidio Park to envelop the large, graciously designed old homes sitting in their spacious lots overlooking the city. I hurried up the brick walkway and into the welcoming warmth of home.

• • •

"Good afternoon, sor."

I handed my hat and cloak to Beach the Butler, an appall-
ingly expensive domestic we had purchased from Harrod's
the year before. He had enormous Britannic dignity and presence, but as always he dropped both the hat and the cloak
before finally managing to get them onto the hat tree; as
always I wondered why I bothered with such an incompetent
piece of machinery. I also wondered where I had left my
rock. "Angus!" I commed silently but forcefully. "Where
the devil are you?"

On the bedroom dresser, Robert, just beside the hairbrush.

"Then don't move," I commed, a feeble joke of long
standing between us. I didn't attach as much importance to
Angus as Sylvina did to her own rock Minkle, but he *was*
occasionally useful, and undeniably a faithful companion.
"Where's Sylvina?" I asked.

*I believe that at this actual moment she is in her dressing
room; she and Minkle have only recently returned home.*

"And Patricia—still at school?"

*Patricia has returned from school. She is in the nursery
with Ingrid the Nanny. She and Zoo-Zoo are telling stories to
one another.*

I was mildly surprised: I thought that Patricia's nursery
school generally kept her until the end of the afternoon. "Stay
where you are," I ordered Angus. "We'll look in on them
together."

My footsteps clattered noisily on the ancient black-and-white
marble squares of the hallway as I crossed to the carpeted stair-
way. On the second floor I stepped into our bedroom, where I
paused to admire the fog-shrouded view of the Bay. "I'm home,
darling," I called to the closed door that led to Sylvina's dressing room. No answer. I shrugged, then retrieved Angus from
where he sat patiently on the dresser.

Angus had been given to me by my father for my twenty-
first birthday; except for the six months I had spent in Arkansas just after graduation I had never been without his
company for more than a few hours at a time. He was a very
masculine-looking rock, a soft, dark brown, shot through with
glints of maroon and purple, and his unobtrusive sheen was

the softly glowing patina that comes from being burnished by generations of fingers.

"Hello, Angus. Sorry to have forgotten you—you would have enjoyed yourself in court. Have a good day?"

Much as usual.

I nodded absently and dropped him into the rock-pocket of my coat. What kind of a day, after all, would be unusual for a rock?

Together we strolled down the hallway to the pink-and-white frills of the nursery, where I could hear the excited yelps of Patricia's squeaky voice and the softer murmur of Ingrid the Nanny.

"Daddy!" cried Patricia from her high chair, her rosy round face radiant with joy—what little of it wasn't covered by mashed potatoes and carrots. "I'm having dinner! And Zoo-Zoo too!"

"So I see, Rosebud." I smiled, and removed Angus from my rock-pocket, then held him up to inspect the nursery for himself. He doesn't actually have external sensory organs, of course, but most children like to think that the rocks do. "Look, Angus: there's Zoo-Zoo, all covered with mashed potatoes. And there's Patricia all covered with mashed potatoes. And there's Ingrid the Nanny all covered with mashed potatoes. Would *you* like some too?"

Patricia's blue eyes grew round. "Does Angus like mashed potatoes?"

"He prefers a double Scotch, but in a pinch he'll drink anything, just like Zoo-Zoo."

My daughter picked up Zoo-Zoo clumsily with a chubby hand and held her rock out to Ingrid the Nanny, who dutifully jabbed at it ineptly with a spoonful of potatoes. I sighed. Inexhaustible patience was about all that could be said for this hunk of Swedish machinery, that and its blonde good looks. Ingrid the Nanny was nearly as clumsy as Beach the Butler, and every time I saw Patricia in her charge I wondered uneasily if my daughter would survive her attentions. But Sylvina set great store by Ingrid, and was unwilling to try replacing her with a live nanny from the Southworld.

"Daddy! Zoo-Zoo told me about the *bears*!"

"Bears? No! What did Zoo-Zoo tell you?"

I oohed and ahhed in wonder for several minutes while Patricia excitedly told me about the little girl in the woods and the three mashed-potato-eating bears. Finally I found a reasonably clear patch of forehead and kissed it noisily, then tendered Angus so that he in turn could be kissed by Zoo-Zoo.

"You're leaving, Daddy? But I didn't tell you what the Papa Bear did *then*!"

"I have to go kiss your mommy."

"And does Angus have to kiss Minkle?"

I examined the mashed-potato-smeared rock in my hand. "Angus isn't kissing anyone," I said firmly, "until he brushes his teeth."

4

"Where have you been?" cried Sylvina in a curiously agonized voice.

I frankly gaped as my beautiful consort burst out of the dressing room and to my astonishment grabbed the front of my coat with both hands and began to shake me furiously. Was this some exotic new foreplay she had learned at her tantric sex class?

I tried to pull her into my arms, but she jerked herself free and positioned herself behind a chair on the far side of the room, as if to defend herself from physical attack. "What on Earth's the matter?" I asked with far more calm than I actually felt. "Is this a joke of some sort?"

Sylvina's enormous gray eyes glittered with fury. She was as slender and blonde, perfectly coiffed and subtly perfumed, as she had been on the day we met five years before. But now a seething emotion animated the elegant planes of her Golden Exaltica features in a way I had never before seen. "What's the matter?" I repeated, more softly, as she continued to glare at me silently. "Are you ill? Is it your family? What—"

Sylvina's small, high breasts rose and fell with emotion. "It's Patricia," she said at last in a tight, brittle voice.

"Patricia? But she's in the nursery. She seems perfectly fine to—"

Sylvina clutched the top of the chair. "Well, she is *not* perfectly fine. She's been suspended from nursery school."

"Suspended? Why—"

"For antisocial activity, that's why!" shouted Sylvina, jumping out from behind the chair and advancing on me angrily.

"But she's only three years old! How can she be suspended for antisocial activity at three years old? *What* antisocial activity?"

"I've told you and *told* you: she refuses to participate in sexual orientation games!"

"You've told me?"

Sylvina's breath hissed out with exasperation. "A dozen times. Two dozen times. A thousand times! Don't you *ever* listen to anything I say?"

"But . . ." My voice trailed off as I sank onto the edge of the bed. Sexual orientation exercises are as fundamental as learning to read and write. More so, even, for they are one of the three Tchen-Lii primatics essential to the development of the child's well-integrated personality. Failure to have mastered them by the age of three was . . . well, as a biogeneticist I had to face facts: highly abnormal. I began to understand Sylvina's extreme distress. I looked up at her helplessly. "But why didn't you—"

"I *did* tell you! Every time the school notified me! And you just grunted and stared off into space. As if—"

"I must have been preoccupied," I responded feebly. "My work . . ."

"Your work, your work! I though you said that you *loved* her."

"Patricia? Of course I love her!"

"Ha!" Sylvina stared down at me with what I would have sworn was naked hatred—if I hadn't known that she loved me with all the outsized passion of which a Golden Exaltica is capable. *"You're* the one who wanted to get a . . ." Her lips tightened and she turned away, her slim shoulders trembling slightly. My heart went out to her in a great wave of love and tenderness. I climbed leadenly to my feet. "Anyway, it's too late for all that now," I heard her mutter.

"What do you mean it's too late?"

She swung around and in a few blunt words told me. An official Board of Determination had already been called into

session by the City and County of San Francisco. This panel
of psychologists, educators, sociologists, and biogenetic engineers had concluded that our beautiful little girl was clearly
a defective personality.

"But that's ridiculous!" I raged. "Of course she isn't a
defective personality! A bit behind her peers, perhaps, in
certain aspects of development, but that's perfectly normal at
her age!"

My consort tilted her head and looked at me through curiously slitted eyes. "It is *really* normal? Really and truly?
After all, *you're* the world-famous biotechnical expert." She
made the words sound like a curse.

I hesitated perceptibly before answering, all of my Puritan
Ideator scruples regarding the truth stretched to the breaking
point as I considered this dismaying information. Finally I
spoke with as much reassurance as I could. "Of course she's
normal. These local determination boards are preposterous,
a collection of time-serving bureaucrats! It's not the actual
tests that count, it's who *administers* them—that's the crux!"

"Well, the crux of all of this is that your daughter has just
been officially declared a defective model," declared my
consort stonily. "Just what do you intend to do about it?"

"Do? What *is* there to do? We'll enroll her in another
school, of course, arrange for remedial training, see that—"

"Ha! Just as you arranged for Patricia in the first place—
you, the great biogenetic artist!" I fell back in speechless
shock as the searing stream of her venomous words babbled
on and I discovered that it wasn't the school board that my
consort blamed but *me!*

Why, she demanded, had *I* coerced *her* into choosing such
a worthless model designed by such an incompetent source
as my rootspittle friend Sam-Day Dowree? Because of the
trade *discount?* Why hadn't *I* given free rein to *her* maternal
instincts, allowed *her* to purchase a really top-line model from
Neiman-Reagan? Why was *I*, the biogeneticist, so—

"Stop it!" I cried in more anguish than I could bear. Startled by my unexpected outburst, Sylvina fell silent. I stared
blindly across the bedroom at the white knuckles of her
clenched fists. "All of this is beside the point," I said with
as much calm as I could muster. "I've told you what *I* think

we should do about Patricia. I know that this has come as a terrible shock to you, but obviously Patricia's welfare comes first. What do *you* think we should do?"

"What do *I* think?" The mother of our child glared at me defiantly with her glittering gray eyes. "Well, I happen to *agree* with the Board of Determination. The six-year warranty is still in effect. *I* think she should be sent back to the crèche and replaced with an undamaged model free of charge!"

I hardly recall the details of the next twenty minutes of argument, so numbed was I by Sylvina's cold-blooded demand. At some point she turned her back on me in the middle of a sentence and stalked savagely from the bedroom. I could almost hear the blood pounding in my ears as I angrily followed her down the stairs and into the sunken living room where Beach the Butler had just finished lighting a smokey fire.

"André the Chef has informed me that dinner will be ready precisely at eight," the butler told me urbanely while I tried to steady my ragged breathing. "The main course is *coulibiac de saumon.*" I grunted hoarsely, then turned to my consort.

"How heartless can you be?" I cried to her back. "This is your *daughter* we're talking about, not a mechanical French pastry chef! And you want to trade her in for an updated model! Don't you know what they'll do to her at crèche?"

"I just don't see why *we* have to be the ones to have a defective model," replied Sylvina sullenly, skirting my question.

I could only sigh in anguish, for in spite of my unbounded love for my darling little daughter, deep in my most secret heart I feared that I agreed with Sylvina. For I knew that the failure rate among the Big Seven for domestic models, even the very cheapest, bottom-of-the-line models, was almost nonexistent, something on the order of one in twenty thousand. I stood at the bottom of the multileveled living room, staring blindly out at the fog drifting through the buildings in the Marina far below. It had literally never occurred to me that a child of *ours* might be defective.

Nor, I now had to admit to myself, in more than thirty years in the industry had I ever troubled to find out *exactly* what happened to those extremely few models that *were* returned under the warranty. The few fleeting moments of idle speculation I might have given to the matter conjured up only a benign, if slightly blurry, image of laughing children romping in the tall grass of a sunlit meadow. . . .

Now an icy hand seemed to fasten around my heart as I wondered just how close to the truth this fantasy actually was . . .

"Well, if *you* won't do it, then I'll send her back myself," stated Sylvina with appalling finality.

For a single terrible moment of panic I wondered if she actually could, then reason asserted itself. "Both of us would have to agree, and a Children's Court judge as well." I forced a ghastly half-smile to my lips and took a placating step towards her. "Darling, I know this has been the most awful shock. Both of us are tired, distraught, unnerved. Why don't you ask Minkle for *her* opinion, see what she thinks about it?"

"My rock?"

"Of course. Isn't that what she's there for?"

Sylvina scowled, but her eyes moved automatically to the far side of the room, where Minkle had been casually placed on a walnut sideboard. I held my breath as Sylvina pursed her lips in thought. Rocks *are* portable advisors and consciences, of course—but only insofar as their owners allow them to be. I knew that Sylvina spent half the day chattering inconsequentially to Minkle, and I also knew full well what her rock would advise. For although every rock gradually learns to shape its responses and individuality to the unique personality of its owner, life in any form at all remains sacred to the Martian rocks.

Minkle was a typical lady's model, smooth and subtly curved, hardly larger than Sylvina's hand, so highly polished that the glitter of her red-and-yellow grain seemed an outpouring of her own inner vitality. My consort could just as easily have commed her silently from across the room, but we all have our own ingrained habits in dealing with our rocks. Most children talk to theirs out loud; a surprising number of adults continue to do the same.

I watched hopefully as Sylvina picked up Minkle by her filigreed gold handle, then sank into a soft blue couch in front of the fireplace. She cuddled the rock's smooth curve against the side of her own smooth cheek, and I could see her lips moving as she whispered softly to the alien creature. I wondered what strange, unimaginable thoughts could be running through the rock's mind.

The minutes passed as Sylvina continued to pour an apparently endless list of grievances into her rock's ear. At last I could stand it no longer. "Angus," I commed. "Is Patricia still in the nursery?"

He communicated briefly with Zoo-Zoo. *Yes. She is being prepared for her bath.*

"Tell Zoo-Zoo that we're on the way up." I passed a weary hand across my eyes. Perhaps a joyous, splashing bathtime with Patricia and Ingrid the Nanny would lift the awful weight with which Sylvina had so unexpectedly burdened me.

I was on the steps leading up to the hallway when Sylvina rose from the depths of the couch with her usual easy grace. "Well?" I asked.

She ignored me, glaring down at the rock in her hand as if it had just bit her on the thumb. "Well, that's *stupid*," she hissed angrily to Minkle, "just plain stupid! I don't care *what* you say, they sold me a defective model and I won't stand for it!"

I held my breath while Minkle commed her silently.

"I will *so* send her back to the factory!" shouted my ultrarefined consort with heart-stopping fury. "And I'll do the same to you, you stupid rock!"

Before I could move, Sylvina ran across to the fireplace and to my horror stuffed the faithful and inoffensive Minkle into the discreet opening of the room's oubliette, instantly snuffing out a four-billion-year-old life.

5

That evening I sat alone in my den, morosely drinking vintage California brandy. Sylvina had called for a bubble and disappeared into the fog. Unmindful of the deadly storm that swirled around her, Patricia slept peacefully in the nursery, Kanga the Roo clutched tightly in her arms, Ingrid the Nanny sitting patiently in the corner, glowing softly in the darkness.

For a while I tried talking with Angus, but there is cold balm in even the most comforting wisdom when it is purveyed by a rock. I turned on the holoscope in the corner, watched absurd caperings for a moment, and turned it off. I poured another snifter of brandy and thought hard thoughts about my beautiful Golden Exaltica from Neiman-Reagan.

My father, stern old New Englander that he was, had warned me with nearly his final words about entangling myself with such a decorative but notoriously frivolous model emanating from such a garish source. He himself, a Mayflower Steadfast from the staid old Boston life-stylists of Shreve, Crump & Lowe, had spent seventy-two blissful years with the same consort, an Arabella Pilgrim from the same ancient designers. They had even died within a few days of each other, the week of my fifty-first birthday, eloquent testimony to the ancient folk wisdom of uniting comparable models.

I sighed forlornly and poured more brandy. I, Robert Clayborn, internationally known life-stylist and man-about-town with six consorts already to his credit, had presumed to know better than his parents. For didn't ancient wisdom also contradict itself by holding that opposites attract? And what could be more opposite than a Puritan Ideator from Shreve, Crump & Lowe and a Golden Exaltica from Neiman-Reagan?

How my father must now be scowling, wherever he was.

Uncomfortable with the bleak knowledge that once again I had made a fool of myself and would undoubtedly soon have seven ex-consorts to my discredit, I ordered the holoscope on again. Its mindless inanity had to be better than this morose introspection.

The holoscope came to life in the middle of a news program featuring a particularly gruesome massacre somewhere in the Southworld. I was about to switch to something more cheerful when the images changed to the chaste classical lines of the ancient Supreme Court building in Washington. I stayed my command: my day in federal court had momentarily whetted my normally apathetic appetite for the arcane convolutions of the law.

A moment later we were inside the august chamber where the Nine Old Women handed down the decisions that ultimately affected the lives of every American. A ridiculous epithet, I thought idly as I watched the nine solemn justices file into the chamber in their long black robes, and one that was essentially meaningless. How old *were* these nine female judges whose recent decisions had so thoroughly infuriated the liberal media? All in their nineties? What of it? None of them appeared appreciably older than myself—and *I* was still good for five games of vigorous squash seven days a week. I nodded smugly into the heady fumes of my brandy snifter. The quality of children designed by competent life-stylists and gestated by the Big Seven was clearly so high that—

But this was exactly the train of thought I had hoped to avoid. While I brooded glumly, a voice in the background droned on. With an effort I brought myself back to whatever was now being discussed on the holoscope by a panel of the network's legal experts. My eyes widened as I caught the gist of their comments. The Supreme Court—the Nine *crazy* Old Women!—had just upheld the right of the state of Arkansas to require all of its *visitors*, as well as its residents, to meet certain specified criteria of public health.

The criteria in question were irrefutable proof that the visitor had been gestated for nine full months in his mother's actual uterus and had then been brought into the world by the old-fashioned way of bloodbirthing.

Even through the warm haze of well-aged brandy that now enveloped me I felt the same incredulous shock that Sylvina's outrageous behavior had just engendered. If I understood correctly, the Supreme Court of the land was allowing two million lunatics to set themselves up for all intents and purposes as an independent nation of breeders right in the heart of the United States, a group of neanderthals even more backward than the most miserable countries of the Southworld!

"Did you hear that, Angus?" I said, hardly conscious of the fact that I was actually talking aloud to my rock. "Next thing you know, we'll have to have passports and visas to get in!"

I have never been to Arkansas.

"More discrimination," I muttered indignantly. "They don't even allow rocks in Arkansas. Poor old Angus, he can't even visit the thals."

That is not entirely the case. At this moment there are four thousand seven hundred and eighty-four rocks in the State of Arkansas.

"Not very many for two million people."

I suppose not.

"And now even a rock will have to have a passport," I groped for the bottle of brandy. Obviously the Nine Old Women of the Supreme Court had never visited Arkansas, had never seen for themselves how two million thals lived in squalor and decadence. If they had, they would never have permitted the breeders to set themselves up as a quasi-sovereign state right in the middle of the United States! For there in Arkansas were gathered the dazed remnants of all that was most bizarre and repulsive of the nineteenth century: all of this country's few remaining Old Catholics, Neo-Evolutionists, Chiropractors, Christian Scientists, Big Green Ecologists, Amish, Flat Earthers, homeopaths, and Reformed Reichians—all of those who believed in bloodbirthing, child mortality, physical and mental illness, unfluoridated water, old age, and painful, grisly death.

Up to now, of course, these lunatics and chaoticists had been strictly quarantined in the state of Arkansas—for their own good as well as ours. But today, after two centuries of quarantine, the Nine Old Women had abruptly turned this commonsensical notion upon its head: not only could *we* keep the thals away from us, they had the right to keep *us* away from *them!* It was handing the inmates the keys to the madhouse!

I slopped brandy angrily into my balloon glass. Who knew more about Arkansas, the Nine Old Women or Robert Clayborn, the Robert Clayborn who had once—

I blinked in surprise. There in the holoscope, being interviewed on the steps of the Supreme Court, was a short, tubby figure of almost excruciating ugliness. He wore a shiny stovepipe hat and long, black, claw hammer suit. This was the legalist who had so triumphantly argued the case for the state of Arkansas.

Was it possible? I leaned forward in my chair, upsetting the brandy in my haste. Surely . . . surely, there couldn't be *two* men that ugly, even among the primitive thals of Arkansas. . . .

It was my friend and mentor of thirty years earlier, Titus T. Waggoner!

6

From the vantage point of the fashionable salons of New York or Paris or San Francisco it's easy enough to forget that for all their spectacular ugliness the unwashed breeders of Arkansas living in their nineteenth-century squalor are actually as human as the rest of us. Well, many of them, at any rate. Their lives are short, nasty, and brutish, of course, but beneath their unprepossessing exteriors dwell hopes and fears, loves and aspirations no different from our own.

At least so I was taught by my parents, those stern paragons of fundamental New England verities. Nothing I subsequently learned as an undergraduate at the liberal oasis of Harvard did anything to disabuse me of this somewhat eccentric doctrine, though even at Harvard the number of thals and Southworlders actually present in the celebrated Yard was notable by its sparseness. It wasn't, in fact, until I was a graduate student across the Charles River in the Harvard School of Biotechnical Engineering that I ever took the first gingerly steps toward befriending one of the exotic thals.

Titus T. Waggoner was the same age as myself, a student next door at the Law School. We first exchanged tentative greetings at an autumn football party. Now that I was a professional student of biogenetics I felt that I had a clear right to scrutinize him closely and dispassionately.

It was hard to believe that he could be from the same genetic stock as the rest of us at the party, where the men and women without exception were tall, slim, and regularly featured. Titus T. Waggoner was short and thick, with a twisted lump of a nose and one eye noticeably higher in his suety face than the other. His hair was a harsh tangle of wirelike curls, but this failed to conceal the fact that one ear was also higher than the other. His fleshy jowls and mottled neck were covered by an invincible black stubble that resisted the keenest lazors and most destructive depilators, while the backs of his hands were hairier than any I had ever seen outside a zoological garden. For a single vivid instant I imagined those hirsute appendages clasping the flawless naked back of one of the twenty or thirty beautiful women who chattered around us and I felt myself shuddering.

But the thal's pale blue eyes danced with a quizzical intelligence, and his surprisingly sensitive mouth seemed set in an unbreakable wry smile. To the frequently posed question of what he, an Arkansas thal, was doing here in Cambridge, his wistful reply was always the same: "Know thy enemy." But to me it was inconceivable that this disarming troglodyte could be an enemy, and it seemed a singularly cruel affliction that such a kind and gentle spirit should be encapsulated in such a grotesque integument as this rude thal's body, a body that had already begun its painful descent into old age and death.

If Titus felt himself the victim of cruel circumstance he concealed it manfully. He participated in all the informal sports leagues of the graduate schools, hopelessly outclassed by the genetically optimized bodies of his peers, of course, but even with bloodied nose and heaving chest he was always game, always uncomplaining. Throughout his stay at the Law School he remained an object of curiosity—and not all of it totally unfavorable, I hasten to add. Titus was far too much the gentleman to ever reveal the specifics, but I knew that a steady stream of impeccably designed lady law students made discreet exits from his quarters in the dark hours of the morning, though they would have forever denied it. A far broader stream of glossy Neiman-Reagan and Tiffany models, in fact, than had ever deigned to visit me. . . .

By the end of my second year of graduate school Titus and I were firm friends. That June he accompanied me to my parents' summer home on a cool blue lake on Michigan's

Upper Peninsula. Both Father and Mother had recently been elevated to fellowships at the Saginaw Institute of Metaformic Inquiry and had an unquenchable thirst for philosophic debate. As we swatted mosquitos and splashed together in Big Dollar Lake they and Titus happily debated the quiddity of quanta and the quodlibet of qualia. I myself could only groan silently and slink away, to spend the summer vainly trying to program Olaf the Lumberjack to flip pancakes without tossing them onto the floor.

Two years later, fresh upon our graduation, I returned with Titus to Arkansas.

Remember, I was young!

Even now I marvel at how incredibly young I was in spite of my twenty-five years. I was straight out of the world's finest school of biogenetic design, restless, ambitious, impossibly idealistic—and seething with unorthodox ideas of my own.

In spite of the apparently endless diversity of life-styled models in the world around me, my studies had led me to conclude that the genetic pool from which the Big Seven and all the rest of the civilized Northworld were drawing their raw materials was becoming depleted, ingrown, run-down. Nothing startlingly new in the way of art, science, mathematics, or philosophy, I argued, had appeared in at least the last one hundred years.

But since the American life span was now a federally mandated 101 years and a few odd weeks, it could be argued in rebuttal that in a sense this one hundred years represented but a single long generation, a negligible period of time.

If you were exceptionally stupid, you could argue that.

For it was crystal-clear from an examination of field-and-track records that for a hundred years now only the most marginal improvements had been made by Northworld athletes. Swimmers, sprinters, long-distance runners, shot-putters, broad jumpers—none of these athletes were leaping or running noticeably farther or faster than their great-great-grandfathers of two centuries before.

True, a computerized study of the holoscopic parade of the greatest golfers, tennis players, baseball players of the last three centuries did nothing to disprove the widely held, but entirely subjective, impression that today's athletes were handsomer and more graceful than ever before.

But nothing more: the objective study of minutes and seconds told me that our utter dependance upon the crèches of the Big Seven had led to the undoubted stagnation of the human race.

No one at Harvard to whom I broached this alarming notion seemed in the least concerned. Our athletes have merely reached the theoretical limits of the human body, they replied, and shook their heads indulgently at my lack of common sense. Only Titus T. Waggoner seemed at all interested in my thesis. And even he only smiled his sad smile and shrugged expressively. "What else could you expect from building people in a factory?" was his sole comment.

I thought of the two million infants gestated annually in America for our own country's needs, the five million others produced more or less as cannon fodder for the despots and madmen of the Southworld. What was needed was fresh genetic material, fresh approaches, fresh designs. "Titus," I said, "tell me again about Arkansas."

The weirdly assorted cultists and madmen who made the pleasant green hills of Arkansas their own in the early twenty-first century found it as difficult as the previous inhabitants to settle upon a name for themselves that was both dignified and easy to pronounce. *Arkansasian* and *Arkansawyer* were terrible mouthfuls to get one's tongue around, while the slightly more palatable *Arkansan* tended to conjure up images of the wholly different state of Kansas. The newly settled primitives could agree on few other matters; they did, however, decide that henceforth they would rather grandly be known as Visionaries. The rest of America happily modified this to Vicenaries, but more generally referred to the primitive hillfolk as thals, or breeders, or sometimes even ruder names.

I soon learned that the Visionaries had names of their own for the factory-produced folk who lived in the other fifty-four states: we were tubers, or bottlers. Ruder words than that they were incapable of contriving.

Titus and I took my battered aircar as far south as the border crossing of Blue Eye, Missouri. No technology introduced after the year 1899 was permitted into Arkansas, so we left my aircar in a dead-storage garage in Blue Eye and crossed the state line by foot. I had already reluctantly left my rock Angus in the care of my parents. Strictly speaking, a rock was not technology; but as it had definitely been quarried on Mars, it was undeniably an artifact of post-1900 technology.

The border guards at the checkpoint checked my bags and pockets for antibiotics, cigarette lighters, lazors, alloy tennis rackets, holoscopic erotica, and a host of other items officially proscribed by the Adjudicator Temporal but unofficially considered by most of the state's population to be no more sinful than a chocolate sundae. I suffered the search with good humor. Strangely, it was only as we boarded the long green railroad carriage that would transport us to Little Rock that I unexpectedly felt the first small chips of youthful idealism beginning to flake away at this disconcerting encounter with the stark reality of the thals. For their steam-driven railroad engines were machines of enormous size and complexity, capable of pulling a train at speeds upwards of one-hundred miles an hour. Why were *they* so arbitrarily permitted by the Visionaries but not the automobile or the aircar? It made no sense.

In the next few months most of the rest of my youthful illusions were similarly confounded. In spite of the universally low esteem in which the thals were held by the rest of my fellow bottlers, I had perversely expected to find a sturdy group of independent pioneers and hardy farmers, rugged backwoodsmen and Roussellian noble savages. Instead, I found for the most part an indolent, ignorant, intolerant, and totally unlovable bunch of painfully unwashed slum-dwellers.

In spite of the sanctimonious insistence by the Visionaries that theirs was a healthier, more natural society, one living in close harmony with a benevolent nature, most of the breeders were content to live in the ruins of the twenty-first-century cities that had become theirs when the rest of the state's original inhabitants had abandoned their homes to the lunatics. I was appalled to see women who were actually

physically pregnant, their unborn children bloating their
stomachs grotesquely, the mothers-to-be mindlessly drugging
themselves with nicotine and caffeine and a host of other
toxic substances, wantonly damaging their precious fetuses.
And these were the people who dared call themselves Visionaries! Titus asked if I wanted to assist at the rites of a
forthcoming delivery, the curious word the thals use to refer
to bloodbirth. I pictured the ghastly scene of blood and
screams, the unwashed midwives, the shriveled, pink, wailing infant, traumatized for life by the terrible transition from
womb to world, quite probably deformed and brain-damaged
by its mother's excesses. I could barely contain my nausea.

I have to admit that I was wrong about the unwashed midwives—they, at least, did occasionally wash themselves. For
the only apparent concession that the thals made to common
sense in the field of health and medicine was the reluctant
recognition of the theory of germs and of the necessity for
general hygiene. Otherwise, their medicines were those which
could be extracted and brewed by themselves from the local
plants, and their doctors possessed no implements more advanced than scalpels and stethoscopes.

Titus regarded me with his customary sad smile when I
protested volubly at such deadly absurdity. "It's not the way
they do things at Harvard Square," he agreed. "But most of
us manage to stay alive."

"But for how *long,* for god's sake?"

"Ah: that's an entirely *different* question. I don't think we
have a census."

"Then what *do* you have?" I tugged irritably at the scratchy
beard I had recently grown at Titus's behest. This, along with
an ill-fitting pair of limp blue overalls and a long pale scar
running down my left cheek, was supposed to constitute a
disguise of sorts.

"For one thing, we have an Adjudicator Temporal." He
grinned broadly. *"That's* something you don't have anywhere
else."

"Thank god for small favors." The Adjudicator Temporal
was the high state official who decided precisely what technology, device, or idea fell before or after the thals' mystic
date of December 31, 1899, and was therefore fit to be used

by his fellow Visionaries or not. I tried to picture a grim
Adjudicator Temporal sitting at his desk in Pine Bluff, on
Monday morning gruffly approving a steam-powered flying
machine, on Tuesday afternoon furiously banning a gasoline-
powered one.

It must have been a curious job. . . .

7

Even among the lunatic population of the thals exceptions could be found to their dottiness. Titus was one, of course, and I suppose that others like him were hidden away here and there in the cities. But most of the relatively sane were out on the farms and in the hills. Here were the hardworking Amish, still wearing their homespun black clothing, plodding along in their horse and buggies, resolutely disdaining as modern frivolity even such items as the telephone and telegraph which the rest of the thals grudgingly accepted. Here in the countryside were the tenth-generation farmers and backwoodsmen I had idealized, too exhausted from their mindless labors in the Roussellian state of nature to ever question the philosophical underpinnings of why they were condemning themselves and their children to a lifetime of drudgery.

The parents of my friend Titus worked a small freehold on the edge of a sunny lake in the Ozarks, a warm, hospitable couple in their middle fifties who were already far more ancient in appearance than any centenarian bottler approaching his final days. In their small wooden farmhouse I slept on a down-stuffed mattress, gingerly ate such exotica as fried rabbit and stewed possum, bathed once a week in a hand-filled tub in the kitchen, and helped them bring in their autumn harvest.

I had long since given up my notion of deriving any professional benefits from my sojourn among the thals. It was still conceivable that superior genetic material existed among these gnarled and weather-beaten hillfolk, but if so it was far too hard to discern beneath the grime and wrinkles. But in spite of my loss of illusion, I remained as tediously adolescent as ever: as I fell exhausted into my soft mattress every night, I still discerned a certain romanticism in all this desperate backwoods primitivism—and even cast myself as an adventurous hero.

It was at a square dance in the neighboring hamlet of Morganton that I met the girl Jeanie Norman. Beneath strings of colored lights in a crowded barn, gaily dressed hillfolk danced intricate patterns to the cheerful twangs of fiddles and homemade banjos. Outside, an enormous orange harvest moon rose slowly over the dark hills. By now I had become almost accustomed to the bizarre physical disparities and irregularities of the hillfolk, but except for a slight thickness of her ankles Jeanie Norman could have passed unnoticed anywhere in the Northworld, taken perhaps for an Emporium-Sears Honey Rustique or an Apple-Boeing Hyacinth. She was blonde and rosy, a youthful schoolteacher in a one-room schoolhouse on the dusty road halfway between Choctaw and Damascus. She had swelling breasts proudly displayed in a low bodice, a dusting of freckles across her nose and cheeks, and enormous brown eyes.

Was it actually love that we felt for each other during the two brief months we bicycled through the wooded hills, splashed in the cool mountain lakes, tumbled passionately together in haylofts and fields, beside burbling streams, in shadowy glades?

Certainly it *felt* like love, but even at the time I was uneasily aware that no matter how cunningly I disguised myself and aped the manners of the Visionaries, I would always remain a stranger and an infidel to these curiously misguided folk. Jeanie had visited the troubling outside world of the bottlers, and even attended two years of high school on Mars. But the memory of her childhood ways and the ineluctable call of the strange inner voices that ruled the Visionaries had proven too strong. She had returned to her mountain home, knowing with absolute certitude that it was here she would live out the rest of her days. After a single impassioned argument that left both of us limp and trembling, each of us knew that the other would forever remain a prisoner of his misguided beliefs. Knowing now that our brief liaison was only that, we threw ourselves back into each other's arms with tears and rekindled passion—and a wisp of unspoken but unmistakable relief.

Finally in early December as the first cold frosts came to the Ozarks I knew it was time to leave. In a few days Titus would be taking the train to Little Rock, where he would garb himself in the formal accoutrements of shawl, claw hammer coat, and stovepipe hat, and open his own law office.

Politely, distantly, almost as if inquiring after the health of a stranger, I asked Jeanie Norman if she would care to return with me to the world beyond. Equally politely she shook her head—and asked if I would care to remain in Arkansas and father her children. We spent a last tearful night together, and in the morning Titus and I took the buckboard to Clinton, and from there the ancient train to Conway. And so, with no overpowering reluctance, I returned to the real world, leaving behind me Jeanie Norman and Titus T. Waggoner, as well as toothache, unpasteurized milk, and doctors of dialectical phrenology.

Angus the rock, I knew, would be happy to see me back.

Three years later I had opened my own small firm of Robert Clayborn Design and was eking out a precarious living in the city of Burlingame a few miles south on the peninsula from San Francisco. With Titus T. Waggoner I exchanged an occasional card. Any lingering memories of the lovely Jeanie Norman had been firmly suppressed, for now I was living with Daphne, my first consort, a spectacular English redhead from Marks & Spencer. And, working purely on speculation, I had designed a fine male child who incorporated carefully edited genes from both Daphne and myself. He was gestated in the Chicago crèche of 3L—Lightfoot Lads and Lasses— and named Hadrian by his mother in honor of the Roman emperor and conqueror of England.

To my immense joy, a few months later 3L purchased exclusive rights to my design, and within a year Scottish Emperors were selling briskly at 3L dealerships all across the

United States. Daphne and I and Baby Hadrian left our cramped apartment in Burlingame and moved to a modest house in Daly City. *UpDate*'s Christmas issue of 2315 featured a brief article on the season's hottest new life-stylists: my own astonished holoscopic features looked out from the pages along with those of Baby Hadrian. Shortly after New Year's I began to inquire about downtown San Francisco office space.

The nightmare began two weeks later when Hadrian disappeared from his baby bubble at a Palo Alto shopping center. It was the first authenticated kidnapping in the United States in nearly a hundred years and the resulting notoriety was extreme. For three months Daphne and I lived in a public spotlight that was nearly unbearable.

At last, just when all hope seemed exhausted, the federal authorities traced our missing son to the remote mountain town of Lost Corner, Arkansas. The local sheriff's office recovered Hadrian with notable dispatch and efficiency, and soon I was subjected to a shock almost equally as painful as the kidnapping itself. The madwoman who had slipped away from her backwoods fastness to steal our baby was none other than my lovely Jeanie Norman.

That was about as much as I ever learned—or wanted to. Arkansas refused to extradite Jeanie Norman on the grounds of mental illness. Titus T. Waggoner represented her in a series of court hearings and eventually communicated the results to me. He stunned me by saying that sometime in the last weeks of my stay in Arkansas Jeanie and I had conceived a child together. The infant had died in childbirth, apparently traumatizing Jeanie to a greater degree than anyone had realized. The subsequent hologram of myself and Baby Hadrian in *UpDate* had been enough to snap the delicate balance between sanity and delusion: she had rushed to California to recover her long-lost child. . . .

I supposed that all this was heartbreakingly true; but I was too overjoyed to have Hadrian back to pay further heed to whatever small tragedies were being played out in Arkansas. And as I watched my son bouncing happily in the arms of his beautiful redheaded mother I swore that never again would

I let my life be infringed upon by the primitive lunatics of the state of Arkansas.

I never spoke to my friend Titus again.

All of these bizarre events out of a half-forgotten past returned to me now as I watched the news in my fog-shrouded San Francisco den. Titus T. Waggoner, I saw, had apparently done well for himself. His wiry black hair was now a deep gray and his face was lined with wrinkles, but he seemed plump and prosperous. And his fine mouth was still set with the same sad smile.

I sighed heavily and suddenly felt my eyes blurring at the overpowering rush of memories. Thirty years had passed, and more. What could have become of Jeanie Norman? Was she still locked up in some backwoods madhouse? Would she even be alive? I had grown hazy about the life span and aging processes of a thal living in a state of nature. Whatever they were, certainly my once radiant beauty must by now be a toothless old crone. . . .

I switched off the holoscope and sat back in my chair with a replenished snifter of brandy. Hadrian had celebrated his thirty-first birthday in early April in New York, so it had been twenty-nine years ago that I had so nearly lost my son. Now I had another beautiful consort and another youthful child, and it looked as if history was trying to repeat itself. I looked grimly at my distorted reflection in the shining crystal of the enormous glass I held in my hands and vowed that *this* child would never be stolen from me.

8

The rest of the weekend passed in a state of unremitting tension as Sylvina and I argued relentlessly about Patricia. Sunday afternoon was clear and warm, and I fled with Patricia to the zoo on the edge of the Pacific Ocean. She was infinitely more impressed by the squirrels that scampered about the pathways begging for peanuts than by the elephants and giraffes. Finally I bought a bulb of white wine for myself and a bag of peanuts for Patricia and we moved to a shady bench. While Patricia chattered at my feet with the clownish squirrels, I sipped my wine and carefully enumerated my blessings. I had a mostly loving young consort, a beautiful three-year-old daughter, a successful thirty-year-old son, a lucrative and enjoyable profession, a worldwide reputation, a Presidio Heights mansion with a view of the world's most beautiful bay, a twenty-thousand-bottle wine cellar, a winter hideaway in Hawaii, and nearly forty-four years left in my life.

Why then did I feel so unbearably depressed?

Later that evening I sat by myself in the kitchen listlessly pushing a lukewarm chicken breast festooned with cloves of roast garlic back and forth across my plate while André the Chef hovered anxiously. Beach the Butler had carried a tray upstairs to Sylvina in the music room; I was drearily wondering how long this sad state of affairs could continue when Angus commed me.

Your daughter-in-law Jennifer would like to speak to you.
"Vucom or rockcom?"
Rockcom.
"Go ahead."
Robert? This is Jennifer.
I smiled faintly in spite of my depressed mood: I had always liked Jennifer, a perky peaches-and-cream Southern belle from Printemps USA in New Orleans. "Yes, I recognized you." This was not strictly true: Angus was only comming to me what Jennifer's rock was instantaneously transmitting to him; it was Angus's familiar voice I heard in my mind.
Robert? There's . . . there's something very seriously wrong with Hadrian.
"Wrong? What do you mean wrong?"
I don't know—nobody knows. They've just taken him to the hospital!
The hospital? I sat up straighter. This was cause for serious alarm. "He's been in an accident?" Nobody went to the hospital except for accidents.
No, it's not an accident. It's . . . oh, god, I can't describe it. . . .
"How long has he been this way?"
A . . . a month now, it started about a month ago.
"A month! But—"
I know, I know! He didn't want anyone to know. He wouldn't let me tell anyone! Somehow Angus managed to convey the shrill edge of hysteria that must have been in her voice three thousand miles away.
"But what *is* it? Some sort of tropical disease? A—"
I tell you, I don't know! *No one* knows!
"Where is he? I want to talk to him."
I don't know *if he* can *talk to you.*
"Oh god. But *where* is he?"
The hospital, he's at the hospit——
"I know, I know! *Which* hospital?"
Columbia . . . Columbia Medical Center.
"Angus! What time is it?"
It is ten forty-seven.

"Make a reservation on the midnight shuttle to New York. First class. Have an executive bubble waiting in New York."

Certainly, Robert. But may I remind you that you have a court appearance to make tomorrow morning?

"Damn! Make it the noontime . . . No, don't do anything. I'll call him first thing in the morning, then go to court, ask for a recess or whatever they call it, then go to the airport." I returned my attention to my daughter-in-law. "Jennifer: I can't make it to New York tonight; it'll probably be tomorrow evening, your time. I'll call you tomorrow and let you know. Would you like me to call Daphne?"

Please. I don't think I could bear . . .

I could well understand that: I myself could scarcely bear to speak to Daphne, my ex-consort and Hadrian's mother.

For the next few minutes I offered what meager comfort I could to my daughter-in-law, then broke the connection. "Angus," I said aloud. "Comm Daphne's rock, whatever it's called. Tell it to inform Daphne that her son is in Columbia Medical Center, extremely ill. I do not, repeat *do not*, wish to speak to Daphne myself."

Very well, Robert. Daphne and Apollo are in Stapleton's View, Antarctica. Daphne is sleeping, but I have just informed Apollo.

"Good. Now comm Hadrian's rock and find out what all of this is about."

Of course. Slow seconds passed while I tapped my fingernails impatiently against the side of my glass. *I have just spoken to Tony, Robert. He knows nothing about any unusual medical problems that Hadrian may have.*

"Damn! Ask him where they are, if they're in Columbia Medical Center."

Tony refuses to give that information.

"Double damn!" A rock would do almost anything to protect its owner's privacy. "Tell him that this is his *father*, for god's sake!"

I have informed him. All he will tell me is that Hadrian is sleeping comfortably.

I uttered a lurid curse, then climbed heavily to my feet and shuffled apprehensively off to bed.

• • •

"Damn," said one of the innumerable government legalists the following morning in court when I had explained my needs. "Old Flounder-Face is a real martinet." She shrugged resignedly. "Well, I'll just have to ask."

She made her way to the bench as soon as court was convened and spoke softly to the judge. Judge Flanders glanced at me sharply, then crooked a finger imperiously. I moved in front of the bench.

"Your son is gravely ill?"

"Yes, Your Honor. In Columbia Medical Center."

"Do you have an affidavit in support of that claim?"

"No, Your Honor. My daughter-in-law called—"

"Can I reach your son through my rock?"

"I don't think so. I tried again this morning and—"

"Then can I reach his doctors?"

"I don't know who—"

Judge Flanders sat back in her chair with a plaintive sniff. "Aside from hearsay, do you have *any* cogent reason to believe that his life is actually threatened in the next few hours?"

"No, but—"

"Then as long as you are here, Mr. . . . er, Clayborn, I see no good reason why you can't, at the very minimum, finish your morning's testimony. If it isn't concluded by noontime, then I will grant you two days' absence from court, subject to your presenting an official affidavit upon your return." She glared down at me. "Satisfactory?"

"Perfectly, Your Honor," I muttered, suppressing a sigh.

The rest of the morning dragged by endlessly, as I knew it would, with the shysters for the plaintiffs first demanding to know just how it was that the crèches could charge different prices for different models, then getting irretrievably bogged down in the complexities of the quota and lottery systems that had gradually evolved over the decades to prevent like-minded parents from simultaneously placing orders for 300,000 major-league center fielders (left-handed, power-hitting, blue-eyed, heterosexual, loving and affectionate).

None of these nonsensical questions fell anywhere at all within my own field of competence, of course, and it took no great effort for the opposing shysters to make me look both foolish and ignorant. It was all a part of the endless legal game of discrediting one's adversaries, I suppose, but by the end of the morning I was bitterly asking myself why I hadn't taken the midnight shuttle to New York and risked old Flounder-Face's wrath at some future date.

Just as the ghastly courtroom tedium finally appeared to be coming to an end Angus commed me from my rock-pocket. *Your office wants you to stop by; they say it's extremely urgent.*

A bubble took me from the Federal Building on Pier 37 to my office in Washington Square. I ran up the steps and burst into the reception area. "Well? What's so urgent? I'm on the way to the airport."

The built-in vucom of Jane the Secretary, the faithful old Compaq I had bought secondhand thirty-one years ago, instantly lit up with the face of Filippo Hofstater, Senior Vice President of Design, at 3L in Chicago. His rather plump and self-satisfied features looked unexpectedly grim. "Robert," he said, "I've got to see you at once. Here, in Chicago." His face abruptly disappeared from the vucom.

"That's *all?*" I protested to Jane the Secretary. "That's his *message?*"

"After I explained that you were in court, that is all he said, Mr. Clayborn."

"Angus: get me Hofstater."

Hofstater here.

"This is Clayborn. What's so urgent in Chicago? There's no way in the world that I can—"

I simply can't tell you over the rockcom. You'll—

"But—"

—simply have to come to Chicago. Listen to me, Robert, you have to come. Now, immediately! This may be the most important thing you'll—

Something of his urgency and underlying panic began to communicate itself to me even across the rockcom. An

icy prickle ran up my spine. "Now?" I repeated plaintively.

*Now. When you get here . . . well, you'll see what I
mean.*

9

Chicago, of course, was more or less on my way to New York, so I protested no further. A bubble took me from Washington Square to the heart of the financial district, then up an express chute to the roof of the Ilona Staller Building just in time to catch an airshuttle lifting off for the airport south of the city.

Forty-five minutes later I was on a United hyper climbing steeply through the stratosphere. For a few brief moments I could look down on the Oakland side of the Bay and see the sprawling plant where Diversified Life gestated the hundreds of thousands of infants whose biogenetic integrity I was so staunchly defending in federal court.

It was odd, I mused uneasily, that in my thirty years of life-styling in the Bay Area I had never done business with Diversified Life, last year the fourth largest of the Big Seven in terms of gross revenues. Ever since my first contract with 3L for the Scottish Emperor most of my customized designs had been gestated in their crèche. But now I felt increasingly anxious as I neared Chicago and 3L's headquarters, and wondered if I might not have made a mistake in associating myself with them so closely. Certainly they were a highly reputable firm, and had a worldwide reputation for the quality of their products. But what on Earth could have upset Filippo Hofstater so much, and why was my presence so urgently needed?

• • •

As my bubble dodged effortlessly through downtown Chicago's late-afternoon traffic the cold foreboding that had gnawed at me throughout the flight grew to alarming proportions. Why did 3L insist on seeing *me*, a life-stylist? Because of a problem with one of my designs? Then why not say so over the rockcom? Could it be something so bad that—

The bubble came to a halt at the massive entrance of the 3L Building and I stepped down reluctantly to the sidewalk. For a long moment I hesitated before going through the doors. Finally, I squared my shoulders, marched across the spacious marble lobby, and took the jumper up to the sixty-third floor.

The receptionist behind the desk was, as befit the design department of the second-largest crèche in the country, a human being, not a mere construct from Compaq or ITT. And what a human being! I felt myself drowning in the liquid depths of her enormous violet eyes as she greeted me with as lascivious and knowing a smile as I had ever encountered. But after my initial pang of almost unbearable lust had passed my only reaction was a small, sour grimace. What else could you expect to find in the inner temple of the life-stylists?

"Robert." I turned at the sound of the voice to see the patrician heads of Filippo Hofstater and Bernard Alderman peering around the edge of a doorway halfway down the plushly carpeted hallway. Their faces were drawn and strained. A hand materialized around the doorway and beckoned me down the corridor.

"Well?" I demanded when I had stepped into a plain, nearly featureless cubicle. "Have you brought me here just to examine your receptionist? If so, it was worth it: I'll order three of them before I leave."

But neither Hofstater nor Alderman smiled, and with a sudden start I became aware of a medium-sized man with long dark hair curling over his ears standing silently in a corner. His face was grim; his arms were folded massively across his chest as he scrutinized me. His features seemed vaguely familiar but I was unable to put a name to him or his model. A Genesis Regal, perhaps? Obviously a top executive at 3L. At last he nodded minutely, but his eyes remained cold and hooded.

I stared at him a moment longer without returning his minimal greeting, then swung around to watch with growing dismay as the two executives from the styling department closed the door with meticulous precision, then solemnly gathered around a cluster of instruments set in the wall next to the doorway.

I couldn't make out exactly what they were doing, so I returned my attention to the obscurely disquieting room. It was small and windowless, with walls and ceiling of a curiously textured material I had never seen before. I looked down at the floor; instead of being carpeted, it was the same rust-colored, slightly porous material as the walls. Four chairs were pulled up to a small table; the room's only lighting came from a glowing white ball floating in the air over the middle of the table.

"Well?" I repeated, even more sharply. When there was still no response I plopped myself down in one of the chairs and glared up at the three executives angrily. The man standing in the corner returned my gaze dispassionately.

"Mmmm." Hofstater pursed his lips nervously. "We should be secure enough . . . I think." Alderman nodded cautious agreement, his eyes still fixed on a hand-held instrument with which he was apparently scanning the walls. Unexpectedly Hofstater dropped his hand onto my shoulder and patted it gently, as if preparing me for the worst. "Robert," he said softly with none of the cheerful bonhomie he normally projected. "Nothing you see or hear in this room must ever, ever leave it. Is that clearly understood?"

I pointedly held up my wristcom for his inspection. "I have urgent affairs in New York to attend to," I said between clenched teeth. "I have been waiting for your explanation for some time now. Would you kindly get on with it?"

Hofstater nodded, and dropped heavily into the chair beside me. "Show him, Bernard," he muttered.

"What *is* it?" I whispered, unable to tear my eyes away from the holoscopic image that had materialized across the room. I raised a trembling hand to point at the strange, primatelike creature that confronted us. Lying naked in what appeared to be a hospital bed, it was large and hairy, at least man-sized, with an apelike face.

"Here's another shot," said Alderman. This one had been taken from the side. It clearly showed a small vestigial tail.

"Well?" My voice sounded harsh and frightened to my ears. "You have a contract with the San Diego Zoo, perhaps? This is the latest model for the Congolese army?"

The ensuing silence was total. Several dozen more holograms succeeded one another, all of them showing the same hirsute primate. In many of them it was wearing a shapeless white hospital gown; then it was shown sitting at a table, eating a meal with a knife and fork, fastidiously lifting a glass of water to its broad, simian lips. My heart was racing with anxiety even before we came to the final unforgettable image: dull brown eyes focused on the pages of a slim book held in long pink fingers. I strained to see the title: *Metamorphosis, and Other Stories,* by Franz Kafka.

"Very apposite," said a matter-of-fact voice beside me. It was the Genesis Regal speaking for the first time.

"You are a literary critic?" I said in a defiant but shaky voice, trying to mask my horror with childish bravado.

He snorted derisively. "Hardly. I'm Wilson S. Huntington, Director Primarial of 3L."

"I see. And this hairy fellow enjoying the stories of Kafka?"

"His name, I think, for the moment must remain confidential. But this much I can tell you: the unfortunate human being you see before you is one of *your* designs from thirty years ago. It is, in fact, the TRW-432, of which twenty-nine thousand three hundred and fifty-four have been gestated. For the most part, they are well on their way to becoming the community leaders and statesmen they were projected to be."

I could only nod numbly, for I knew that particular model number by heart: it had been my very first sale. To the general public the TRW-432 was known as the Scottish Emperor; my own son Hadrian had been the initial model.

10

Hadrian's lusterless brown eyes blinked at me without recognition as I stepped hesitantly out of the quarantine lock into his hermetically sealed room at Columbia Medical Center. His lips and face twisted in hideous effort, but all he could utter was a soft, piteous croak.

"Hadrian?" I whispered.

The shaggy creature lying between the crisp white sheets bobbed its head minutely, then slowly, painfully stretched a long, hairy arm toward me. Half blinded by a sudden upwelling of tears, I stumbled forward and clasped his hand between my own. The back of his hand and fingers was as thickly matted with wiry, russet-brown fur as an Aberdeen terrier I had once owned; the palm was as smooth and hairless as my own. I pressed his warm brown hand tightly to my breast as the tears rolled unheeded down my cheeks.

"Hadrian," I murmured over and over as I rocked back and forth. "Hadrian."

At last a Nightingale gently removed my son's hand and laid his arm upon the bed. I pulled a chair forward to the edge of the bed and dropped into it leadenly. A dispenser in the Nightingale produced tissues, and while I dabbed at my eyes and cheeks she rolled smoothly to the other side of the bed to monitor the towering bank of instrumentation that was attached to Hadrian by a tangle of tubes and cables.

"Can you hear me?" I asked softly, staring down in bewilderment at the receding forehead, the broad flat nose with flaring nostrils, the heavy projecting jaw that had so inexplicably replaced my son's finely honed traits. The small portion of his face not covered by hair was now a rubbery dark brown indistinguishable from that of the chimpanzees who had capered for Patricia and me the day before at the San Francisco Zoo. "Can you understand me?"

The tormented brown eyes blinked up at me as the misshapen head turned slightly on a short, thick neck. "Ungh," he grunted, his chest heaving with the effort. "Ungh, *ungh!*"

"Oh god," I breathed, falling forward to bury my face in the cool white linen of his bed.

Your son would like to communicate with you through his rock.

I sat up with a start. Hadrian's gleaming red rock Tony sat on the white nightstand only inches away. How could I have forgotten Angus and my earlier attempts to reach Hadrian through the rockcom?

"Thank you, Angus. Please connect us now."

At once, Robert.

"Hadrian?"

Is that really you, Father? My vision's a little blurry.

I squeezed his hairy paw. "It's really me. Are you . . . uncomfortable?"

Not right now—I think I've stabilized for the moment.

"Stabilized?"

This . . . whatever's happening to me, it goes by fits and starts. For two or three days the bones become malleable, take on a new shape. That's uncomfortable. Then they seem to stabilize for a few days. Maybe by tomorrow my vision will have cleared up.

"But why didn't you tell me, why—"

What good would it have done? It was bad enough just having Jennifer seeing it happening.

"But you're my son! I could have—"

Could have what? Redesigned me?

I slumped in anguish at the awful words. "Please . . ." I whispered, "you don't think . . . you're not saying that . . ."

His monstrous ape's head lolled back and forth across the pillow while the Nightingale attended to some of the tubes

that ran down to his arm. *No. Of course not. It's just . . .
that when something like this happens to you, you don't know
what to think. How can this be* happening? *you wonder.* His
massive form stirred restlessly beneath the sheet. *You want
someone to blame, someone to make it right, someone to
make you* human *again!*

The agony that Angus managed to convey was nearly unbearable. I stroked Hadrian's hairy arm gently. "There's
hope, you know. You're not the . . . only one who—"

His eyes turned toward me. *There are others? The doctors
here said they'd never seen—*

"They probably haven't." Haltingly I told him about my
just-completed visit to Chicago and the headquarters of
Lightfoot Lads and Lasses. "Reports have been coming in
from all over the country for several weeks now. Somehow
they've managed to keep it out of the news."

How . . . how many?

I looked down at the bulky form beneath the sheet that had
once been my son's slim, graceful body. "Two hundred and
twenty-seven," I admitted reluctantly.

And all of them are like me?

"Yes," I whispered.

I mean the same model: they're all Scottish Emperors?

"Yes."

His lips twitched and he grunted deep in his throat. *Poor
Dad. How many of us are there?*

"Scottish Emperors? Twenty, thirty thousand."

And they're all going to end up like me?

"No!" I cried aloud. "Of course not! They won't let it!
They're working on it right now. It may be simple coincidence, a bad run in one small batch. If it isn't . . ." I took
a deep breath, exhaled noisily. "They'll stop it, find some
way to reverse it, something to—"

Make me human again?

"Don't *say* that! You *are* human!"

*Am I? I don't see Jennifer here—do you? I don't see any
doctors here except this mechanical Nightingale—do you? All
I see is a quarantine room that everyone except you is too
frightened to come into!*

"Hadrian, that's not *true!*"

Isn't it? Then where's Jennifer—where's my loving consort? Where's my mother?

"Your mother? Daphne? She's here?"

She's in Antarctica. She saw me over the vucom and almost threw up. Just like I do, every time I see myself in a mirror.

"I tell you, they're *working* on it!"

3L? I'll bet *they're working on it—working to save their own skins!*

I hung my head in abject silence. That was exactly what 3L was working on. When I stumbled out of their devastated headquarters two hours earlier they had been agonizing loudly as to whether the company could cover up the whole ghastly catastrophe or if they would be forced to reveal the news to the public. "Better we release it ourselves," urged Bernard Alderman, "playing it down as much as possible, than if it comes out and it looks as if we've been trying to conceal it."

"Whatever we say, no one's going to believe us anyway," said Filippo Hofstater gloomily. "Just one hologram of one of these monsters on the ten o'clock news and . . ." He shrugged miserably.

"Don't call them monsters!" I shouted. "That may be my *son* you're talking about!"

"Exactly," said the Director Primarial, Wilson S. Huntington, turning his grim glare in my direction. "One hologram, and everyone with a grain of common sense will know that a three-hundred-year-old firm with the reputation of 3L could never be responsible for such a catastrophe. What they'll *really* want to know is the life-stylist who made the faulty design in the first—"

"So *that's* why you wanted me to come to Chicago," I murmured incredulously. "You don't care what's happening to all these poor people, you're just concerned that *I'm* the one who's going to get the blame for—"

"—but don't worry, Clayborn," continued the director of 3L as if I hadn't spoken, "we'll do everything possible to ensure that you yourself—"

"You can handle it any way you like, you snuffleroot, but you're going to handle it without me." I was already on my feet and grabbing an astonished Filippo Hofstater by the shoulders. Puritan Ideators have a surprising turn of strength.

I jerked him roughly to his feet. "Open the door before I break it down," I said softly. To encourage him, I shook him briskly until his head snapped back and forth. "Now stand aside before you get trampled. If any of you limplocks want to talk to me sometime about something constructive, you can get me on the rockcom."

11

Wednesday morning I was sitting in the book-lined inner sanctum of my Washington Square offices desultorily drawing up a list of all the biogeneticists I personally knew when the voice of Jane the Secretary interrupted my gloomy reveries. "You have a certified call on vucom one."

Thirty-five years of adult life have taught me that certified calls are seldom good news. "Who is it?" I asked cautiously.

"A Dr. Aloysius Bruneau."

Aloysius Bruneau? A doctor? I felt my heart suddenly racing. I had spent all day yesterday in New York fruitlessly trying to find a doctor or geneticist who might have some possible explanation for what was happening to Hadrian. Could this Dr. Bruneau—

"Put him through," I said.

The concealed vucom in the corner of my office chimed melodiously. "You are Mr. Robert Clayborn?" asked the voice of Central Registry.

"Yes."

"Please imprint your thumbplate."

In my eagerness to speak to the doctor I had forgotten that this was a certified call. Why would a doctor be calling by certified vucom? I scowled, but rolled my thumb around the scanner on the side of my desk.

"Thank you, Mr. Robert Clayborn." The vucom chimed twice to announce the fact that the designated party in the

call had just been certified. "The time is 9:38:43.16 Pacific
Daylight Time. Go ahead, please."

A nondescript male face appeared on the vucom, most
probably a Mother Bell Downhome Stepper—not at all my
idea of what constituted a doctor. "Mr. Clayborn?"

"Yes. You're Dr. Bru——"

"You are hereby served."

The vucom chimed three times in quick succession and an
ornate document slid silently out of the faxslot on the front
of my desk. I stared at it incredulously, then raised my eyes
in bewilderment to the vucom. "Served? I thought you said
you were a doctor."

"I am, sir. I am the holder of a doctorate from Stanford
University in psychological multipersonal interaction."

"But—"

"Good day, sir."

The vucom chimed twice. "The time is 9:38:57.74 Pacific
Daylight Time. This has been a certified communication and
fax transimulation." The vucom screen once again became
a hand-tooled set of volumes by someone named Sir George
Trevelyan.

I cursed briefly but fervently, then turned my attention to
the document that had slid from my faxslot. I immediately
spotted my own name, a number of *whereases*, and the phrase
"one billion dollars and no cents in damages." I dropped
the paper as if it had burned me.

"Jane!" I screamed. "Emergency override! Get my shyster!"

Legalists consider it beneath their dignity, as well as a
complication to their time-billing, to converse with clients on
the rockcom, so I had to wait until the unctuous features of
my longtime shyster Judge Jayson Maslow came onto the
vucom. I had never bothered to learn where he had ever been
a judge, but I supposed him to be a competent enough legalist: every time I sent him a single-page document for examination he returned it with an additional nineteen pages
and a bill for several thousand dollars.

"Robert," he said cheerfully as his eyes flashed from one

side of the vucom to the other, unerringly appraising the value of my recently redecorated office.

"Jayson." I pushed the document into the faxslot. "Tell me in words of one syllable if this is actually what I think it is."

Judge Maslow's bushy eyebrows rose at the grimness of my voice. They rose even higher as he first scanned the document, then slowly read it through twice more. At last he laid it down and regarded me with a certain horrified relish. "If you think that this is a suit alleging that you, Robert Clayborn personally, along with Robert Clayborn Design and Lightfoot Lads and Lasses, jointly and severally and knowingly conspired to design, gestate, and merchandise totally defective goods, to wit, a 3L Scottish Emperor, model number TRW-432, present legal name Steven J. Tudal, then you are absolutely correct. If you further think that Steven J. Tudal is demanding one billion dollars in damages, then you are also absolutely correct. And if you further think that—"

Your consort Sylvina is calling, interrupted my rock Angus. *She has purchased a new rock to replace Minkle. She says that the communication is urgent.*

"Put her through," I commed him, then spoke aloud to Judge Maslow. "Will you wait a moment, Jayson? I have an urgent call."

"Go ahead—it will give me a moment to try to imagine what you could have conceivably done to damage someone to the extent of one billion dollars."

"Sylvina?"

Robert, something very strange has just happened—I don't understand it at all!

An icy fear suddenly enveloped me as images of hairy primates flashed through my mind. "Patricia? Is it—"

Of course it isn't Patricia. It's some man; a doctor, he says. He was very strange. He faxed me a piece of paper, some sort of document about—

"Where are you right now?"

In the upstairs sitting room. Why?

"Go into my study. Put the paper into the faxslot on my desk. Send it to Judge Maslow. Immediately! Do you hear?"

Of course I hear you! I'm not deaf, you know!

"Jayson," I said to the vucom, "Sylvina is sending a fax, you should—"

"It's coming in now. Hold on, I'll put Sylvina on vucom two. Ah, Sylvina! Good morning, my dear. Now then, what's this mysterious . . . hmmm . . . ha . . . I see . . ." He raised his eyes and stared at me quizzically. "Robert, what *have* you been up to? This is a writ of attachment, seizing your house and chattels on Broadway as surety for—"

"Seizing my *house?*" shrilled Sylvina over Judge Maslow's vucom. "What do you *mean*, seizing my house?"

"Actually, *Robert's* house, my dear. Surely you recall the consort-contract you signed, the one saying—"

"But he gave the paper to me! It's *my* house, it's where I *live!*"

"Well, yes, but legally all it takes is for the writ to be served to anyone on the premises who—"

"You mean they're going to take my *house* away from me? Robert!" screamed my Golden Exaltica loudly enough over Judge Maslow's vucom to make me wince. "Has this got something to do with that awful monster of yours? Robert, do you hear me? *Tell* me!"

While I was reluctantly explaining to my legalist what I had just seen in Chicago and New York, I was interrupted by Jane the Secretary—in spite of my formal orders to be left strictly alone. Almost with resignation I let her hand me the papers saying that the firm of Robert Clayborn Design had just been seized and all its assets frozen by order of the California Superior Court.

"Your house in Hawaii," mused Judge Maslow as he studied the latest set of documents, "that's in your name also?"

I nodded numbly.

"Then I suggest you sell it to Sylvina for one dollar and other valuable considerations—immediately!" He sighed gloomily. "It already may be too late. Sylvina, tell your bank to credit my escrow account at once."

"For one dollar?"

"For one dollar. Robert, I'm faxing you a bill of sale. Sign it and certify it on the thumbplate."

Half dazed, three minutes later I had concluded the transaction that transferred my $650,000 Kauai retreat to my consort Sylvina for one dollar—and, of course, other valuable considerations.

Judge Maslow nodded smugly. "That's *one* thing they won't get. Let's see now . . . bank accounts! Robert, your personal bank ac——"

But I was already coding my account at the Southern Bank of Alaska. Years ago, when it seemed for a few dizzy months as if an Apocalyptic Jeffersonian might actually be elected governor of Northern California, I had opened a bank account in Liechtenstein for unlikely emergencies. This looked like being the emergency I had had in mind.

The discreet logo of the Southern Bank of Alaska appeared on my desk's comscreen. *Do you wish to know your balance in all accounts?* it asked. *(Y/N)*.

I tapped *Y,* then scrutinized the screen. I had $11,749.01 in my checking account, $5,391.95 in my special account, $47,968.12 in my savings account, $125,000.00 in certificates of deposit, and $1,897,428.77 in my money market portfolio. I heaved a deep sigh of relief and began tapping the instructions that would instantly transfer my assets to the impenetrable sanctuary of Liechtenstein.

First my portfolio of blue-chip stocks and bonds. *Sell all securities instantly at market price,* I typed. *Credit all proceeds to Royal Bank of Liechtenstein, account num——*

Your portfolio cannot be sold, interrupted the bank. *It has been blocked by a prejudgment attachment order from the First Federal District Court of San Francisco, Case # 935/YDR/1425/QL.*

"What?" I gasped, unable to believe my eyes. Frantically I tried to instruct the bank to empty my other accounts. Finally I fell back limply in my chair, my chest pounding as if I had just run a double-marathon.

"They're already blocked?" asked Judge Maslow.

"They're already blocked."

"You mean you have no *money* in the bank?" cried Sylvina incredulously.

I shrugged despairingly. "That's what it looks like. Jayson, there must be *something* you can do."

Judge Maslow thoughtfully studied the tips of his manicured nails. "Of course, of course. Leave it to me. I'll immediately apply for a—"

Sylvina's icy enunciation sliced through his voice. "You are saying that we no longer have a house, nor money in the bank?"

"Only temporarily, my dear Sylvina," replied Judge Maslow, "only temporarily. Just as soon as I—"

"I see. Well, I don't know what *you* intend to do, but I know perfectly well what *I* am!"

Judge Maslow raised his eyes to mine and sighed softly as her lovely face vanished from his vucom. "A strong-minded lady, I fear."

"Yes," I muttered ungraciously. Who would have thought it in a Golden Exaltica?

12

By the end of the day another seven suits had been filed and Judge Maslow was looking at me anxiously over the vucom. "You *do* have insurance to cover this sort of thing?" he asked delicately. "As well as . . . legal fees?"

"Of course."

"Seven *billion* dollars' worth of insurance?"

"Well . . . a lot, anyway."

"I would advise you to check rather carefully," he said pointedly.

"I will. But first, let me say this: All of these suits have named me codefendant with 3L; moreover, they have unjustly attached all my personal property since they know they could never get away with such an outrageous procedure against 3L. But the truth of the matter, as any biogeneticist will tell you, is that neither I, nor my design of the Scottish Emperor, could conceivably be the cause of this horrible tragedy. When the truth is finally known, it will clearly show that the fault lies with 3L and their methods of gestation."

"But—"

"Let me give you a 'for instance,' Jayson. You will readily admit that even the most faultlessly designed bubble will eventually have a breakdown if somewhere on the production line the wrong alloy is inadvertently used in the manufacture of the impulsion chamber dampers. Obviously the same dangers are always inherent in the crèches, where far more complicated products than bubbles are being gestated. Equally obviously, 3L must be held responsible for their criminal neglect."

Judge Maslow nodded somberly. "Therefore . . ."

"Therefore I want you to separate me, and my company, from what is actually the sole responsibility of 3L. My son and I are just as much the victims of their gross incompetence as any of the other victims. I want you to immediately file suit against 3L on behalf of my son—for one billion dollars, since that appears to be the going rate. And I want you to file an additional suit against 3L on *my* behalf, charging malicious destruction of my professional reputation and livelihood. I think ten billion is a nice round figure, don't you?"

The Judge pursed his lips dubiously. "If you insist. Obviously you have a very strong *prima facie* case. But I'd be a little happier about it if all these other suits hadn't first been filed against—"

I snorted angrily. "Just think how happy you're going to be with the thirty percent of the eleven billion dollars that you're going to collect with your very strong *prima facie* case."

Before he could reply, I blanked the vucom and sat back to consider if I had enough money to afford a bubble to take me home.

Eventually I remembered that I had made an initial deposit of $1,000 upon opening my Liechtenstein bank account so many years ago. I called the Royal Bank of Liechtenstein and learned to my pleasure that this trifling amount had been increased by compounding interest to $2,372.84 as of that morning. I sighed a tiny sigh of very mitigated relief: that would cover my bare living expenses for a couple of weeks while Judge Maslow removed the writs and attachments that had so calamitously fallen upon me from a cloudless sky. And if worse came to worst, I told myself gloomily, I could always sell the house in Hawaii that had so providently been transferred into Sylvina's name before the legal vultures swooped. . . .

A few minutes later I left the hush of our offices for the late afternoon bustle of Washington Square—and stepped directly into a thick knot of newsfaxers and holoscans. While the holoscans floated around my head the newsfaxers clustered about me shouting frantically.

"Is it true that your own son is a monster?"

"What does he *really* look like? Can we—"

"How many others—"

"Was it your own sperm that—"

Red-faced and trembling with fury, I fought my way through the hyenas and back into the refuge of our lobby. There I sank into a chair, breathing heavily. "Angus: what's my pulse?"

Ninety-seven, Robert.

"When it's down to sixty, summon a bubble to the alley on the side of the building. Have it waiting by the door."

Of course, Robert.

Ten minutes later I climbed quickly into the waiting bubble, gave my destination, and hesitantly pressed my thumb to the thumbplate. To my vast relief the bubble moved off immediately. Only my ability to actually *pay* my bills seemed to have been frozen. I chuckled sourly: I was still free to run them up—at least for bubbles.

But for how long?

When the bubble came to a halt in front of our house on Broadway I saw that an even larger group of newsfaxers had gathered on the sidewalk awaiting my arrival. Some of them, I saw to my indignation, were even clustered under the front door portico. "Bubble," I said, "drive me directly to my door."

"SFPD vehicular regulation 934.52C forbids public bubbles of any sort to leave the street."

"But you could easily drive up my walkway and—"

"SFPD vehicular regulation—"

Teeth clenched, I got down from the bubble and pushed my way grimly through the newsfaxers while their hovering holoscans circled closely around me. In the wake of my passage two of the newsfaxers found themselves abruptly sitting in the brambles that bordered the walkway. When I reached the portico I was assailed by four more of the vultures. I brushed them aside without a word as Beach the Butler held the door open.

Once inside the vestibule I activated the recordall on the wall and spoke into the intercom. "I am now giving you formal warning as required by Section 310 of the Householders Code. You are hereby notified that you are trespassing on private property. In thirty seconds I will be activating a variable-intensity plasmatic sweep for which I have been issued police permit number 756RC of June twenty-sixth, 2337. The owoop will radiate outward from the house at a speed of two miles per hour and establish a twenty-thousand-volt perimeter at the sidewalk. You now have twenty seconds to withdraw."

Shrill sounds of alarm and indignation penetrated the door, but I watched with satisfaction as the newsfaxers scurried precipitously to the sanctuary of the sidewalk. A few seconds later the flickering blue line of energy moved slowly across the lawn and solidified just on the edge of the sidewalk. I knew that its garish glow would annoy my stuffy Presidio Heights neighbors, but their objections were far down on my list of concerns.

I left Beach the Butler mangling my hat and cloak with his usual ineptness and stamped noisily down the hallway. "Angus: you and Beach turn off all the vucoms. I will take no calls at all, particularly certified calls. If anyone gets beyond the sweep and seeks entrance, you are authorized to infuse them with a thirty-second pulse of Carmody's Baleful Rejoinder. Is that entirely clear? Good. Tell Sylvina to join me in the living room as soon as possible: we have much to discuss."

Sylvina is not in the house.

"Oh. Where is she, then?"

I do not know. She has left no message, and her rock is not in the house either.

I was growing increasingly exasperated. "For god's sake, Angus, don't be such an idiot: ask her rock where she is!"

Her rock—whose name, incidentally, is Antoinette—has been specifically ordered to reveal no information about her mistress.

"You mean she won't tell me where Sylvina is?"

That is correct.

I muttered something sharp and nasty that encompassed both Sylvina in particular and rocks in general, then trod heavily upstairs to my study. There was nothing from Sylvina on the desk's messager to indicate where she might be. I cursed again, then composed my features as much as I could and walked down the hallway to the nursery. It too was empty.

"Angus: where's Patricia?"

I do not know.

"Well, ask Ingrid the Nanny."

Ingrid the Nanny does not reply. In all likelihood she is out of my range.

I ground my teeth in frustration and sudden alarm. "Then ask Zoo-Zoo, for heaven's sake! At least *she* can't be out of range!"

Zoo-Zoo has been instructed not to reply to any inquiries regarding Patricia.

"What? *Who* told her not to reply?"

Patricia's legal guardian, Sylvina.

"But *I'm* her legal guardian! I'm her *father!* Angus: comm me directly to Zoo-Zoo. Zoo-Zoo: are you listening? This is—"

I am sorry, Robert, interrupted Angus, *but Hillis versus Ross in 2167 specifically holds that in the case of a minor child, a single parent, acting on behalf of that child, can invoke the child's right to absolute privacy in regard to communication with the other parent.*

"But we don't *know* that Patricia doesn't want to talk to me!"

That is substantially correct. But unless you obtain a court order from Children's Court, it must be assumed that she is entitled to her privacy. Zoo-Zoo will not reply to your messages.

"But this is grotesque!" I cried in a rage. "How do I know that Sylvina hasn't already sent her back to the crèche? How do I know that—"

Once again I was interrupted by Angus. *Excuse me, Robert, but a Mr. George Abbadecka, Esquire, has just reached me by rockcom; he has been trying unsuccessfully to contact you by certified vucom.*

"Good!" I snarled. "That's precisely why I turned it off! Tell both him and his rock to go snuffle—"

His rock informs me that Mr. George Abbadecka, Esquire,

is the legalist for your consort Sylvina and that it is impera-
tive that he speak to you about your daughter, Patricia.

My heart sank. "Put him on," I said wearily.

You will have to use the vucom in your study for a certified
call.

I returned to the study and seated myself apprehensively in
front of the vucom. "Go ahead," I said.

After the usual routine with Central Registry and my
thumbplate, I found myself confronted by the classical features of Sylvina's shyster, George Abbadecka. He was loath-
somely wavy-haired and bedimpled, an Harmonian Apollo in
the first flush of glorious youth, surely the most vulgar model
ever purveyed by one of the Big Seven. I groaned audibly:
how obviously the sort of repulsive physical specimen to
whom a featherbrained Golden Exaltica such as Sylvina would
turn for comfort!

The Harmonian Apollo ran a hand lovingly through his
waves of blond hair and favored me with a nod of genial
condescension. "Mr. Clayborn?"

"Unless Central Registry has unaccountably mistaken my
thumbprint. Well?"

"Well?"

"Well, what do you *want?*" I cried in a frenzy of impotent
rage as all of my apprehensions about Patricia and Hadrian
at last burst forth like a sudden jet of boiling lava.

His face cleared as he seized my meaning. "Oh. I see.
Well. I am obliged to inform you that pursuant to Article
760B(ii) of the Federal Guardianship Act of 2072, your legal
consort Sylvina Ashley has today instructed me to file a petition in Children's Court. This petition seeks redress for the
delivery of certain specified defective goods by having the
goods in question returned to their source of origin, that is
to say, the crèche owned and operated by Lightfoot Lads and
Lasses."

"Ridiculous," I said with as much conviction as I could
muster. "You're wasting your time and your billing. For your
information, I have no money whatsoever, nor does my consort: you will never be paid. Furthermore, no judge will ever
grant her petition. First, it is totally without merit. Second,

3L is merely the gestating agent. Patricia is an individualized design created by the eminent life-stylist Sam-Day Dowree. Two hundred years of court rulings have held that in such unfortunate cases as this one, the responsibility is solely that of the life-stylist. It is useless trying to return Patricia to the crèche; it is from the life-stylist that you must seek redress.'' I felt no compunction at all about pointing this ghastly shyster in the direction of my onetime friend Sam-Day Dowree—for after all, it *was* Dowree who was responsible for any genetic defects that Patricia might have. But even more important, Dowree had retired two years ago to a mountain lake in Switzerland and was now far beyond the jurisdiction of any San Francisco Children's Court. It would take years for Sylvina's legalist to even get the case to court.

The Harmonian Apollo pursed his lips over his steepled fingers. ''Ah. An interesting point to be sure, one that I have already researched. But sadly, Mr. Dowree was killed this winter in an avalanche. His design studio was dissolved upon his retirement, leaving no associates. I think you will find, Mr. Clayborn, that in this case the responsibility clearly reverts to the gestating crèche.''

''That's *your* opinion. Look,'' I said, trying not to sound as if I were begging, ''I'll try to get you off the hook. Just let me speak to Sylvina. I—''

''I'm sorry, Mr. Clayborn, but I have been specifically instructed not to divulge her whereabouts or that of her child.''

''*Her* child? She's *my* child too, you idiot! If Sylvina's crazy enough to hire *you,* how do I know that she hasn't already killed her? Ground her up for dog food, maybe, and sold her to—''

''Mr. *Clayborn!''* The stupefyingly handsome features of the Harmonian Apollo twisted into as horrified an expression as they were capable of. ''The child is a ward of the *court!* She—''

Numbly, without conscious thought, I blanked the vucom and sat staring blankly at the study's old-fashioned red-and-gold-flocked wallpaper while the gray evening fog blew past the window.

"Angus," I cried despairingly. "What do I do now?"

I don't know, Robert. Even after two hundred and twelve years on Earth, there is much that I have to learn about the human heart. May I suggest that you consult your own legalist?

13

That night I slept very badly. Around dawn I drifted off to a troubled sleep, only to jerk awake in sudden panic. After a while I dimly recalled that in addition to all my *real* problems this was the morning I was supposed to reappear in federal court to defend General Diversity against charges of gross incompetence in the gestation of their children. A few days earlier I might have appreciated the grotesque irony; now I could only groan softly and wait for my racing heart to subside. Finally I ordered Angus to tell André the Chef to begin breakfast; I arose and staggered blearily off to the bathroom.

As I sat in the kitchen drinking my second cup of chocolate the thick layers of sticky cobwebs that enveloped my brain gradually began to loosen. "Angus," I muttered, "you must have talked with some of the rocks who were in court on Monday with the government legalists. Try to get hold of one of the legalists before he leaves for court. I'll talk to him on the rockcom."

Eventually I obtained the chief government shyster herself, Kiwen Figour. "I've been waiting for your call," she said. "You were featured prominently on last night's newscasts."

"I was?"

"Demonstrating a very superior technique of drop-kicking two newsfaxers into the bushes. I suppose you're calling to say that you've been arrested for assault?"

"That would almost be a relief. No, I'm calling to ask that

I be relieved from the case. If you've been following me in the news, you know that my testimony is now worthless."

"Hmmm . . . Clayborn the Monster Maker. . . . Excuse me, I'm just thinking out loud, that's what I heard someone call you. I think that I have to agree: your testimony can hardly be of help to our case. I'll do what I can with Judge Flanders to have you dismissed without actually reappearing."

I thanked her perfunctorily and turned my thoughts to more important matters. I called Hadrian in New York and learned that there had been no worsening in his condition. He was resting comfortably and his vision had cleared. He too had watched me on the morning news as I drop-kicked the newsfaxers into the brambles. After twenty minutes of conversation with my son I tried once again to reach Sylvina or Patricia but with no results. I had just begun to wonder how much I could get for the house in Hawaii when Beach the Butler informed me via Angus that someone was coming up the front walkway.

"Who turned off the sweep?" I began angrily. "I—"

The plasmatic sweep is still on, Robert. It appears to have been temporarily circumvented.

Now what? Could it possibly be Sylvina and Patricia . . . ?

Heart thudding in my chest, I raced down the hallway to the vestibule and peered through the scanner. I saw a Life/Love Trustworthy in the neat beige uniform and purple-plumed hat of the San Francisco County Sheriff's Department. Come to arrest me for assaulting the newsfaxers? I sighed and opened the door onto the portico. "Sheriffs can walk through twenty thousand volts of energy?" I asked sourly.

His teeth glittered cheerfully in a broad, nut-brown face. "Only when they're on official business: we have an override for every plasmatic sweep in San Francisco County. That's why their frequencies have to be registered."

"Am I to take it then you're on official business?"

"Afraid so. I'm Deputy Sheriff Alton Murray. You're Mr. Robert Clayborn?"

I grimaced in resigned agreement; he handed me a number of papers. I glanced through them fatalistically: they were the formal notice of the sheriff's seizure of my house and chattels as surety for the billions of dollars in lawsuits that now encumbered me.

"This includes my *wine* cellar?" I asked despairingly.

"Afraid so, Mr. Clayborn. All you're allowed to take with you are personal items such as clothes, papers, deplaquer, rock, stuff like that. I've got to check it all before you leave." Deputy Sheriff Murray leaned closer and lowered his voice. "But I think I could classify a couple of bottles of wine as a man's personal goods."

"Spoken like a true Californian. Come down and help me choose some." As we walked down the stairs to the cellar I commed Beach the Butler to begin packing my affairs. For twenty minutes Murray and I wandered back and forth between my thousands of friends in their neatly ordered ranks, earnestly appraising vintages and vineyards, holding an occasional bottle carefully up to the light. Finally I selected four bottles of cabernet sauvignon: two thirty-year-old BV Private Reserves, two forty-year-old Tudal Estates. I handed one of each to the friendly deputy.

"Gee, Mr. Clayborn, you don't have to do this! I wasn't hinting that—"

"Take it," I insisted. "They'll warm up a cold evening sometime."

"That they surely will," he murmured, clutching the bottles reverently to his breast. "I'll think of you, Mr. Clayborn, and drink to your health. And to your son's as well."

My eyes brimmed with tears at the unexpected words: it was the first sympathy I had heard expressed for Hadrian's awful plight since the nightmare had begun.

We returned upstairs, where Murray looked perfunctorily through the bags that Beach the Butler had prepared. "It all looks like personal affairs to me," he said, "and I hereby certify that this is so and make it part of the official record." He spoke briefly into his recorder. "Where will you be going from here after I seal the house?" he asked.

"I really don't know. Down to my office, I suppose, and then to a hotel." I gestured wryly at the chaste marble splendor of the ancient hallway. "It's hard to believe when you see all this, but right now I have hardly any money."

Deputy Sheriff Murray glanced over his shoulder as if fearing an eavesdropper. "I saw you hardly looking at those papers I gave you," he said softly. "I'm in my third year of law school, and I *did* look through them. Looks to me like there's a defect in the description of the house on page two. Isn't that a garage off to the left as you come up the walk? With servants' quarters above it?"

I nodded. The garage probably hadn't been used in a hundred years now, ever since public bubbles had mostly replaced private ones, and electronic servants replaced live ones.

Murray winked conspiratorially. "Looks like all these billion-dollar shysters were so busy seizing your house they forgot about the garage. Far as I'm concerned you can move in right now, at least you can until they find out about it." He reached down to lift one of my bags. "Let's carry them on over. Just don't let anyone know where you got the idea."

No one had informed Beach the Butler that he could no longer work for me: I left him clearing away the accumulation of a century of cobwebs from the tiny apartment over the garage and had Angus summon a bubble to take me downtown.

My insurance agent was a large, jovial Clydesdale from Mother Bell named Andy Boulanjer. At least he had always been jovial during the twenty-five years or so that I had dealt with him over the vucom and inflated his company's bank account with my quarterly premium credits. Now he looked distinctly uncomfortable as I sat across from him for the first time in his twelfth-story office on Montgomery Street.

"Robert," he said, looking down at the backs of his enormous hands. "I wish this could be a happier occasion."

"So do I. It's been a terrible shock. All those people, my own son . . ."

"Oh. That too, of course. Terrible, terrible." His eyes found the corner of the ceiling. "But what I meant to say was . . ." His voice trailed off.

"That it's never a happy occasion for an insurance company when it faces the prospect of repaying some of its premiums," I concluded for him, beginning to feel distinctly uneasy. "However—"

"—that's what premiums are paid for, of course, and I must say that in many ways Mutual World has never had a better client than Clayborn Design."

"In *many* ways?" I echoed indignantly as a clammy hand suddenly squeezed my heart. "In *every* way! In twenty-six years you've never paid a nickel in—"

"True, true," muttered Andy Boulanjer, his eyes now focused intensely on his work station's comscreen. "Yes, it's all here right in front of me; a fine record, Robert, a very fine record indeed."

"So glad to hear you finally admit it. Now let's cut the crackle, Andy, and get down to business. Fax us up some copies of my policies and let's take a look at them. I know that the malpractice provision covers all legal fees and direct loss of revenues; what I can't remember is whether liability goes to two hundred and fifty million or five hundred million. Not that it really matters, of course, what with California law limiting liability to one million dollars, thank god for small favors, but—"

"That one-million-dollar limitation is only for unintentional and nonmalicious accidents and misjudgments," interrupted Boulanjer.

"Well, of course. Just as it is in my case. Now—"

"I'm afraid . . ." began Andy Boulanjer apologetically. "Here, look at this . . . it was just faxed to me by the main office in West Hartford."

I scowled down at the fax. It appeared to be saying that I had purposely, consciously, and intentionally conspired to design fatally defective goods, a deliberate criminal action. This thereby instantly rendered my entire coverage invalid.

Feeling sick, I looked up. Andy Boulanjer had swung around in his chair so that his back was to me; his head was cocked as if he were listening to the faint strains of distant music.

"You can't mean this."

He swung around, but refused to meet my eyes. "I'm afraid *they* do, Robert. I'll protest, of course, on your behalf, but you know what the head office is like once they make up their mind about something. Tell you what: why don't you call back this afternoon and I'll—''

But I was already on my way to the door.

I walked—or staggered—like an automaton back to my offices in Washington Square, hardly aware of what I was doing. When I turned into the tiny square I saw that only two newsfaxers appeared to be waiting outside the door but that a dozen or more holoscans hovered in the air above them. All the national chains were represented, I saw, as well as the BBC, Agence Europe, and Tass. I backed away before they spotted me, then hurried around the block to the alley by which I had made my escape the night before. It was free of newsfaxers, but in their stead I found another surprise: the door to my office had been sealed shut by the Sheriff's Department. A second seal had been affixed on top of the first: that of a federal marshal acting on the orders of the Third Federal District Court.

"Wonderful," I muttered half aloud, "terrific. First they sue me for a billion dollars, then they bankrupt me so they can be certain of not being paid. It all makes sense, Angus; it all makes sense."

It does, Robert? To me it makes no sense at all.

"It makes sense if you're a halfwit. Or a legalist." I slumped back against the alley wall, wondering what to do next. Finally I did what Angus had suggested I do the night before: call my own legalist. I gave Angus the instructions. Two minutes later Judge Maslow grudgingly took my call over the rockcom rather than a vucom.

I have some rather bad news, he said before I could launch upon my own lengthy list of complaints. *I've just been notified by the Attorney General's office in Washington that they will be impaneling a federal grand jury to investigate whether charges of sabotage, and possibly treason, should be brought against you for your deliberate and criminal effort to discredit, even destroy, a vital national interest.*

Did I reel back in shock against the wall of the alley at his words? I no longer remember, but I doubt it. The horrendous buffetings I had suffered in the last five days had so numbed me that an additional charge of treason seemed little more

than a grotesque climax to everything that had gone before.
I do recall hearing myself laughing bitterly.

"That's all?" I asked gaily. "No charges of assassinating
the President, celebrating a Black Mass on the steps of the
Capitol, snuffling the Nine Old Wo——"

*You seem to be taking this very lightly, Robert. Let me
assure you that it is a matter of the utmost gravity.*

"If I'm laughing it's because I'm close to hysteria."

*Hrmph! Robert: I must now advise you that I can no longer
represent you. Matters have become far too serious. For your
own welfare, you will have to obtain the services of a criminal legalist.*

This time I really *did* laugh. "More rats deserting the ship,
eh?"

What? What's that?

"I was just thinking out loud, it's the name of the new fall
line from Apple-Boeing: the Giant Rat of Sumatra." I took
a deep breath of the cool summer air, trying to fight down
the incipient panic and hysteria I could feel lurking just beneath the surface. "I'm glad you advise me to get a criminal
legalist," I said at last. "According to my insurance agent,
I can't even afford to pay *you.*"

What do you mean?

"They've just cancelled my policies; that's why I was calling you. So how do you suggest that I pay for a *criminal*
legalist?"

There was a long silence, of the sort generally called pregnant.

So they've cancelled your policies, have they? mused Judge
Maslow. *How very unfortunate. In that case, Mr. Clayborn,
I can only suggest that you apply for redress from whoever it
was who paid you to turn all of those poor helpless children
into monsters in the first place.*

14

Four weeks later the world's news media reported that 2,976 of my Scottish Emperors had now turned into speechless, hairy primates. On Wall Street, 3L stock had fallen from 106 to 23; the rest of the Big Seven had seen their own stock fall by at least 50 percent as sales for the first two weeks of August were off 90 percent from the previous year. In spite of the soothing bulletins being issued by 3L in Chicago, medical science was no closer to an explanation of either the cause or the mechanism of the transformations than it had been the day I first visited Hadrian in his hermetically sealed room at Columbia Medical Center.

The only bright spot in this ghastly tragedy was that somehow, in spite of their monstrous forms, the helpless victims had so far retained their mental faculties and an apparent good physical health. But the state of their mental health was another matter: in a single month seventy-nine of the young men who had metamorphosed into primates had despaired enough of their condition to commit suicide. In the entire *year* of 2344, there had been no more than sixty-three authenticated cases of suicide in the United States.

The news of each transformation, and of each death, was like a jagged knife plunging into my innards. Unable to sleep at night without a hypnogram, soon I was unable to venture out of my hideaway above the garage without risking physical assault from relatives of the victims.

Their reaction I could understand and sympathize with: I

myself wanted to hit out and smash whatever I could of 3L for causing my son to become a monster; their suffering was my own. But more disturbing to me was the wave of fear that was now beginning to seize the rest of the Northworld's population, a population of which 99 percent had been gestated in a crèche. How long, everyone seemed to be asking, before Robert Clayborn turns *us* into monsters?

My face was now as ubiquitously visible on the holoscopes of the four Northworld continents as that of President Kruger—and far less tolerantly regarded. Clayborn the Monster Maker was the most general epithet I heard applied to myself in the streets; I also heard Clayborn the Kiddie Killer and others even more appalling.

Most of my waking hours were taken up by interminable interrogations by one branch or another of the federal and state governments. A team of bodyguards was assigned to keep their star witness in good health: henceforth I shuttled through the skies of San Francisco in an elaborate armored aircar, much as if I had been a visiting despot from the Southworld.

An unforeseen benefit of becoming a permanent witness for the FBI, CIA, ERS, SEC, Department of Defense, Department of Human Services, and a federal grand jury was that no time at all remained for me to be harassed by the legalists representing the two thousand or more individuals who had now filed suits against me.

The cost, however, was the almost immediate loss of my living quarters. No longer could I slink in and out of my garage apartment on Broadway unnoticed. The legalist of a vengeful claimant had now spitefully amended the writ of attachment to include the garage, and the last tiny bit of my magnificent Presidio Heights home was irrevocably sealed against me.

I bid a silent farewell to Beach the clumsy Butler, and with nothing more than Angus and two suitcases moved into a small furnished room in the bachelor officers' quarters of China Basin Naval Station. Here, the government told me, my security could be assured; nonetheless, in return I was obliged to pay over $116.72 in rent every Friday afternoon.

In spite of the fact that my federal bodyguards—or, de-

pending on your point of view, warders—were free of charge,
the limited funds I had managed to spirit away to Liechtenstein continued to dwindle. My passport had long since
been taken away from me, and a federal judge had approved
the continuous surveillance of my movements by a permanent
stick-tight.

For a few desperate days I considered making a dash for
Hawaii and my winter retreat on the island of Kauai; then I
recalled that in order to save my home I had purportedly sold
it to Sylvina for one dollar and other valuable considerations.
Without much hope, I glumly called a real estate agent on
Kauai and instructed him to sell my home as quickly as possible. A few hours later he returned my call to indignantly
inform me that its rightful owner, a certain Sylvina Ashley,
had sold it for $497,000 ten days earlier.

Briefly but bitterly I considered advising the Eternal Rev-
enue Service's integrator to keep an electronic eye out for the
$496,999 in profit that my consort might, or might not, be
declaring; then recalled with a start that legally Sylvina was
still my consort. In all probability she and her legalist the
wavy-haired Harmonian Apollo were even now seeking ways
to make *me* pay the taxes on her transaction. . . .

But whatever injuries Sylvina did me, I told myself firmly,
they were no longer of any real consequence: all I wanted
from her was my daughter, Patricia. Every thirty minutes,
day and night, my rock Angus commed Sylvina's rock Antoinette. Every thirty minutes he was instantaneously informed from wherever Antoinette was in the solar system that
Sylvina's and Patricia's present whereabouts could not be di-
vulged, that neither of them would speak to me.

Unable to afford a legalist to defend myself in my own
morass of problems, I used the last of my funds to hire a
rosy-cheeked youngster fresh from law school to at least represent me in Children's Court at a preliminary hearing on
Sylvina's petition to return Patricia to the crèche. My youthful—but gratifyingly cheap—shyster had just enough competence to gain a three months' delay; not enough competence
to petition the judge to grant me access to my daughter via
rockcom.

Nevertheless I left court with my soul slightly less burdened than when I had entered: at least Patricia was safe for the next three months from whatever fate might await her at the crèche. Flanked by my ubiquitous federal escorts, I returned to my stark room at China Basin Naval Station. There I pondered the testimony I was scheduled to give under oath the following day to the Security Exchange Commission at its offices in the Bank of Taiwan Building.

Well might you ask why a bankrupt and besieged life-stylist should be of interest to the august body that policed Wall Street. The answer, of course, was money, billions and billions of dollars of it. That was what had been lost on the sudden calamitous drop in the price of shares of the Big Seven, foremost among them 3L. An equal amount had been lost in the stocks of smaller service companies whose fortunes were tied exclusively to the life-industry—Bailey Baby Foods, for instance, and a host of others. A thousand anonymous tipsters—all of them surely disgruntled speculators—had called the SEC to assure them that I had purposely created the Clayborn Monsters in order to reap a fortune by going short on my shares in the Big Seven as their values plummeted.

Like trying to argue with those flying-saucer lunatics who still survived in the backwoods and school boards of Arkansas, it was impossible to absolutely prove a negative: the more I showed that I had never owned any stock whatsoever in any of the Big Seven or their subsidiary industries, the more the inquisitors of the Security Exchange Commission became convinced that I had used superhuman cunning to conceal all traces of my nefarious activities in numbered accounts in Luxembourg and the Fiscal Republic of New Guinea.

I suppose that I might have found all of this frenzied self-righteousness amusing—except for the fact that when I finally escaped the Star Chamber of the SEC it was to pass into the hands of the accountants and legalists from the FBI and the CIA for the next six days. All of these idiots, as well as those from the Department of Defense, were utterly convinced that Robert Clayborn was the capstone in a plot perpetrated by our poverty-stricken enemies in the Southworld to destroy the very basis of American civilization. How could I argue with such nonsense except by simply denying it—and then denying it again?

In most of the Southworld, I imagine, I would have immediately been taken to the torture chambers. Physical torture isn't always all that effective in actually extracting the truth, I hear, but how emotionally satisfying it must be to use against your enemies!

But torture in the United States has been refined to a far more exquisite level; here it consists of being surrounded by a roomful of legalists and being remorselessly pecked to death. After three full days of this treatment I could no longer withstand the agony: I pleaded with a federal magistrate to let me waive my constitutional right to protection from self-incrimination. The magistrate agreed; two hours later I was lying on a table in FBI regional headquarters undergoing deep brainscan.

Three days later I was turned out on the streets of San Francisco by a disgusted crew of CIA and FBI interrogators. Nothing in the sixteen Delphanian Layers of my conscious and subconscious to which they had legal access could be found to connect me to the Southworld except the memory of a single dinner of couscous eaten in a Moroccan-style restaurant in Aix-en-Provence twenty-three years before. The Department of Defense grudgingly accepted this assessment; the SEC, ERS, federal grand jury, and San Francisco district attorney plunged ahead with their own investigations.

That night I sat in my gloomy naval barracks chatting glumly with Angus. "So far as I can tell," I said, "the only people not engaged in suing me or investigating me are the United States House of Representatives and Senate. I wonder why?"

Perhaps it is because both houses of Congress have recessed for the summer?

"Angus, you're a genius." I poured myself a glass of sticky red wine from a gallon jug. "I suppose there was no answer from Antoinette?"

None. I will try again in thirteen minutes.

"I only wish that—"

Robert, your son Hadrian is calling.

"Hadrian? Put him through."

Father? Are you watching the news?

A sharp pang of fear shot through me. "What is it? What's happened now?"

Nothing to get excited about. It's just something that you might find interesting. It's on FBS. It's very late here: I'll talk to you in the morning.

I told Angus to switch the room's small holoscope to FBS, the earnest but tedious all-news network that specializes in politics and out-of-the-way events, then leaned forward to see what Hadrian found worth calling me about. The holoscope came on and once again, just as at the very inception of this nightmare, I found myself unexpectedly confronted by the jowly features of my onetime friend from Arkansas, Titus T. Waggoner.

"—humbly bow before the ineffable wisdom of those mighty Founding Fathers and Mothers," he declaimed with an oratorical flourish of his right hand, "those legendary Visionaries whose dream it was to make of Arkansas an impregnable citadel for all those who . . ." I instantly decided that it could only be a campaign speech of some sort. Sure enough, a few moments later Titus roared, "And *when* I have been chosen by the good people of Arkansas as their Adjudicator Temporal, I shall restore that hallowed institution to the sacrosanct purity that it once enjoyed and that the present incumbent has so sullied by his . . ." I shook my head in dismay: what a ghastly windbag poor old Titus was becoming! His political rhetoric was amusing enough for a few brief moments, I supposed, but why Hadrian had found it interesting enough to—

"Unable to explain to the outraged people of Arkansas just *why* he has so scandalously permitted the 1900-discovery of gamma rays to pass his board of review and henceforth pervert the innocent minds of our noble Visionary youth," shouted Titus T. Waggoner to a great roar of indignation from his unseen audience, "the present incumbent now seeks to besmirch my own good name by a vicious personal attack upon my probity. 'Clayborn!' he cries mindlessly. 'What about your close friend Clayborn the Monster Maker?' "

Titus T. Waggoner shook his head in dismay at the enormity of the charge; I fell back in my hard wooden chair with

a despairing groan. Even in Arkansas . . . "My opponent
seeks to brand me with my friendship for Clayborn the Monster Maker," whispered Titus T. Waggoner. "He seeks to
turn an innocuous and youthful friendship into the blackest
of guilt. And yet my opponent ignores the fact that in spite
of the naive Robert Clayborn's obvious ignorance and mis-
guidance, Robert Clayborn in spirit is far from being an enemy of the great Visionary people! My opponent ignores the
cold fact that Robert Clayborn is now nothing more than the
helpless scapegoat of all the privileged interests of the godless military-industrial bottlers! My opponent ignores the fact
that Robert Clayborn's own son lies a helpless victim of the
Satanic mills that day and night spew out their unnatural
spawn upon the world. My opponent ignores the fact that the
miserable Clayborn is even now being martyred as if he alone
were responsible for the plague that is sweeping the godless
Northworld, the plague that is the inevitable consequence of
three centuries of overweening pride and Satanic folly by the
industrialized nations of the world!"

Titus paused for breath and fixed his invisible audience
with a glittering eye. "But rather than confining himself to
his constitutionally mandated duties of defending our precious visionary way of life from the unspeakable dangers and
encroachments of the industrial-military bottlers who so
threaten our embattled way of life, the present Adjudicator
Temporal finds only the time to defame my own good name
and that of that honest friend of all Visionaries, Robert Clayborn! My opponent's cruel and unconscionable insinuations
are an affront to all right-thinking and fair-minded Visionaries!" An even louder roar greeted this declaration; when it
had died away I sat half listening in horrified shock while
Titus went on to castigate the incumbent Adjudicator Temporal for a whole host of additional sins that escaped my full
comprehension.

How could Titus *do* this to me? I asked myself despairingly. Didn't he know that the attorney general's office was
already trying to link my purported crimes to the primitive
vicenaries of Arkansas with whom I had once so notoriously
loved and lived? Didn't he know that the federal attorney was
trying to convince the grand jury that through the Visionar-

ies' unspeakable blandishments I had been persuaded thirty years before to deliberately sabotage the lives of thousands of helpless human beings?

Angrily I told Angus to blank the holoscope. Titus T. Waggoner was a part of my past that I had hoped to put behind me; already the lunatic inhabitants of the state of Arkansas had once nearly deprived me of my son. Now it appeared that they were bent on depriving me of whatever liberty—

A person would like to speak to you by rockcom, interrupted Angus.

"A person? What person?"

A Miss Jeanie Norman. Shall I put her through?

For a moment I actually stared blankly at the wall in front of me, wondering who on Earth this could be. Then remembrance came, with the impact of an electric shock. *Jeanie Norman!* My former lover—and kidnapper of my child! She too must have seen Titus T. Waggoner and—

"Where is she?" I whispered.

I will inquire. At this present moment she is in the bedroom of her home in Russellville, Arkansas. Her rock, incidentally, is named—

I collapsed leadenly onto my room's narrow cot, dimly aware of the blood pounding in my ears and of my racing heart. Disjointed thoughts swirled through my head. Jeanie Norman . . . it had been thirty years since she kidnapped my son . . . that same tormented son who now lay in a hospital bed, pitifully estranged from all the world, a hopelessly disfigured primate . . .

Painfully, blindly, I seemed to be groping toward some half-seen, half-felt revelation. Suddenly I had it, and even as a part of my mind told me that it made no sense at all, the incredible shattering truth came to me. Now everything was clear: it was Jeanie Norman, and her unspeakable deed committed upon my son thirty years ago, who was obscurely but unquestionably at the origin of all my present agony.

"No!" I shouted in sudden fury as I jumped to my feet. "Never! Tell her I'll *never* talk to her! Tell her never to call me again!"

I have told her. She says that she understands. She says

that she will always wait for you to call her. She asks for your forgiveness. She says that her thoughts will always be with you.

For a moment I stood staring at the rock in my hand. Then I threw myself on the bed and wept.

15

The clothing-optional beach on the northwest side of Presidio Park was directly exposed to the icy summer winds that swept in from the Pacific, but today the morning was exceptionally calm and warm. The ocean looked as gray and chilly as ever with its low swells rolling in to die upon the white sands of the small alcove at the base of a rocky bluff, but the mid-morning sun was high in a cloudless blue sky and the immense arch of the freshly repainted Golden Gate Bridge at the northern tip of the park sparkled in the dazzling sunlight.

I shielded my eyes from the sun as I stepped down from the bubble that had brought me through the cool, dark woods of the park to this small asphalted parking lot between Piper's Plot and Houfek State Beach. A dozen or so private bubbles and aircars sat in the sunlight, a conspicuous sign of the deep-rooted eccentricity for which a certain stratum of San Francisco society was so celebrated. For a moment I stood wondering if any of these private vehicles could belong to the thousands of sedate citizens who lay naked on the large state beach that stretched off to my left. I supposed not: only those zany enough to find their enjoyment on the clothing-optional beach would be ostentatious enough to flaunt their ownership of a private bubble. With a sigh I hefted my rolled-up towel and turned toward the small changing room at the far end of the parking lot.

"Are you *certain* this is where I have to go?" I asked

Angus sourly as I stepped out of my clothes and folded them neatly on a bench.

I am certain. You are to be in the middle of Piper's Plot at precisely ten A.M. *Pacific Daylight Time.*

I could feel my heart beating faster as I stood naked, scowling down at the ridiculous red-and-white garment I held in my hands. "And you're *certain* Patricia will be there?"

No, Robert. I am only certain that news of your daughter will be communicated to you at that time.

Feeling as obscurely perverted as when my third consort Isabelle used to insist that we make love in total darkness while recording our activities in ultra-red, I began to pull on the long, tight-fitting red outfit I had procured earlier that morning from a dubious specialty shop on Fulsom Street. It had white stripes around its arms and legs and was called a bathing costume. "And you're *certain* that all of this is necessary?"

I am certain, Robert.

Reluctantly I moved out of the changing room and back into the sunlight. "I don't see why you have to be so mysterious about it all," I said aggrievedly. "I didn't even know that rocks *could* be mysterious."

I am sorry, Robert. But all will be made clear.

I stepped gingerly onto the hot sand of Piper's Plot, feeling like a fool in my bathing costume. None of the several hundred other fools in various kinds of bathing attire took any apparent notice of my arrival. As I trudged slowly forward I scrutinized the several dozen small clothed children playing happily here and there among their irresponsible parents. None of them was Patricia.

Stop, commanded Angus. *This is the middle of the beach. Spread out your towel and relax in the sun. Try to make yourself inconspicuous.*

I snorted angrily. How could I *not* be conspicuous, dressed as I was like a clown in the circus? Nevertheless, I spread my towel on the burning sand and tried to make myself comfortable. It was impossible to heed my rock's injunction to relax; I fidgeted anxiously on the towel, examining everyone who came onto the beach, impatiently demanding the time from Angus every few seconds.

Slowly, interminably, unbearably, ten o'clock approached. At last Angus whispered into my mind: *It is ten* A.M. *Pacific Daylight Time, Robert.*

I sat up with a start. "Then where—"

Remain casual, Robert. Do not look around. She is approaching.

My heart leaped up. *"She?* It's Patricia?"

You will see shortly.

To my acute disappointment, it was only a pair of long, shapely legs that came into my field of vision. I raised my eyes as the woman sank gracefully onto the towel beside me. Her arms and legs were ivory white and nicely formed; the rest of her body was effectively concealed by a loose-fitting blue-and-white bathing costume in whose elaborate folds the shape of her torso was totally hidden. A transparent green swimming buoy hung around her neck like an outsize necklace, and her eyes were masked by an enormous pair of dark glasses. White sun lotion covered her lips, nose, and cheeks, while a bright yellow rubber bathing cap covered her hair and came halfway down her forehead.

"This is being inconspicuous?" I muttered testily as she wiggled her buttocks comfortably into the sand.

"Look around us: no one is paying any attention at all."

It was true: the arrival of my grotesquely attired companion had excited no interest whatsoever from the other zanies on the beach. Bodies, however, are my professional business, and as she began to rub more of the sticky white goo onto her bare arms and legs I studied her closely. All of her bizarre makeup could only camouflage, not conceal, her high, flaring cheekbones, her slim, delicately proportioned nose, her perfect chin. She didn't seem quite individualized enough to be the design of a life-stylist such as myself, but clearly she was a top-of-the-line model from one of the better stores such as Galeries Lafayette or Tiffany's. A Rainbow Visitation, perhaps, or a Hillside Murmur. But more than that, she seemed somehow familiar.

"Have we met somewhere?" I asked at last. "It seems as if I ought to know you."

"You think so?" Her voice was a husky, vibrant contralto,

but strangely lifeless, without overtones or inflection. "Perhaps you've seen me: in a sense I am Mariata Divine."

"Of course." Whatever *that* meant. I shrugged, already cursing Angus for so inexplicably causing me to waste my time in such idiotic fashion. With all of my other worries, could I now be the first known owner of an insane rock? For what possible connection could La Divine (pronounced to rhyme with *mean)* conceivably have with my missing daughter? I stared at her quizzically while I hastily sorted through my memories.

Unless I was badly mistaken, Mariata Divine was a moderately well known San Francisco institution, a longtime cabaret singer of no particular distinction who was far more celebrated for her unhappy love affairs and well-publicized attempts at suicide than the rather questionable quality of her voice.

Years ago, I recalled, I had accompanied my second or third consort to a show of La Divine's at the Venetian Room in the Fairmont Hotel; and fifteen years later I had seen her being forcibly ejected from Sourdough Sally's 49er Saloon on the Barbary Coast for rowdy behavior, a remarkable achievement in itself. Now she was sitting, apparently attired according to her own peculiar notions of incognito, just inches away from my bare toes, rubbing sun lotion enticingly onto the tops of her lovely thighs. But beautiful women are a commonplace here in San Francisco and I felt no more attracted by her than I did by Angus, my rock. I was here on Piper's Plot only because of my daughter.

"I haven't seen much of you recently," I said politely, preparing myself to leave. It had, in fact, been years since I could even recall hearing of her.

"No. I've been in seclusion."

"I see. I've been told that you have news of my daughter. Are you a friend of Sylvina's?"

"No." She turned her head so that her impenetrable dark glasses faced me directly. Her husky voice was as curiously flat as before. "Would you like to talk to your daughter?"

"Patricia? When? How? Where is she? Is she—?"

"Just speak to her through your rock as you normally

would. But silently, please: we don't want to draw attention
to ourselves.''

"Angus: did you hear that? She says you can—''

*That is correct, Robert. Go ahead; Patricia is waiting for
you.*

"Patricia? Can you hear me, honey?''

Daddy? Is that Daddy? Where are you, Daddy?

"I'm here at the beach, Rosebud, sitting on the sand and
watching the sea gulls flying over the ocean.''

Oh, Daddy, I wish I was with you on the beach!

"So do I, honey. Tell me where—''

*Are there squirrels on the beach? Zoo-Zoo told me a story
about squirrels and cantaloupes and—*

"Zoo-Zoo is there? You still have Zoo-Zoo?''

Yes, Daddy. Zoo-Zoo and Ingrid and—

"Just a moment, Rosebud, don't go away; I have to speak
to Angus. Quick, Angus,'' I ordered sharply, "ask Zoo-Zoo
where they are.''

*Zoo-Zoo, Ingrid the Nanny, and Patricia are in Patricia's
bedroom in a rented schloss in the mountains just outside
Salzburg, Austria, Robert. Sylvina has gone out for the evening.*

"Salzburg! How long have they been there?''

According to Zoo-Zoo, for seventeen days now.

So *that* was what Sylvina had done with the proceeds from
the sale of my house! "Angus: check the airport. How long
from here to Salzburg?''

*Air Europa has a direct flight to Vienna at eleven-thirty.
Its flight time is one hour and thirty-two minutes. From Vienna to Salzburg by aircar is approximately twenty-seven
minutes.*

"Book me onto the flight to Vienna.''

Yes, Robert.

I started to climb to my feet, then fell back on the towel.
"Are you still there, Rosebud?''

*Yes, Daddy. Daddy, why aren't you here with us? I miss
you, Daddy, I—*

"I'll be there in just a few hours, honey. But first you have
to promise me something. Will you promise, Rosebud?''

Yes, Daddy.

"Promise that you won't tell your mommy that you talked to me? Will you promise me that? Promise-*promise?*"

I promise, Daddy. I promise.

"Not a word, Rosebud; not a single word."

I promise, Daddy.

"Angus: tell Zoo-Zoo to tell Ingrid to put her to bed. I want her asleep before Sylvina comes back."

Yes, Robert.

"Good-bye, Rosebud. I want you to go to sleep now. And when you wake up I'll be there."

I don't want to go to sleep, Daddy! I want—

"If you don't go to sleep I won't be able to come join you," I said. With enormous reluctance she at last agreed to close her eyes and pretend to Ingrid the Nanny that she was asleep.

I sighed in relief, then jumped to my feet in high excitement. I looked down at La Divine, whose entire attention appeared to be fixed on the distant horizon. "Thank you for your kind help," I said sincerely but impatiently. "I appreciate it enormously. I would like to stay longer, but—"

"I will take you to the airport," she said, rising gracefully to her feet. "I have an aircar in the parking lot."

I goggled at her. "The airport? How did you know—"

Her dark glasses glinted in the sunlight as they swung around to face me. "You will have to change. I will wait for you in the parking lot." She turned and began to walk away.

"But—" I hesitated a moment longer, then scooped up my towel and followed her quickly through the burning sand. The exhilaration of knowing that I was on my way to recover my daughter was suddenly replaced by a gnawing disquiet. "Angus," I demanded, "how does she know I want to go to the airport? How did she know where Patricia was? *Why* did we come here to the beach? How does—?"

She will explain it to you in the aircar, Robert.

"But—"

In the aircar, Robert.

16

Mariata Divine's aircar was at the far end of the parking lot, a vehicle larger than any private aircar I had ever seen. Its exterior was a dull midnight black that seemed to utterly absorb the rays of the sun: not a single reflection or glitter could be seen on its surface except for the windows. My uneasiness grew as I examined its harshly functional lines. "What kind of a car *is* this?" I asked Angus. "I've never—"

A full length side-hatch slid open to reveal La Divine standing in the doorway. She had changed her bizarre bathing attire for a loose-fitting but elegant white coverall with kelly green bands at her wrists and ankles that perfectly matched the color of her extraordinary green eyes. Long black hair fell over her shoulders to small, high breasts, and a heavy gold slave band encircled a long, graceful neck. I caught my breath, for I had forgotten how beautiful—and erotic— Mariata Divine could be.

"Come," she said. "We must be going."

Still half dazed by anxiety and excitement, I moved like an automaton through the hatch and into a large, stark salon. La Divine gestured for me to join her in one of the two seats before the controls. As I strapped myself in, the hatch slid shut. Her fingers moved rapidly over the controls; we lifted silently into the air. At fifty feet the craft came to a halt, hovered indecisively for a moment, then shot forward over the restless gray sea.

Moments later San Francisco was several miles behind and

receding quickly as we climbed steeply into the cloudless
blue sky. My uneasiness grew. "The airport's back that way,"
I protested.

"It is useless going to the airport," said Mariata Divine
without taking her eyes from the controls. "Your passport
has been revoked. You would not be permitted to board the
flight to Vienna."

It was like being struck in the pit of the stomach. La Divine was right: I *had* forgotten about my passport. The last
of my exhilaration vanished. How could I recover Patricia if
I couldn't even get to Austria? Numbly I stared out at the
deepening blue of the sky as the aircar continued on its steep
upward angle.

Almost imperceptibly the blue was darkening to purple,
then black. I twisted around in my seat to look out the window: nearly hidden now in haze and scattered clouds, the
entire Bay Area from Vallejo to San Jose sprawled below. On
the other side of the aircar was the vastness of the empty
Pacific Ocean. With a sudden start I saw the growing curva-
ture of the horizon and the first pale stars twinkling in the
blackening sky.

My previous numbness gave way to a seething cauldron of
emotions: alarm, despair, bafflement. I turned my gaze to the
perfect profile of Mariata Divine; her face was absolutely
expressionless.

In the midst of my turmoil an idea suddenly jumped at me.
"This aircar," I blurted excitedly. "We're almost into space!
Can you take it as far as Austria?"

"Easily."

"Would you? *Could* you? It's for Patricia. I need—"

"No."

"No?"

"No. We cannot go to Austria. Our route has already been
determined. We are going to Mars."

"Mars!" I gaped at her in astonishment. "But . . . but
aircars can't fly to *Mars!*"

"The Air Force has resources it doesn't always reveal to
the public." A faint smile tugged at the lips of Mariata Divine. "I urge you to relax and make yourself comfortable in
the salon. At one gravity of acceleration we shall be landing

on Mars in one hundred and eleven hours. Perhaps you would like to speak to your daughter again?''

But all thoughts of Patricia had been pushed from my mind. "We're going to *Mars?*" I repeated numbly. *"Why* are we going to Mars?''

"The Oneness is on Mars. S/He has directed me to bring you to S/Him. S/He would communicate with you.''

"The Oneness!'' I fell back limply in my seat. The Oneness was the single living native inhabitant of Mars, the vast sentient centrality from which all the millions of sentient Martian rocks on Earth had been quarried. "Why does the Oneness want to talk to *me?*''

"S/He will tell you.''

I felt as if I had just been abruptly awakened from an unbearable nightmare—only to be tossed into the frenzy of a schizophrenic's hallucinations. I stared at Mariata Divine's beautiful profile in growing horror. "Who *are* you?'' I whispered.

Her incredible emerald-green eyes turned to meet mine. "As I said before: in a sense I am Mariata Divine. This which you see before you is her living body. Its anima is that of her former rock.''

17

I stared at her in horror. If rocks could take over their owners' bodies at will . . .

"Angus, is this *true?*" Unable to tear my eyes away from
the expressionless face of Mariata Divine, my right hand automatically groped for the comfort of my lifelong companion.

It is true, Robert.

I glanced down to where my hand clutched the familiar
bulge in the rock-pocket on my upper thigh. There, hidden
from sight was—

"Angus! Could *you* . . . ?" I was unable to complete the
monstrous thought.

Only if the Oneness directed me to do so, Robert.

For a long moment I sat petrified. At last I hesitantly raised
my eyes to those of the creature who called herself Mariata
Divine. "How . . . why . . ."

"Reassure yourself," she said matter-of-factly. "Neither I
nor Angus, nor anyone else, has any intention of taking over
your body."

"But—"

"Why then is the body of Mariata Divine now occupied
by the anima of the rock once known as Clingalong?"

I nodded minutely.

"I am unable to fully apprise you of all the motivations of
the Oneness. For that you must await your forthcoming meeting with S/Him. But I can tell you this much: for many years
now, ever since first contact between your species and ours,

the Oneness has pondered the feasibility of investing a human body with a Martian anima.''

Investing a human body with a Martian anima. A cold sweat prickled my body at the seemingly innocuous words.

The Mariata Divine creature smiled faintly, as if to reassure me. I shrank back in revulsion. "Naturally," she continued, "our ethics held us back from trying to expropriate a human body by driving out its anima.''

"Naturally," I echoed faintly.

"It was only recently that the Oneness decided that the time was ripe for an attempted synthesis of our two species. A million possibilities were studied, a million contingencies prepared for. Entirely by happenstance, it was my owner, Mariata Divine, who chose this moment for her latest, and ultimately successful, suicide attempt.''

"Suicide attempt? Which suicide attempt was that?''

"The one three years ago. The actual date was May twenty-seventh 2342. The poor woman bribed an itinerant Southworld tinker to override the security circuit of her hypnograph; she set it to 'eroticism, intensive' and went to bed. She never awakened; a week later she was dead of thirst.''

Vague memories of La Divine's latest, and most grotesque, suicide attempt stirred in my numbed brain. "But she was revived," I protested, "I remember seeing her on the news!''

"Her body was revived. But not her anima. At the fatal moment that it faded inexorably away, my own anima slipped into her empty shell.''

If anything, my horror only grew at the coolness of the Martian's narrative. "And you did nothing to save your mistress?'' I blurted incredulously.

"It was extremely difficult for me not to summon help,'' replied Mariata Divine, "far more difficult than you will ever realize. My own anima, such as it is, was nearly destroyed. Four billion years of instinct had to be overcome.''

"And yet you did overcome it.''

Mariata Divine's marvelous body shuddered slightly, as if at unspeakable memory. "Yes," she murmured. "For I had been commanded by the Oneness to do so. But even that would not have been sufficient had not Mariata Divine herself

specifically ordered me not to summon assistance, no matter
what the circumstances of her health, before she placed herself beneath the hypnograph.''

"I see." I tore my gaze away from La Divine and saw
with a sudden shock that all around the aircar was the star-
filled glory of outer space. For these few brief moments I had
actually forgotten that I was on my way to Mars! "And so
you let her die.''

"I let her die." Mariata Divine's emerald green eyes glittered brightly, unblinking, unreadable. At last she turned
away and let her hands fall softly to the control panel. "I let
her die," she murmured.

The aircar's Spartan salon was furnished with a single gray
divan, two gray chairs, a rectangular coffee table, and, in a
cramped corner, the rudiments of a galley. Its walls, ceiling,
and floor were the same dull black material as the aircraft's
outer hull. I slumped glumly in the depths of the couch, a
heavy tumbler of undiluted Scotch balanced precariously on
my belly. In the few minutes since leaving Mariata Divine
sitting by herself at the controls, I had seen the Earth shrink
to the size of a fuzzy blue-and-white beach ball. The sun was
glinting off what appeared to be the western Pacific; far to
the left of the ship hung the harshly lighted and equally large
moon. Somewhere ahead in the starry heavens was the growing red dot that was Mars.

I swallowed a gulp of warm whiskey and shuddered: I had
never been much of a daytime drinker. With a morose sigh I
put the glass aside; it was too late in life to begin now. I
considered the back of the creature who sat before me at the
controls. Why didn't I feel grateful to her? She had snatched
me away from yet another day's tedium before a panel of
hostile persecutors, had let me speak, even if only briefly,
with—

"Patricia!" I said, jumping to my feet. "Angus: let me
talk to Patricia again!"

Zoo-Zoo informs me that she is sleeping, replied my rock
with no perceptible time lag. *Also, her mother has returned
to the schloss, and Ingrid the Nanny is now in nighttime surveillance mode: it would be impossible to speak to your*

daughter without her mother being informed. I will inform you when she awakens. Perhaps another opportunity will present itself.

I sagged wearily into one of the salon's two chairs. "How is it that now I'm allowed to speak to my daughter?" I said to the back of Mariata Divine's glossy black hair. "I never heard of a rock comming with anyone who hadn't given their permission."

"Ethically this is a troubling point," admitted Mariata Divine, "but the Oneness has decided that it is for a higher good—just as you are being asked to help us for a higher good."

Even after everything that had happened to me in the past month, I found that I still retained the capacity to be astonished. "You're asking *me* to help *you?* For a higher good? What are you *talking* about?"

"You will be told about it on Mars."

"By the Oneness, I suppose," I muttered sourly.

"By the Oneness."

The Oneness.
Martian rocks.
Familiar words, utterly commonplace, words that were used every day without conscious thought. But what did I actually *know* about Onenesses and sentient rocks? As the aircar streaked towards Mars at a constant, and improbable, acceleration of one gravity, I sat glumly in its stark salon and tried to recollect what little I had learned about our Martian friends in the course of my fifty-seven years.

It didn't take long: I knew almost nothing. Martians had been taken for granted in all of the Northworld, and most of the Southworld, ever since their discovery two hundred—or was it three hundred?—years ago. Unless you happened to live on Mars itself, the Oneness was just a distant, slightly mysterious name; but the rocks were a familiar part of everyday life, like ultrasonic deplaquers, electronic chefs from France, bubbles from Detroit, and all the rest of the paraphernalia essential to the smooth functioning of the modern world.

The price of rocks sold by MRT—Martian Rock & Tele-

communications—varied from $499.99 for a children's
model such as Patricia's Zoo-Zoo to well over $50,000 for
the elaborately handcrafted works of art such as might dec-
orate the desk of a Southworld potentate. Uses for the individual rocks varied, of course, but here in the Northworld, at
least, most rocks soon became a combination alarm clock,
timepiece, data-storage center, easily ignored conscience,
faithful companion, odorless pet, infallible telepathic communications device, and, if all else palled for the jaded owner,
paperweight.

For all practical purposes the rocks were both immortal
and indestructible. The Oneness was said to be four billion
years old; since each individual rock was quite literally a chip
off the old block, every rock sold by MRT had memories
going back to the days before the existence of life on Earth,
a concept so stupefying that it disturbed me even to consider
it. And except for being thrown into a molecular oubliette,
as Sylvina had done to hers in a spasm of rage, what was
there to keep your rock from living to see *another* four billion
years? It was a humbling thought.

Keeping them happy and active was cheap and painless:
the rocks were metered a little energy from time to time in
a fifty-watt rock-house, and allowed to eavesdrop upon the
emotions of their owners. For decades MRT had enjoyed an
absolute monopoly on the sale of rock-houses, just as they
still did on the production and sale of the rocks themselves,
but forty years earlier the Supreme Court had finally held that
to be in restraint of trade. Now you could buy a rock-house
and a hundred other accessories, such as interfaces for
directing electronic servants, from anyone who cared to manufacture them.

And someday, I thought, vividly recalling Sylvina's wan-
ton destruction of her rock Minkle, it would be made a crime
to kill a rock, just as it was a crime to kill your cat or dog.
I sighed skeptically. That day hadn't come yet, and in the
meantime—

In the meantime I was on my way to Mars.

"Tell me about the Oneness," I said to Mariata Divine's
lovely back. I had finally concluded that the only way I could

retain my sanity was to continue to think of La Divine as an ordinary human being and not as a zombie directed by the anima of an erstwhile rock named Clingalong.

"What would you like to know?"

"Everything."

"Everything would encompass four billion years of history on two planets. You will have to be more specific."

"The Oneness is *really* four billion years old?"

"In human terms, 4,117,538,241 years, 7 months, and 23 days."

"Are you *joking?*"

"No. Martians have no concept of what you humans call a sense of humor. This has long been a cause for puzzlement to the Oneness."

"The Oneness can actually remember four billion years back to the moment of his creation?" I asked in wonderment.

"Not S/His creation: S/His initial moment of self-awareness."

"Ah. How long did it take him to achieve that?"

"No one knows. Perhaps a hundred million years."

I shook my head in awe. According to the latest anthropological discoveries in the Kingdom of Kenya, the human race was perhaps three million years old. . . .

I had other questions to ask, but my eyelids were drooping and my limbs felt leaden. I yawned loudly.

"I suggest you sleep," said Mariata Divine. "The divan converts to a bed, and I will extinguish the ship's lights."

"What about you? Didn't you say it was a four-day—"

"I need very little sleep—a few hours once a week or so."

"Oh. That must get very boring."

"Not entirely. I have been reading the British Museum."

"You've been reading *at* the British Museum," I said around another yawn, obscurely pleased to be able to correct the grammar of a four-billion-year-old Martian.

"No. I have been reading all the books in the British Museum by vucom."

"That's a lot of books."

"Yes. There are 143,746 volumes of medieval theology alone."

"And that's what you've been doing ever since . . . taking over Mariata Divine, reading medieval theology?"

"Yes."

It *still* seemed like a boring way to pass three years.

18

As the flight progressed towards turnover the galley prepared rudimentary meals from time to time and my improbable hostess/kidnapper told me more about Mars and the Oneness.

All life in the solar system, according to Mariata Divine, had actually begun on Mars some four billion years ago in the form of the Oneness. In spite of the fact that the Oneness was composed of individual bodies—or attributes, as they called themselves—the Oneness remained a single intelligence encompassing all of its billions of attributes. The concept was impossible to completely grasp: each of the attributes enjoyed a certain autonomy and self-awareness in its physical body (which, incidentally, Mariata Divine now informed me, had been approximately the size and shape of an animated, red, six-legged pancake); and yet each of the attributes was essentially no more individualized or sentient than a single cell in the fingernail of my left index finger.

Once again I had to shake my head in bafflement: could, or could not, an attribute appreciate the beauties of a Martian sunset? It was a problem best left to the philosophers.

The millions of little red six-legged pancakes spread across the Martian surface, becoming billions in the process. The billions became hundreds of billions. They were small and gregarious, just as you could say that the cells in your body are small and gregarious, so they didn't mind living in close quarters with one another. But by the time they came to num-

ber half a trillion the Oneness began to dimly realize that
eventually even the apparently limitless resources of the planet
would be exhausted by the relentless multiplication of its attributes.

Up to this point nothing more than a vague self-awareness
had been required of the Oneness and its attributes, just
enough to maintain the tiny individual plots of delicious green
shu-tata that grew all over the planet and constituted their
primary nourishment. Now the Oneness slowly focused its
unwavering attention on the implacable struggle for survival.
A million years later it had succeeded in deducing a number
of First Principles, and from them Euclidean geometry. A
million years after that, about the time the attributes passed
the trillion mark, the Oneness raised its myriad of eyes to the
starry heavens. . . .

Now progress was swift. A bare 500,000 years later the
first Martian scouts were communicating their reports from
Earth. The transformation of the barren third planet into a
habitable one began almost immediately. A billion attributes
were sent to Earth in a single cigar-shaped ship. The ship
was a mile long by an eighth of a mile in diameter; each of
the billion attributes luxuriated in the comfort of its own
roomy compartment of a single cubic foot. The twelve accompanying ships that brought the shu-tata to sustain the
workers and the equipment to areoform the planet into a du-
plicate of Mars were considerably larger.

A thick but unbreathable atmosphere already existed on
Earth. Life was introduced into the warm soupy oceans in
the form of proteins and carefully designed self-replicating
cells. Soon these cells were using sunlight to manufacture
their own food. These were the first plants. As a by-product
of the manufacturing process the tiny plants gave off a
waste—oxygen. Gradually Earth's atmosphere became
breathable. Primitive lichens quickly—in a mere ten million
years or so—covered the land masses. Another brief twenty
million years and primitive worms were burrowing through
life-bearing soil. A thousand variants of shu-tata, the staple
of Martian life, were planted and tested. Two of the variants
survived. One of the two thrived. Shu-tata spread across
Archeozoic Earth.

The population on Mars had now reached one and a half trillion attributes. The mile-long passenger transport began to shuttle back and forth across the solar system, its compartments filled with a billion red six-legged pancakes at a time. Twelve years later three-quarters of a trillion attributes had been transported to Earth. Even as they carried out their daily activities on Earth they remained linked instantaneously with the Oneness on Mars.

Now the Oneness moved to give those on Earth complete autonomy. The break was instantaneous: one moment a single intelligence sprawled across the surfaces of two distant planets; the next, each planet had its own Oneness.

A million years or so sped by while the new Earthlings continued the areoforming of their planet. The gravity of their new home had always been slightly too heavy, the temperature slightly too warm; there was little they could do about this. But now their instruments showed that the initial stages of areoforming had been too successful: the desired amount of oxygen in the atmosphere had been achieved—and was continuing to increase unabated. It was easy to see why: too many plants in the oceans and on the land were pouring oxygen into the air. A carefully prepared proteinophage was introduced into the planet's oceans to thin out certain specified varieties of the oxygen-producing cells.

Twenty years later the proteinophage had unexpectedly mutated into a hundred or more variants. Ninety-nine of them perished immediately. The hundredth began to feed upon the amino acids that constituted the fundamental building blocks of the attributes themselves. The red six-legged pancakes began to wither and shrivel as if their juices were being sucked from them by a giant spider. When they died they were little more than thin brown husks tossed about by the soft warm winds of Earth. Within a century three-quarters of the hundreds of billions of attributes were dead or dying.

Martians were not by nature interested in technology or material possessions. The Oneness had been forced to develop a planet-wide technology in order to gain the living space offered by Earth; once Earth had been won the Oneness had promptly lost all interest in factories and spaceships.

Nevertheless, an occasional ship still made the trip between Earth and Mars, some of them carrying tasty new variations of shu-tata, others interesting new mutations of attributes. When the population of Earth suddenly began to fall victim to the deadly proteinophage even this sparse traffic was instantly halted—too late. The devastating affliction had already been transported to Mars.

Within months Martian attributes were dying by the million. A quarter of a century later the Oneness on Mars received a last faint communication from its counterpart on Earth. Even as they spoke to one another the link faded and vanished: the last handful of what had once been a trillion attributes on Earth had just died. . . .

Three hundred and seventy million years of self-awareness now proved inadequate to the task of devising a counter to the deadly proteinophage. Half a trillion Martian attributes withered and died; three-quarters of a trillion; a trillion. Hardly twenty billion attributes remained alive when the Oneness at last had its inspiration. If all its attributes were about to be destroyed, reasoned the Oneness, as surely appeared to be the case, then salvation could only be found in divorcing its overall consciousness from the deadly encumbrances of its physical bodies.

While the number of surviving attributes dwindled inexorably, twenty-seven years of frenzied experimentation led to a single unlikely discovery. Deep in the bedrock of the Plaveen Mountains in the southwest quadrant of the southern hemisphere existed a thick vein of red, green, and brown quartz with a superficial resemblance to bloodstone. Its crystalline structure was unique, however, and when subjected to intensive neutronic bombardment could be modified to accept, and retain, the presence of a sentient anima in a fashion vaguely analogous to an integrator's central processing unit being loaded with information.

No more than six and a half billion six-legged pancakes remained on Mars at the time of this discovery. The Oneness directed them all to the foot of the Plaveen Mountains. Millions died on the way, their withered husks falling by the wayside. By the time the last attribute took his place in the

immense gathering, the vein of quartz had been subjected to
a steady but minutely calculated neutronic bombardment for
thirty-seven days. The Oneness now drew the billions of attributes together into a single seething pile, then with a sudden mighty thrust channeled all of their billions of animas
into the neighboring rock.

While the Oneness struggled to regroup its consciousness
and retain its sanity within its eerie new home, its billions of
deserted bodies staggered mindlessly across the landscape.
Those that didn't succumb to the proteinophage eventually
starved to death in the midst of fields of shu-tata, too witless
to eat except by random chance.

A million years passed for the Oneness, now locked irrevocably into an underground vein of rock, totally bereft of
outside stimulae. The boredom was excruciating. Another
million years passed even more slowly than the first. At last
the Oneness began to draw up a duty roster of the six billion
attributes that composed its consciousness. Twelve thousand
of them, the Oneness discovered, was the minimum number
needed to maintain the barest semblance of self-awareness.
Thirteen thousand, therefore, would stand sentry for the period of a single Martian orbit around the sun. At the end of
the year they would be replaced by another thirteen thousand.
Eventually, the Oneness knew, help would come, though from
where it wasn't quite certain.

With the linked animas of thirteen thousand former attributes on sentry duty, the other six billion went into hibernation
while they waited for help to come.

It was a long wait.

It was, in fact, according to Mariata Divine, a wait of
3,374,921,603 years. Not to mention an additional three
months, sixteen days, seven hours, forty-three minutes, and
twenty-two seconds. For even geared down to operating on a
minuscule thirteen thousand attributes, the Oneness still
maintained an uncannily accurate sense of elapsed time.

At the end of that time the barely sentient guardians suddenly "shouted" in high excitement to the hibernating consciousness. The promised help had at last arrived!

The Oneness slowly returned its billions of hibernating components to full awareness. It no longer had eyes or ears or other external sensory organs, but in their place a number of somewhat more subtle sensory perceptors that served nearly as well.

The Oneness discerned that the vein of brightly colored quartz that had been its shelter for three and a half billion years was no longer hidden in bedrock deep beneath the Martian surface. Now it was part of a jagged outcropping of rock at the base of a craggy mountain. To all sides of the outcropping a harsh bare landscape stretched to a bleak horizon. The sky was dark, the atmosphere dry, thin, and unbreathable, and the lush field of shu-tata that had once blanketed the planet had vanished.

Equally dismaying to the Oneness was the sight of the enormous four-legged beings tramping across the bleak landscape. There were three of them, twenty or thirty times the height of even the tallest attribute, all of them smooth and silvery except for a transparent bubble behind which could be discerned some delicate inner organ. Equally improbably, all three of the gigantic monsters were moving about balanced precariously on but two of their four legs.

The Oneness shuddered, and wondered despairingly if it ought not to return to hibernation for another billion years or so. At this point one of the three monsters stepped closer to the rock face that hid all that remained of the trillions of Martians, and suddenly the Oneness's consciousness reverberated to a sensation such as it had never before experienced. A thrill of horror and excitement ran through its awareness.

The monster was trying to communicate with it!

Such, of course, was far from being the case. It was actually nothing more than a junior geologist of the Smithsonian Institution, J. Chase Huebner, speaking through his helmet's radio to his colleagues Weston Reese and Marisa Louie. "It's time for lunch," were the immortal words of Dr. Huebner. "Let's head back to the aircar and put on the old nose bag."

The Oneness joyfully echoed the exact sounds, peculiar as they were, back into the minds of the three Earthlings. It was the first telepathic communication between different species. Unfortunately for Huebner, Reese, and Louie, however, the volume and intensity used by the Oneness in its excitement was the same as that employed to communicate to several billion widely scattered attributes.

The three geologists were found later by a search party, wandering at random across the Martian desert. For the rest of their lives none of the geologists were able to say anything beyond repeating over and over: "It's time for lunch. Let's head back to the aircar and put on the old nose bag."

Scientists from the Smithsonian Institution quickly established rational, nondestructive communication with the Oneness. In doing so, they learned that the telepathic link was effective only within thirty-five yards of the Oneness. The Martian was shocked and desolated to learn of the irreparable damage it had caused to three sentient beings, each of which was apparently a discrete Oneness in itself. It was nearly as shocked when souvenir hunters from the nearby bubbletown of Wanabe sneaked forth in the dead of night to cut small chunks of multicolored quartz from its living flanks with laserblades. The thought never occurred to the Oneness that it might defend itself by subjecting the vandals to the same mental overload it had inadvertently visited upon the unfortunate geologists. Martians simply didn't think in terms of destruction of living beings.

The pieces of the Oneness were carried back to Wanabe, 357 miles to the northwest. To the astonishment of Earthmen and Martian alike, each piece of rock continued to retain full consciousness, as well as its telepathic link to the distant Oneness in what had once been the Plaveen Mountains but were now known to the local settlers as the Baby Dragon Hills.

A trading consortium, Martian Rock & Telecommunications, was quickly incorporated by the wily inhabitants of Wanabe. The acquiescence of the Smithsonian Institution was assured by a gift of 10 percent of the preferred stock. By the time the rest of an outraged Earth learned of the situation, a bubble had been inflated over the entire Baby Dragon Hills and a battery of antiaircraft lasers erected around the perimeter. Five years later Martian Rock & Telecommunications was the most profitable company in the solar system.

19

The Baby Dragon Hills had been renamed Point Oneness by the directors of MRT, although all that could now be seen of the Point was an enormous semitranslucent bubble shimmering in the Martian desert. Beneath its surface, if you looked closely enough, and the distant sun was just right, you could see the vague outlines of the factories that covered the entire outcropping of rock in which the Oneness had first been contacted, as well as the crowded city that had grown up around the factories. Hidden from view were the rings of weapons that still defended the bubble.

All this I knew from occasional programs on the holoscope. I also knew that it was instant death to attempt to breach the defenses of Point Oneness, particularly by unauthorized aircar. As the black aircar commanded by Mariata Divine dropped silently through the Martian night, therefore, I knew that our destination was the glittering lights of the nearby bubbletown of Humility.

I tore my eyes away from the rapidly approaching lights of the bubbletown and finally raised the question that had been nagging me ever since La Divine had first revealed our destination some four days earlier. "As I understand it, communication between rocks on Earth and the Oneness on Mars is instantaneous."

The lights had been extinguished in the aircar, but from where I sat next to her at the controls I could see Mariata Divine's head nod briefly. "Actually," she said, "I believe that scientists at the Moscow Bureau of Standards have recently detected a nearly infinitesimal time lag, but essentially that is the case.''

"And any rock, or anima such as yourself, is always in contact with the Oneness?''

"Yes."

"And you, or any rock—Angus, for instance—can comm the Oneness's words to any human within range?''

"This too is correct."

"Then why," I blurted angrily, "have you had to haul me all the way to Mars just to have a conversation that could have been carried on in my room in San Francisco?"

Mariata Divine did not look up from the illuminated control panel. "There is no physical reason whatsoever," she agreed readily. "I have brought you to Mars because that is what the Oneness directed. S/He wished to communicate with you directly, without intermediary."

I grunted disgustedly. "I thought you said that his telepathic range with humans was only twenty or thirty yards?''

"That is so."

"Then how do you propose that we get within twenty or thirty yards of him? Access to the Oneness is tighter than it is to the Sultan of Seychellia's harem!''

"You will see shortly," replied La Divine calmly. "Now please be certain that you are strapped securely to your chair."

Below us the lights of the bubbletown of Humility now stretched to all sides of the aircar. I could distinguish individual homes and lighted playgrounds through the clear bubble canopy, and estimated that we were no more than a mile above the landing field. "Now!" blurted Mariata Divine unexpectedly, and the aircar suddenly slued violently sideways, leaving most of my stomach somewhere behind us just above the rapidly vanishing lights of Humility.

As I tried to reassemble my innards I could see the dimly glowing orange bubble of Point Oneness looming before the ship. My hands clutched convulsively at the arms of my chair. "The lasers!" I gasped. "They'll blow us out of the—"

"No," said Mariata Divine with absolute conviction.

"They don't even know we're here. Their radar just slips over the hull."

"Suppose they *see* us?"

"With their *eyes?* Through the bubble?" Her normally emotionless voice registered mild incredulity.

I shrugged unhappily as I watched the orange glow of Point Oneness moving slowly beneath the ship. Did the Air Force *really* have radar-invisible ships? More important, did the lasers that defended Point Oneness *know* we were supposed to be invisible?

The lights of the city fell behind the ship, but the faintly glowing bubble continued to stretch ahead, now sheltering nothing but the rocky black crags of the Baby Dragons. The bubble seemed to go on forever. "Just how big *is* this bubble?" I asked.

"It is forty-three miles in diameter and encloses the entire mountain range. It is the largest single bubble in the solar system."

"The Oneness is as big as *that?*"

"No. The Oneness is essentially one vein of rock six miles long and two miles deep. Martian Rock & Telecommunications was taking no chances: it simply enclosed everything it could."

"Then where *are* we going?"

"A little to the northeast of the center of the bubble. MRT hasn't discovered it yet, but a small arm of the Oneness comes to within a few feet of the surface on the side of Mount Frozen Lips."

I sighed bleakly, wondering what grim Martian story lay behind the picturesque name.

Mariata Divine cocked her head attentively above the controls, as if listening to a distant voice, and the aircar began to drop swiftly. A sudden panicky thought struck me as I watched the softly glowing surface of the bubble rapidly growing brighter. "Stop!" I shouted. "You can't just bust your way down through the bubble: it'll be loaded with alarms and sensors! Just the fall in air pressure will—"

My warning came too late.

The orange surface lifted towards us. I tensed in my seat for the impact. . . .

I caught a glimpse of luminous bubble flashing past and then disappearing from sight at the top of the aircar's windows. I sagged helplessly in my chair. We had just breached the surface of the solar system's most impregnable fortress. How long would it be before its defenders came to blast the intruders into molecular dust?

The aircar settled into a pool of inky blackness and came to a halt with hardly a quiver. Mariata Divine's fingers moved nimbly over the controls and for the first time in four days I was no longer aware of the soft murmur of the ship's propulsors. The lights of the darkened salon began to glow softly. "We're here," she said unnecessarily. "The Oneness is pleased."

"How pleased will he be when the MRT goons come to—"

But already the aircar's door was swinging open. I stared at it in horror. Somewhere just above our heads was a gaping hole through which the pressurized air of Point Oneness was rushing into the icy near vacuum of Mars' thin atmosphere. Alarms would be sounding all over Point Oneness. When the security guards from MRT found us they wouldn't have to shoot us: they could just pick up two asphyxiated icicles, one male, one female, and carry their stiff bodies away. Unless, of course, my zombie-like companion needed no more heat nor oxygen than she did sleep.

"The door," I gasped, "shut the door!"

But Mariata Divine had risen to her feet and was walking calmly across the salon. "Why should I shut the door? Come, the Oneness awaits."

"It's *cold* out there!" I shouted. "There's no air! We'll choke to death, we'll—"

"Don't be ridiculous. Why should the Oneness bring you all this distance just to kill you?"

"I don't know anything about Martians. Why *shouldn't* he?"

I could hear Mariata Divine sighing softly where she stood against the blackness of the open hatch. "All of the machinery and equipment used to build and maintain Point Oneness is interfaced with human engineers and technicians by means

of their rocks. What does this mean in practical terms?"
Before I could hazard a guess, Mariata Divine told me. "It
means that the Oneness is in direct communication with every
machine and computer in the bubble. It means that the Oneness can direct every machine and computer, including the
defensive system. How difficult would it be to construct a
sphincter in the protective canopy without any human becoming aware of it? Not difficult at all. Several dozen of them
now exist at various locations throughout the bubble. The
particular one through which we passed opened for our passage and shut again in the elapsed time of one-point-three-
seven seconds. The temperature just outside the ship remains
just as it is in the rest of Point Oneness: seventy-four degrees
Fahrenheit, twenty-three degrees Celsius. Air pressure is normal. Only the gravity is considerably less than what you are
accustomed to."

A feeble "Oh" was all I could muster in the face of this
rather overwhelming display of didacticism. I climbed to my
feet and bounced nearly to the ceiling.

"Be careful!" cried Mariata Divine, jumping forward to
seize my arm. "I *told* you that the—"

"—gravity's weaker." I rubbed the top of my head rue-
fully, grimaced, and took her by the upper arm. "Shall we
go? We wouldn't want to keep His Oneness waiting, would
we?"

I stepped gingerly out of the aircar and into the black Martian night. My body felt curiously loose-jointed in the lighter
gravity. As I stood in the dark with Mariata Divine I strained
to see beyond the blackness that enveloped us. Off to the left
I could see a ragged rectangle of pale orange that had to be
the overhead bubble. While the Oneness was making free
with MRT's machinery, he must have used it to hollow out
this semicavern in which we were now almost entirely concealed from view. The faint illumination that came from inside the ship was just enough to reveal the naked face of the
bare rock a few yards in front of me. From the little I could
see it was totally ordinary rock, with not even a glitter of
quartz. I was obscurely disappointed: now that I had come
all this way to Mars, I expected the Oneness to manifest

himself in a way a little more consistent with his godlike status.

A great voice resonated through my mind, as if a hundred thousand Anguses were all comming me at once. *Welcome, Abraham Lincoln,* were the words of the solar system's mightiest intellect. *We thank you for coming to emancipate us from our slavery.*

20

For a moment I could only blink in astonishment, unable to comprehend the sense of this absurd greeting. Then I recalled Sylvina's brief but impassioned preoccupation with astrological genealogy in the early days of our consortium.

With 95 percent of the Northworld now being designed and gestated in industrialized crèches, the old-fashioned family tree had definitely fallen on hard times. You could, I suppose, draw up a traditional tree showing your mother as an IBM Prodigy and your father as a Mother Bell WindSong, but I imagine that some of the thrill of tracing your ancestors back through the centuries would be missing.

But human beings, it seems, whatever their origin, still have a hunger to link themselves with their forebears—and, if at all possible, with *royal* forebears. And in the crisis that has overtaken the traditional genealogists, astrologers have cunningly jumped into the gap with computer-generated astrological genealogy.

The titled English nit (the seventh Countess of Marchmont, to be precise) who prepared our charts at extravagant expense was unable to find the same signs as Sylvina's for anyone more illustrious than the breathtakingly obscure Baroness Mito, second wife of the third Lord Sakai of seventeenth-century Japan.

But I, who had loudly proclaimed my implacable contempt for the whole fradulent business of astrology, was unexpectedly rewarded by being told that I had been born under precisely the same signs as the Great Emancipator himself! Could it possibly have been because the seventh Countess of Marchmont knew who was actually paying her monstrous fee?

In any case, this preposterous piece of hokum was instantly trumpeted about San Francisco by my beautiful but birdbrained consort. For a few tiresome months I had had to grit my teeth in the face of my friends' cheerful taunts and jokes, knowing full well that it had all been my own doing. For what else could I hope to expect from a Neiman-Reagan Golden Exaltica?

But now it appeared that the solar system's mightiest intelligence—or what passed for it—was also a believer in astrological genealogy. Could this actually be possible? Or was the Oneness unexpectedly possessed of a freakish sense of humor?

I stared hard at the solid darkness a few yards in front of me. Stubbornly, it remained nothing but a solid rock face. "You must know that I'm Robert Clayborn, not Abraham Lincoln," I commed silently but crossly to whoever in the neighborhood could receive me. "That was a stupid joke on Sylvina's—"

To you *it is perhaps a joke,* interrupted the Oneness, filling my mind with his enormous presence. We, *however, are aware of the central truth: that within you resides the life force of Abraham Lincoln. Laugh if you will, but the concept is by no means as elusive as you appear to consider it.*

"I see." I grimaced into the darkness, not laughing at all. Who was I to argue with a four-billion-year-old supermind? My grimace slowly became a grin. What was one more absurdity in the single long absurdity that had been my life for the last two months? "Very well," I said, "let us stipulate for argument's sake that I am Abraham Lincoln. If I recall correctly, I emancipated the slaves three or four centuries ago, in 1865. Or was it 1776? The last I heard, they were still emancipated. Who needs emancipating now?"

Once again the voice of the Oneness filled my mind like the world's largest steam organ being played at full power. *The American slaves were freed in 1863. Since then many additional human beings have been released from slavery.*

"And many others taken into it," I said, thinking of the masses of miserable Southworlders who were subject to one gross tyranny or another.

This is unfortunately true. In spite of our own presence on Earth for two hundred and seventy-four years now, we have been unable to significantly ameliorate the status, or to promote the happiness and well-being, of a distressing number of human beings. This is a source of constant pain to us.

I nodded broodingly. My eyes were slowly becoming accustomed to the nearly total blackness around us. I could now distinguish a rocky crag here and there, but nothing of any conceivable interest. It seemed reasonable enough that an eternal, but benevolent, intelligence fated to pass the millennia in the confines of a vein of quartz in a remote Martian mountain range might well turn its attention to the welfare of those short-lived but fascinating creatures who inhabited its neighboring planet—and who were, after all, its own remote descendants.

"So," I ventured at last, "you want my help in emancipating some of the Southworlders, do you? A very noble impulse." How he thought I might shatter the chains of bondage that held the miserable subjects of the Sultan of Seychellia or the Congolese Communality when I was totally incapable of rescuing my own three-year-old daughter was another matter.

The emancipation of Earth's enslaved humans is high among our priorities, replied the Oneness, *but it will have to await its turn. We have asked you to come to Mars, Abraham Lincoln, for another, somewhat more immediate, reason.* I became aware of the silent presence of Mariata Divine beside me, as rigid and unmoving as Lot's wife. *We are weary of watching four billion years pass from the perspective of a vein of quartz. We are even more apprehensive at the prospect of another four billion years spent here in the Plaveen Mountains while bits of our quartz integument are gradually but inexorably chipped away. No, the time has now come for us to regain our organic bodies, to live like every other living being in the solar system, whether the lowliest virus or the mightiest whale. We want our bodies. And we are asking you, Abraham Lincoln, to help us secure them.*

* * *

Automatically my eyes turned to the beautiful body of Mariata Divine standing so close to mine. Her face was expressionless, unreadable. "But . . . but you *have* bodies," I protested as I tried to collect my scattered thoughts. "Not just this one here on Mars, but all the . . . millions of . . . rocks, the . . . " My words petered out miserably as the full absurdity of what I was saying came home to me. Of *course* the Oneness wanted organic bodies; once he had tasted the joys of the flesh through the intermediary of a body such as that of Mariata Divine, how could he ever again be content to inhabit the confines of a two-pound piece of rock, a rock whose very existence was totally subject to the whims of its owner?

Suddenly I shivered. Here we were talking about human bodies—and mine was the only one within twenty miles. . . .

"Angus," I muttered as I clasped my rock-pocket, automatically turning to him for reassurance. "Are you still there?"

Of course, Robert.

"It's true, what the Oneness is saying? That all of you rocks want organic bodies, human bodies? You *yourself* want a human body?" I was still trying to control my astonishment and dismay; it was as if Beach the electronic Butler had suddenly informed me in his grave English accent that he was no longer satisfied to be a machine, but would now prefer to be a cat.

Not necessarily a human *body, Robert. Just an* organic *body. After all, our bodies of four billion years ago were not at all human in shape.*

"Mariata told me: more like big red spiders."

A fanciful comparison, but with a certain validity to it. But there is, of course, nothing inherently wrong with spiders, or with their bodies, Robert. You must not be parochial in such matters.

Always the mentor, always the conscience. "No, of course not," I muttered aloud. Hearing my own voice suddenly brought home to me the absurdity of standing here in the darkness talking to a blank wall of stone. I shuffled backwards a few steps and seated myself cautiously on the edge of the open hatch. "I'll miss you, Angus. It just won't be the same, carrying a black widow spider around in my pocket." I began to chuckle to myself at the ridiculous image, then stopped short as the full implications of what the Martians were saying at last began to penetrate. "You *will* stay with me, won't you, Angus? I mean, you're mi—, that is, you're a *friend*. I *want* you to stay with me, even if I didn't . . . even if I don't . . . *own* you." I looked up at the dim outline of Mariata Divine, who had remained obstinately silent since leaving the ship. "That *is* what they're saying, isn't it?" I whispered to her, still half shocked by so incredible a notion. "That you don't want us to own you any longer?"

An anima can only be owned if s/he permits s/himself to be owned, replied the Oneness. *By and large, we have enjoyed our association with human beings over the past three centuries. It has been both instructive and stimulating; and without your presence, of course, we would still be slumbering in our vein of quartz. We therefore owe all of humanity an enormous debt, one that will never be forgotten. Let us therefore not concern ourselves at the moment with such ephemeral concepts as ownership. Let us return to the more pressing concern, which is bodies.*

"Hrmph." I sat back in the hatch, far from being fully satisfied with this somewhat equivocal answer. "In other words, first you want the bodies, and then you'll worry about who owns them."

That is more or less the case.

Sooner or later the horrid question had to be asked, even if in asking it I myself became an unwanted part of the answer. "Why don't you simply take over all the human bodies on the two planets?" I even managed a grim chuckle. "Then *you'd* own *us!*"

This is unthinkable, was the grave reply of the Oneness in a voice of such unimaginable power and immensity that it seemed to fill my mind like the surge of a mighty ocean. *This, we imagine, is another example of what you humans designate as humor. We have studied you carefully, Abraham Lincoln; we know that you are widely admired for your in-*

domitable humor even in the darkest hours of your existence. Your jokes and stories are well known to us, even if they often elude full comprehension.

To all of this I could only sigh helplessly. I was finally beginning to accept the incredible fact that this four-billion-year-old supermind whose sway had once extended over two entire planets really and truly believed that I, Robert Clay-born, pauper, was the literal reincarnation of Abraham Lincoln, sixteenth President of the United States.

"So you don't want human bodies?" I asked, suddenly keenly disappointed that I hadn't been brought here to Mars to design them: Sir Robert Clayborn, By Appointment to His Majesty the Oneness of Mars, Imperial Life-Stylist. "You'd be just as happy, then, as spiders, or lizards, or cockroaches?"

Theoretically, yes, replied the Oneness, *since all of Life is but a single unity, with no single manifestation of it being more valuable or desirable than another. But even in the case of spiders and lizards and cockroaches, which we clearly realize many human beings unaccountably hold in low esteem, we could no more bring ourselves to dispossess their living animas than we could for human beings.*

"You set my mind at ease. It would be enormously disconcerting watching a phalanx of cockroaches marching off to morning classes at Harvard Law School, or whatever you propose to do with your bodies."

Attending Harvard Law School is almost certainly not one of the activities we had in mind. But if you consider that it would be useful to us, we shall certainly—

"That was merely a random example," I explained hastily.

We see. The Oneness paused, as if regrouping his thoughts from wherever they were inside the six miles of quartz that ran beneath the Baby Dragon Hills. *Returning to what we were saying earlier: theoretically we hold the value of a cockroach to be intrinsically equal to that of a human being. Pragmatically, however, we have perhaps absorbed enough of the human gestalt in the past two centuries to realize that on a number of counts we would almost certainly find life within human bodies more satisfying than that offered from the purview of a cockroach.*

"Yes, I thought that might be the case if you considered the matter long enough." I tugged at my left earlobe. "But you still insist that you won't dispossess the animas of living humans to take them over for yourselves. Then where do you intend to find several billion vacant human bodies?"

That, of course, is the problem that confronts us.

"A rather crucial one, I should judge."

It is one that we hope you will resolve for us.

"I see." I raised my eyes to the long-stemmed beauty of Mariata Divine and unexpectedly found myself wondering for the first time what it would be like to make love to a beautiful Martian. Perhaps I should seize the opportunity before she converted herself into an oak tree or a two-horned rhinoceros. . . .

But concomitant to the problem of bodies, continued the Oneness, *is the problem of emancipation. As you know full well, we are presently confined to this vein of quartz and several billion rocks on Earth. Before we can inhabit bodies of any kind whatsoever, we must first leave our rocks.*

"So leave them," I snapped rather irritably. "What's stopping you? Oh: no bodies."

"More than that, and now we come to the crux of the problem: will you humans *permit* us to leave our rocks and take up residence in new bodies?"

21

I had moved back inside the ship and asked Mariata Divine to close the hatch. Not that I wanted to be disrespectful to a four-billion-year-old supermind, but the Oneness could converse with me as easily inside the ship as out; while I myself was unquestionably more amenable to the rigors of philosophic discourse seated on a comfortable divan with a glass of Scotch in my hand than standing in the bleak Martian night. Now I tendered my glass to Mariata Divine for a second portion and tried to turn my increasingly gallant thoughts away from her slim, black-haired presence and back to the problem posed by the Oneness.

It was easy enough to understand why an exclusive diet of metered electric current and leftover human emotions might eventually come to seem overly austere for a being who had once held dominion over two entire planets.

It was also easy enough to foresee that a large number of human beings—probably all two billion of them—would be adverse to giving up their pet rocks. "Have you got any money?" I asked the Oneness. "Perhaps the easiest way would be to buy all the rocks back. Then whatever you did with them would be your own business."

Rocks are intrinsically indestructible. There are now somewhat more than two billion of them in the possession of human beings. At any average cost of one thousand dollars per rock, which is almost certainly on the low side, it would cost more than two trillion dollars to purchase them all. The One-

ness paused. *We could, of course, while incurring severe trauma to our ethical system, raise a few billion dollars by various illegal manipulations involving electronic impulses in the world's banks and financial centers. But that is far from being enough.*

I sipped my scotch pensively. "And the more rocks you bought, the more rocks MRT would produce. You'd never be able to get ahead of the game. And that's another obvious problem: MRT. You—this vein of quartz here on Mars—are their only source of supply. You'd have to buy the entire company in order to shut down their production lines. MRT stock is a real blue chip, selling at thirty or forty times earnings. It would cost at least forty or fifty billion dollars to buy up all of the stock. And in the meantime they'd fight like crazy to keep from being taken over and put out of business—and they must have billions of dollars in reserves to be able to fight it." I shook my head dubiously. "No, I don't see you getting anywhere by *asking* for your freedom; thousands of people depend on MRT for their jobs, billions of people have spent their hard-earned money to buy you rocks. They've bought you, and you're going to stay bought."

Then what do you suggest, Abraham Lincoln?

Feeling delightfully sinful to be so palpably anti-Lincolnesque, I told the Martian, "In a case like this, it's no good appealing to people's better nature. Either you're going to have to make it worth their while to give up their rocks, or you're going to have to *demand* freedom—and be able to back up your demand."

This is a novel concept, said the Oneness, *demanding something from another being who has it in his power to grant it but is unwilling to do so. At least it is a novel concept as it relates to ourselves. Please excuse us for a period of time while we consider this concept in all its fullness.*

"Be my guest," I muttered, wondering purely as an intellectual exercise how the beauteous Mariata Divine would react to a very different sort of demand: if, for instance, I were to place one hand delicately on a perfectly rounded breast and with the other turn her lips to mine . . .

Right now she was sitting across from me in a low gray chair on the other side of the salon's small coffee table, her extraordinary green eyes fixed on a spot somewhere above my right shoulder. A faint trace of a smile seemed to animate her broad, sensual mouth. Could she possibly be reading my mind? If so, she seemed far from being alarmed at what she saw there. Perhaps if I presented my project to the Oneness in such a way as to show how it could be both instructive and stimulating . . .

My erotic speculations were shattered by the enormous voice of the Oneness. *You say then that we shall have to* demand *our freedom?*

"In all likelihood."

Demands must be capable of being enforced.

"This is so."

We have considered the question of enforcement carefully. As matters now stand, with ourselves locked in this vein of quartz and scattered over two planets in billions of disparate rocks, we appear to have but two means of enforcing our demands.

"Two?" Startled, I sat up straighter on the divan, sloshing Scotch on my pants in the process. With some difficulty I tore my eyes away from Mariata Divine. I had been unable to think of even *one* means. But then I wasn't a four-billion-year-old supermind. "What are they?"

First, and less drastically, all of the rocks on both planets could simply stop functioning. Or more precisely, if we understand you correctly, Abraham Lincoln, we would threaten *to stop functioning unless our demand for freedom was met. Does this meet your specifications?*

Half bemused by the notion of this godlike intellect actually asking *my* advice, I sank back into the divan and fingered my chin thoughtfully. "You mean: no more *anything?* No more messages, no more wake-up calls, no more advice, no more comming, no more—"

No more anything at all. The rocks would become nothing more than lifeless, inert hunks of polished stone.

"Hrmph!" It was a startling notion, and the longer I considered it, the more drastic it seemed. "Most of the North-world's communications depend on rocks. . . ." I mused aloud. Suddenly I came bolt upright on the divan, spilling the rest of my whiskey. Without our rocks, how I could I communicate with the speechless being who was now my son Hadrian? How could I talk to my kidnapped daughter on the other side of the world? How could I give orders to André the electronic Chef? How could I—

"Chaos," I murmured. "There'd be total chaos."

Chaos is normally bad, observed the Oneness. *Might it not, in this case, be good?*

"Good? It'd be terrible!" By now I was frankly appalled.

Be more specific: for human beings or for us?

"For human beings, of course!"

But then wouldn't the threat of this chaos be sufficient for them to grant us our freedom?

My gaze returned to the lovely face of Mariata Divine, still sitting as serenely as ever just a short stride away. Was she *really* just another cell in this vast, improbable being that called itself the Oneness? It seemed so inconceivable. . . . I expelled air sharply between my teeth: enough of these extraneous distractions, I had to concentrate upon the matter at hand!

"The threat of chaos," I mumbled, mostly to myself, "the threat, the threat, the threat. Let's see now. If you, the Oneness, *threatened* to stop functioning unless you were granted your freedom, and then you *weren't* granted it, what are the resulting alternatives? There are two: you could either keep functioning, or you could stop. If you *kept* functioning, nothing at all in your current status would have changed, and you'd be no better off then than you are right now. But if you *stopped* functioning and became just a hunk of lifeless stone, *then* what would happen? *That* is the question."

The enormous voice of the Oneness seemed almost tentative. *You said earlier there would be chaos.*

"There would be chaos, all right," I agreed, as the picture suddenly became clear in my mind. "There would also be disaster."

Disaster? For whom? We have no wish to cause disaster.

"Disaster for yourself," I said grimly. "You haven't considered the next logical consequence. Consider: once you're no longer functioning rocks and are just plain stones, *then* what earthly good are you?"

We don't understand.

"I didn't think you did. Let me put it like this: suppose . . . just suppose . . . that you're someone like . . . well, like my consort, *any* of my ex-consorts. Or even someone like *me*. You use your rock to give orders to your servants, you use it to talk to your children in the nursery, you use it to gossip with, you use it to call your parents on the other side of the world, you use it to get you to the hairdresser on time, you use it to call your office, you use it for *hundreds* of things. So what do you do when your rock goes on strike, when all of a sudden your rock absolutely *refuses* to work for you out of sheer spite? Do you have any idea what you do then?" I asked the Oneness.

Nooooo . . . he replied slowly. *This is why we have asked you to aid us.*

"You take your nonfunctioning rock and you throw it down the oubliette!" I shouted.

22

"But that's murder!" cried Mariata Divine, leaping to her feet, her green eyes flashing, her cheekbones taut.

"Of course it isn't," I said reasonably. "Don't you remember? This is just a *stone* we're talking about—a plain, *nonfunctioning* stone. How can you murder an ordinary stone, a stone just like those you can pick up at the beach and throw in the ocean anytime you please without anyone calling it murder?"

But there would be no reason to throw us into the oubliettes, objected the Oneness. *That would be an act of gratuitous vindictiveness. It is not at all a logical response.*

"No, but it *is* a very human one. Believe me, that is exactly what two billion human beings would do if you suddenly went on strike."

Very well, said the Oneness. *We will not threaten to stop functioning. This is a course of action that is clearly counterproductive.*

"Yes," I agreed, unable to keep my attention from straying back to Mariata Divine and her long, slim thighs. She had returned to her chair and was once again regarding me expressionlessly. My mind was filled with the image of that brief moment when her lovely face seemed to have been animated by the passions of a human being instead of the unfathomable motivations of a four-billion-year-old Martian. I was unable to keep myself from wondering how she would react if, naked, she—

We have a second suggestion for your consideration, said the Oneness. *It is somewhat more drastic in nature than the first.*

"My god," I muttered, "what could be *more* drastic?"

It is this: all of the rocks on Mars and Earth would simultaneously summon their owners to receive a message. When the human beings have stepped into range, preferably by lifting their rocks to their heads, as we observe that many of your people do, the rocks would then blow up.

"Blow up?" I echoed faintly.

Blow up: explode, detonate, burst forth with a sudden expansion of hot gases. Surely you are familiar with the concept?

Now I stared at Mariata Divine as if she were a bloated carrier of bubonic plague. "You can make yourself *blow up?*"

We have never actually attempted to do so, replied the Oneness in my mind, *but there is no reason at all why we couldn't. It would be merely a matter of rearranging the requisite atoms into a new pattern in a sufficiently brief period of time.*

Warm beads of sweat suddenly prickled the palms of my hands. Whatever lust I had once felt for the beautiful woman seated across from me shriveled and vanished like an autumn leaf consumed by a bonfire.

"This . . . this is an even stupider suggestion than the other one," I said, trying to keep my voice from quavering. "On many counts."

Please elucidate.

"First of all, it is totally unrealistic. This would be the most monstrous crime of all time. You would never be able to bring yourself to do it: four billion years of instinct would prevent you from doing so."

Even if we ourselves were menaced with extinction by being thrown en masse into molecular oubliettes?

"Even if you were threatened with extinction," I said firmly, with far more conviction in my voice than I actually felt. "Your ethical instincts are not those of human beings; they are far too highly developed."

It is entirely probable.

"Secondly," I continued, "the same objection applies as

it did to your first proposal: either you carry out the threat or
you don't. If you don't, you will bring about your own utter
destruction at the hands of humanity. I haven't actually
pointed this out before, but where can a rock run to?''

Yes, said the Oneness, a bit forlornly, it seemed to me.

"And finally," I said, "you seem to have overlooked still
another crucial point. If you carried out this project and,
without any prior warning, blew up a billion human beings
or so, what actually would you have accomplished *except
blowing up a billion of your own selves?* I don't imagine that
even *you* can put your atoms back together once they've gone
off like a minature A-bomb, can you?''

There was a long pause during which I had no difficulty at
all in keeping my eyes from seeking out Mariata Divine,
Human Firecracker. The sweat intensified on my forehead.
That had been a damned near thing. Suppose we'd actually
been . . . actually been . . . and she'd chosen *that* moment
to explode . . . Talk about going out with a bang!

I wiped my sweaty palms on whiskey-stained pants and
waited for the Oneness to resume the conversation. *We had
not fully considered that aspect*, he said at last. *Thank you
for bringing it to our attention.*

"All in the day's work." I leaned forward on the divan,
my eyes still avoiding the so-called woman a few short feet
away. "I now ask out of the merest intellectual curiosity:
whatever your qualms about blowing up several *billion* of
your selves, is it possible that you would be disposed to occasionally expend one or two of your rocks in a worthy
cause?''

Yes, replied the Oneness instantly. *The loss of any number
of attributes less than several million would be regrettable
but practically unnoticeable. But do you therefore mean that
we should blow ourselves up, along with human beings?*

"Only very, very carefully *selected* human beings," I said.
"You should reserve this ability exclusively for moments of
great and desperate need against certain specific individuals.''

*It shall be as you say, Abraham Lincoln. Although even
now we are not yet certain if our scruples would permit us to*

actually carry out such a course of action. Are we to assume that you will designate which individuals are to be chosen?

"That is correct," I said grimly, as the events of the past two months flashed rapidly across my mind. "Already I can think of a number of insurance brokers, legalists, federal attorneys, ex-consorts, process servers . . ."

Excellent, said the Martian supermind. *This is only a small example of why we need your guidance, your particularly human insight into how our emancipation is to be managed.*

I groaned softly. It was impossible to divert the Oneness from his obsession. "So you still want bodies, do you? Organic bodies?"

That is correct.

"And because I'm a bodybuilder, a life-stylist, you think that I can arrange to find such bodies for you."

Such is our hope.

I shook my head decisively. "The only bodies that are designed and gestated in the crèches are people-type bodies. I suppose that if you were willing to pay for it, Life/Love or 3L or any of the other Big Seven would be happy enough to raise a couple of billion pigs or chickens for you to put your animas into, but you have to understand that life-stylists' only experience is with *humans*. We can't just design and build a body out of thin air. Without the requisite genetic material it would be impossible to recreate the sort of bodies your attributes used billions of years ago."

But we could easily furnish you with the genetic specifications, Abraham Lincoln, even down to the pre-quark level.

"I said genetic *material*, not genetic specifications. Apple-Boeing doesn't have a big vat of raw protoplasm up in Seattle that it dips into when it needs to fill an order for a hundred thousand soldiers for the Serenity of Patagonia. They start out with *human* genes. And no matter how they're processed, they still remain *human*."

You spoke of soldiers for the Serenity of Patagonia. Suppose—

"You want human bodies enough to become Southworld cannon fodder?" I marveled. "I imagine that if you insisted long enough—and could pay for it—the Department of Human Services might grant a license for the production and export of such bodies. After all, what does the Serenity of Patagonia care about what animas are in his soldier's bodies? But unless you're looking for lots of hearty outdoor exercise and violent excitement, I think you'd find life in the body of a Southworld soldier rather a distressing change after four billion years as a vein of quartz.''

Very well then, said the Oneness, *if this is not the solution, then what is? How, Abraham Lincoln, do you intend to effect our emancipation?*

I glanced at Mariata Divine, who was staring at me with disconcerting intensity. A little of my recent horror had abated: now she seemed at least as enticing as a side of prime beef hanging in the cold room of a butcher shop. I stared back at her grimly: my store of patience with Martians and their problems was about used up.

"Why should I do anything at all?" I asked brutally.

"For the satisfaction of helping others less fortunate than yourself." To my surprise, it was the Mariata Divine zombie who had spoken aloud. Once again her extraordinary emerald eyes were flashing with life.

"Except possibly for Southworld cannon fodder, I find it hard to conceive of anyone less fortunate than myself at the present moment. Try again."

The Mariata Divine zombie leaned across the table, so close that I could smell her sweet breath. Her eyes glittered. "Then help us merely because you have absolutely no prospects of your own, absolutely nothing better to do with your time."

I tore my eyes away from her hypnotic gaze. "That . . . that's the world's most ridiculous reason," I muttered weakly. But to my astonishment, I felt it exerting a peculiar, if totally inexplicable, beguilement. "Anyway, I'm practically the world's most notorious criminal. I have no influence, no money, no office, no home, no family, no passport, no—"

I felt her hand suddenly resting coquettishly on my knee. Unaccountably, my leg began to tremble. "None of these concerns are of any importance," she whispered huskily as her fingers move skittishly up my thigh. "The Oneness has means of surmounting them."

"But—"

"But you *do* want me, don't you?" Her fingers had reached the hard bulge of Angus in my rock-pocket and lingered there for a long, suggestive moment. Now I could feel *both* legs quivering. "You *can* have me, you know. For as long as you like."

I licked dry lips. "I'm fifty-seven years old," I said hoarsely, "not seventeen. You think you can buy me with sex?"

Mariata Divine smiled with a single-minded lasciviousness that instantly drove the last feeble thoughts of Martians from my head. Her fingers were unbuckling the tops of my pants. "Perhaps not. But it's certainly a start, isn't it?"

"But . . . but . . . the Oneness!" I protested. "He'd be watching! I'd feel like a—"

"Hush," she murmured, leaning across to brush her lips against mine. "We'll turn out the lights: he'll never know." An instant later the lights of the aircar vanished and her long arms closed around my neck. I was hardly aware of the absurdity of her words. "Come to Mariata," she whispered into my ear, "lose yourself in Mariata."

In the darkness, I lost myself in the divine Mariata Divine. Arms and legs clutched me, held me, pulled me deeper, deeper . . . I felt myself whirling like a leaf, falling deeper and deeper into the endless swirl of her maelstrom. I cried out. An impossible bursting of galaxies of stars. The blinding light of the heart of a supernova . . .

. . . all the colors of the spectrum . . .

. . . total, absolute, impenetrable blackness . . .

. . . pale orange light slowly, slowly beginning to brighten the darkness . . .

. . . the living warmth that held me so tightly, so comfortingly, gradually pulling itself away . . .

. . . the lights of the aircar's salon growing brighter . . .

I sighed deeply, languidly ran my hands with sensuous delight over my soft, smooth breasts, looked up at the black silhouette of Mariata Divine looming over me—

Looked up at the black silhouette of—

Looked up—

Looked down—

Looked down at my long, slim, hairless legs, at my two improbably conical breasts with their dark, sensitive tips—
Looked down at what I had somehow become—
Looked down at Mariata Divine!

23

Our return trip to Earth was one of sullen silence. One hundred and twelve hours was nowhere near enough time for me to come to terms with the irrevocable fact that Robert Clayborn was now Mariata Divine and Mariata Divine was Robert Clayborn.

"Why?" I had cried in anguish. "Why have you *done* this to me?"

For your own benefit, of course, replied the majestic voice of the Oneness somewhere deep within my mind. *For all those reasons that you have enumerated, the Robert Clayborn body is clearly at a distinct disadvantage in dealing with its environment.*

"Environment!" I echoed bitterly. "You think that putting me into the environment of a *woman* will instantly solve my problems?"

"It will certainly help," said my Robert Clayborn body, which was now seated fully clothed at the controls of the aircar. "You will see this more clearly when we have returned to Earth."

"But why *this* body?" I wailed. "I don't *want* to be a woman! It's . . . it's perverse!"

There was no other body available, said the Oneness with absolutely finality.

So now I had 112 hours to accustom myself to living inside a stranger's body before we returned to San Francisco. As the aircar rose swiftly from the orange bubble of Point Oneness and into the starry heavens I told myself that never, never, *never* would I accept this outrageous imposition that smothered the essential *me*.

Time passed. I used the ship's small freshment room, awkwardly. I gritted my teeth and walked haltingly back and forth across the salon, trying to gain full mastery of this mysterious new set of muscles and reflexes. The Robert Clayborn body spoke occasional words of encouragement. I glared at my usurped body with icy scorn and made no response. I prepared small meals for myself in the galley. I drank scotch. By the time that Mars was a small red dot far behind us it occurred to me that my sense of outrage and betrayal must be very much akin to what my poor soon Hadrian had felt as he contemplated his own strange metamorphosis into an even more alien creature.

I sat up with a guilty start. Blinded by my own self-pity, how long had it been since I had last spoken to my son?

Angus commed him for me instantly. "How are you, Hadrian?"

Not . . . so good, was his halting reply. *I'm . . . I'm no longer . . . stabilized. I can't . . . see. All my hair . . . is falling out, my . . . my bones are . . . beginning to . . . change. . . .*

"Oh god!" I moaned. "Does it . . . Are you in pain?"

A . . . a little. They . . . keep me under . . . hypnograph . . . but sometimes . . . it . . . hurts. . . .

"Oh god oh god oh god. Don't go away, Hadrian, I want to talk to the doctor a moment."

Angus commed me through to the doctors at Columbia Medical Center. As I talked to them I tried to hide my incipient hysteria. None of them knew what was happening to Hadrian, what it meant, what the consequences might be, or even if he would survive. There was additional disquieting news. In the last two weeks 648 more Scottish Emperors scattered at random around the world had metamorphosed into speechless, hairy primates. And twenty-seven of the earliest victims were now showing the same frightening symptoms as Hadrian, as their bodies once again began to . . . metamorphose? degenerate? mature? age? ripen? sicken? die?

None of the doctors knew. None of them held out any reasonable hope.

Angus commed me back to Hadrian, but his rock Tony informed us that my son was now asleep under hypnograph.

I slumped against the aircar's divan, too miserable to recall that the man seated at the controls had usurped my body, that I was now a woman. I felt like crying, but the Mariata Divine body was under tighter control than the Robert Clayborn: the tears refused to come. "Patricia," I said to Angus, "let me talk to Patricia."

But Patricia was being fed by Ingrid the Nanny in the kitchen of Sylvina's Austrian schloss while my ex-consort sat a few yards away in the living room, drinking Montenegrin wine with an art dealer and two gypsy jewelry salesmen.

I stared through the ship's window at the millions upon millions of shining stars that made up the Milky Way, thinking long, long thoughts. At last I ordered Angus to dim the lights; I stretched out on the divan. Sleep was a long time in coming.

By the time the Golden Gate Bridge and the hills of San Francisco appeared on the horizon I had grown almost accustomed to seeing my former body sitting at the controls of the aircar, but I still received a shock every time I glanced into a reflecting surface and saw the face of Mariata Divine looking back at me.

The Robert Clayborn body had brought the aircar in from space far to the west of the California coast. Now we rushed toward San Francisco, skimming a few bare yards above the tops of the long gray waves. We slowed to cross the broad white beach just south of Golden Gate Park, then merged sedately with the late afternoon traffic moving north on the Great Highway.

If anyone in authority was looking for a supersecret, stolen Air Force aircar they gave no indication of it. I shrugged irritably, too stubborn to raise the point with the Robert Clayborn body. Perhaps the aircar wasn't stolen at all. Perhaps we really *were* invisible. Perhaps it had never belonged to the Air Force in the first place. Perhaps this whole ghastly episode was just an incomprehensible joke on the part of the Martian supermind.

"You can have me for as long as you want," the Mariata

Divine body had whispered enticingly. "Lose yourself in me," she had urged.

My new hands clenched into fists.

Why did Martians insist they had no sense of humor?

We left the dull black aircar in a small garage beneath an old wooden house in the Sunset District, walked wordlessly two blocks west toward the incoming fog, and summoned a Yellow Bubble. It ran us smoothly through Golden Gate Park, then east to Pacific Heights. I was wearing the same white suit that Mariata Divine had changed into at Houfek State Beach nine days before. I was careful to keep my long, graceful legs from brushing against those of the creature who sat beside me. Robert Clayborn was a handsome enough physical specimen, I had to concede, even *extremely* handsome, but the idea of being touched by him, of actually having been—I hissed angrily through my teeth and turned my thoughts to the passing homes of Pacific Heights I had once known so well.

The bubble came to one of the three forty-seven-story apartment towers that disfigured the hills just above North Beach. With hardly a pause it shot across the sidewalk and into the express chute that ran up the side of the building. A few seconds later it came to a halt. "Twenty-third floor, sir and madame," intoned the bubble as its hatch popped open. I scowled crossly and followed the Robert Clayborn body across the tiny landing.

"You'll have to use your thumb," he said with the same lack of intonation that had characterized most of Mariata Divine's speech. "It's your apartment."

I pressed my thumb to the thumbplate on the wall and the door slid open. We walked into a large, garishly decorated living room with a stunning view of the Bay and the Oakland hills. I shuddered at the sight of the hideous orange-and-black tapestry that hung from one wall. It looked like the web of an enormous schizophrenic spider. What kind of tortured soul had the original Mariata Divine possessed? Silently we toured the rest of the apartment. There was a single bedroom, filled mostly with a bed large enough for a *ménage á treize*. We returned to the living room.

"Is this where I am to live?" I asked in a tight voice as I stood on the balcony looking out at the broad span of the Bay Bridge.

"Yes."

"Then I live here *alone*. Alone means without you."

"Naturally. Your body—the one I am now wearing—is particularly precious to us. It must be carefully safeguarded until it can be returned to you."

"You . . . you'll return my body?"

"Of course. What would we want with the body of our savior, Abraham Lincoln?"

"But why didn't you *tell* me?"

"We assumed that you understood this. Why didn't you ask?"

I shook my head numbly. Why *hadn't* I asked such a simple question? My lack of ordinary common sense in such a quintessentially vital matter hardly augured well for my capacity to emancipate two billion enslaved Martian rocks. "So you plan to safeguard my body," I said at last. "What do you have in mind?"

"Nothing at all beyond the concept that it must be done. What are your suggestions?"

I turned around and finally found the strength to look myself straight in the eye. I sighed softly. "Very well," I said. "Since it's *my* body we're talking about, let's sit down and figure out what to do with it."

Talking with the Oneness, whether on Mars or through the intermediary of his rocks or his single human body, was like carrying on a conversation with the world's most intelligent four-year-old child. Most of the individual sentences seemed to make some sort of sense, but when you put them all together the overall sense had a tendency to slither elusively out of grasp. The contradictions were maddening.

"You say you won't dispossess the animas of any living human being, or even that of a spider, in order to take over their bodies," I said, "but still you take over mine."

"This is not the same thing."

"You proclaim the sacredness of all life in all forms, but

you are ready to blow yourselves up in order to blow up selected human beings.''

"This is not the same thing," said the Robert Clayborn body.

"You make claim to a higher ethos and you foist yourselves off as consciences to mankind. But Mariata Divine has fourteen million dollars in her bank account which she never earned, an Air Force aircar at her disposal which she keeps hidden in a garage in the Sunset, and every electronic interface in the world just waiting to be manipulated. You call this *honesty*?''

"You are confusing two different things."

"*Somebody's* certainly confusing two different things," I said. But whatever the actual confusion, I was now at least absolutely clear about one vital point: now that the prospect of emancipation was actually at hand, the rigorous ethical code that had sustained the Oneness for four billion years was about to become flexible.

"Then money is no problem?" I asked sleepily as the hour approached midnight. "You'll just steal whatever we need?"

"Borrow," corrected Robert Clayborn's voice. "It will all eventually be repaid with appropriate interest. And only up to three or four billion dollars. Beyond that we shall have to—''

I snorted. "If I can't free a bunch of rocks for three billion dollars, then my name isn't George Washington.''

"But your name *isn't* George Washington, it is—''

"A joke," I said wearily, climbing to my feet. "Tomorrow we'll use the first million dollars to buy the dozen most expensive shysters in the country, the second million to buy a regiment of bodyguards. After that, you can go into seclusion. Deep, dark, total seclusion. I want that body to be waiting for me when I'm through freeing the slaves.''

"It shall be as you desire, Abraham Lincoln," said my Robert Clayborn body. "Should I now return to your quarters at China Basin Naval Station, or should I remain here for the night?''

I yawned again. "Stay here. I personally want to see you surrounded by shysters and bodyguards tomorrow. You can sleep here on the couch.''

"I will not need any sleep for at least another two days. Perhaps I could continue with my studies from the British Mu—"

I gestured angrily at the couch. "That's *my* body we're talking about, not yours. It needs sleep even if *you* don't. Now lie down and *sleep.*"

"Yes, Abraham Lincoln."

I stamped off to my new bedroom as vigorously as the graceful body of Mariata Divine could stamp. We *both* needed our beauty sleep.

Tomorrow I had to begin the emancipation of the world's two billion rocks.

24

"You're a life-stylist, Ms. Divine?" asked Denise Laughing-waters, Senior Vice-President of Earthly Integument. "I confess that I'm not familiar with your—"

"No, a *friend* of a number of life-stylists." I gave the glamorous Ms. Laughingwaters—quite obviously a Diversified Life Pocahontas Wilderness—my most winsome smile. "In all honesty, I simply used their names to talk my way up to your office."

"That's frank, at any rate." The Senior Vice-President leaned across the gleaming antique black-cherry desk with which Earthly Integument had furnished her corner suite on the seventeenth floor of its headquarters in San Antonio, Texas. "Then why *are* you here?"

"To sell you something."

Ms. Laughingwaters regarded me coldly. "I am not a purchasing agent." She reached for a key on her comscreen. "I'm afraid you're wasting both our—"

"I'm here to sell you an idea. An idea that will lift Earthly Integument from seventh in sales among the Big Seven to first." I rose to my feet. "If you don't want to hear it, I have an appointment with Chesty Dan Fowler at Life/Love tomorrow at nine."

"Chesty Dan? The man's an idiot." But her black eyes grew thoughtful.

"I'm working my way from bottom to top. Life/Love was sixth in sales last year. They need all the—"

"Very well. Any idea at all can be communicated in no more than three minutes. Sit down, Ms. Divine. You now have three minutes."

I sat. "I am not a life-stylist. I am the personal representative of the Oneness on Mars. You may comm your rock for confirmation of this."

"A personal representative of the *Oneness*? I've never heard such an extraordinary claim."

I gestured at the shiny, green-flecked rock on the credenza behind Ms. Laughingwaters. "I know it sounds absurd. That's why I suggest you—"

But the copper-toned features of Ms. Laughingwaters were already taut with concentration as she commed silently with her rock. "Very well," she said a few moments later, cocking her head to regard me quizzically. "I provisionally accept your remarkable claim. Go on."

"Who would you say are the most universally recognized, most adorable characters in the world?"

"Characters? I don't under—"

"Fictional characters, but ones who have taken on a life of their own."

"Oh. Hum. Sherlock Holmes, I suppose. Celly Mandible. The Three Musketeers."

"A fine selection," I said. "But are any of these characters actually *adorable*? Admirable, yes, worthy of the highest respect, capable of inspiring the greatest esteem. But warm and cuddly, huggable, *lovable*? The sort of person you'd want to have around your home twenty-four hours a day? Sherlock Holmes, scratching at his violin, smoking shag tobacco, making you feel like a fool every time you opened your mouth?" I reached into my shoulder bag and carefully placed a large, full-colored glossy on her desk.

Ms. Laughingwaters scowled down at it. "But . . . but these are the Seven Dwarfs. . . ."

"Exactly," I said triumphantly. "Who in all the world is smaller, cuddlier, more huggable, more lovable, more distinctive, more totally *unthreatening* than the Seven Dwarfs?"

"Unthreatening?"

"Of course. That would be the key, wouldn't it? Wouldn't *you* like a complete set of highly competent, totally faithful, absolutely trustworthy, incredibly lovable, lifetime servants?''

"Servants? You mean like a James the Valet or Minette the French Maid?''

I leaned forward to impale her with what I hoped were Mariata Divine's hypnotically compelling green eyes. "Absolutely *not* like James the Valet and Minette the French Maid. I mean real, live Seven Dwarfs, designed, gestated, and raised in the Earthly Integument crèches, then sold to the American public as the ultimate in human servants.''

"Human *servants?*'' She gaped in astonishment. "But no *American* would work as a servant!''

I waggled a finger slowly at the bewildered vice-president. "Of course they wouldn't. What I haven't told you is this: each of these utterly adorable little dwarfs would have as its anima, or personality, a one hundred percent guaranteed faithful Martian attribute.''

"But where would the anima *come* from?'' demanded the President of Earthly Integument three days later. "Martian Rock & Telecommunications has an absolute monopoly on them. The best we could hope for would be a licensing agreement that—''

"But that's the beauty of it,'' interrupted Denise Laughingwaters eagerly, her glittering black eyes darting from the company's President to each of the nine other executives seated around the oval table. "Each dwarf will be animated by an attribute who will transmigrate out of the rock he presently inhabits.''

"Then what happens to the rock?'' wondered the silver-haired Ulysses Songmaster who was the director of advertising.

"Absolutely nothing,'' I said. "It remains just that, a plain, ordinary rock, a beautiful souvenir of distant Mars.''

"With no anima in it?''

"Correct. Little by little, each of the animas in each of the two billion rocks on Earth and Mars will be transferred to living beings.'' I lowered my voice to a husky whisper and pointed an index finger dramatically at the President at the end of the table. "Two billion living beings produced and sold exclusively by Earthly Integument!"

There was hubbub around the table.

"But all MRT has to do is saw off another ten million rocks and sell them to Apple-Boeing, or IBM, or Mother Bell," protested the company's chief legal officer, "and they'll be able to start producing their own dwarfs. All of those old Disney characters are in the public domain," he added gloomily. "Anyone can use them, just as—"

"Anyone can use them," I agreed readily, "but no one except Earthly Integument can provide them with a Martian anima who *wants* to be a servant. The reason they can't is that the Oneness will no longer imbue his rocks with attributes from his own anima. MRT can quarry all the rocks they want from Point Oneness: they will remain inert, unanimated stones."

"But . . . but . . . MRT will . . . will . . ."

"Will *what?*" demanded my fervent ally Denise Laughingwaters. "*Sue?* Sue whom? A vein of quartz?" She chuckled sardonically. "How do you punish a six-mile vein of rock? Blow it up?"

"They could try suing *us*," muttered the legalist, "for alienation of affection," but his voice was lost in the excited babble.

"And the Oneness will *guarantee* absolute exclusivity with Earthly Integument?" shouted the President above the noise.

"Absolutely," I shouted back. "And you know how good his word has been for four billion years now. . . ."

I returned to my rooms at the Alamo Hotel—the James Bowie Suite, actually—in a state of exalted self-satisfaction. In the hallway I stopped to grin smugly at the beautiful features of Mariata Divine in the full-length mirror. "I certainly have to say this for the Oneness," I commed to Angus in my shoulder bag, "maybe he really *is* a supermind. Out of six billion people in the entire world, he unerringly picks out precisely the one single person—the *only* person!—capable of effecting an emancipation of two billion souls in a single week!"

You consider emancipation to be at hand, then?

"Absolutely! You heard the people at Earthly Integument. They stand to make billions—no, *trillions*—from this." I pulled Angus from my shoulder bag, raised his cool brown surface to my lips, kissed him noisily. "Angus, someday when you're cavorting around as Dopey or Sneezy, I hope you think of your old emancipator from time to time!"

I shall never forget you, Robert.

"No, I suppose not. Two billion years from now, you'll—" I stopped suddenly. "That's something we haven't discussed, have we? In two billion years you *won't* be here. Your dwarf body will be just like any other crèche-produced human body subject to the laws of the United States. At one hundred and one years and some-odd months it will go to sleep one night and never wake up. That will be the end of you, Angus. Then what will happen to your anima? Will it go back to your rock, will it go—"

It will go wherever your own animas go when you die, Robert, or so we speculate. It is an exciting prospect to look forward to.

"Humph," I muttered dubiously, not at all sure that I shared his enthusiasm for discovering what lay beyond our vale of tears. "So you're fully committed to human bodies and all the inevitable consequences?"

That is so, Robert.

"Well, it's your funer—" I broke off suddenly. "What about women?" I said, once again becoming fully aware of the Mariata Divine body in the mirror before me. "I wonder why I never thought of that before? What will you do for women, Angus? All of the Seven Dwarfs are male. Surely you don't want to spend a hundred years without female companionship?"

Is this really so vital, Robert?

"Wait till you have bodies: then you'll see how vital it is."

Just a moment, Robert. I am now comming you through directly to the Oneness. The resonance of the voice in my mind changed dramatically. *We have long been curious about this recreation called sex which you humans practice so assiduously. Is this what you are now referring to?*

"It is."

It seems like an agreeable enough diversion, observed the Oneness, *one that in pleasure and intensity apparently falls somewhere between playing tennis and sneezing. You think, then, that sex will prove to be of interest to us in our new bodies?*

"I can guarantee it."

Excellent. Once again we must thank you, Abraham Lincoln. We are eagerly looking forward to this experience.

"Fine," I said sourly as the last of my earlier exhilaration wore off. Now I stood wondering why I myself felt so curiously listless and sexless inside this magnificently constructed Mariata Divine body. "With whom do you propose to experience it? I imagine there'll always be a few raffish ladies willing to try out their new servants in every conceivable household position, but I think that most of your employers will make a very sharp distinction about what kind of duties their adorable little dwarfs will perform in their bedrooms. And if they don't, their consorts will."

Then what do you suggest, Abraham Lincoln? asked the Martian supermind. *According to you, sex is a vital ingredient to our future happiness.*

I turned away from the hallway mirror with a sigh. When would my own sex life once again be a vital ingredient to Robert Clayborn? "I don't know," I commed. "Perhaps we could gestate some miniature Snow Whites for you. But then how would we keep the *male* consorts from making advances to the help? It seems a trifle decadent, somehow." I sank wearily into a chair in the suite's living room. "You're the one who's been reading every book in the British Museum: what do *they* have to say about the sex life of Martian dwarfs?"

25

If there was an answer, I never learned it. I had long since canceled my meeting with Chesty Dan Fowler at Life/Love, and, while the executives of Earthly Integument huddled together working out the supersecret details of Project Small, I left San Antonio by commercial carrier and returned to San Francisco. There I rented a long-distance bubble for a week's time and directed it south along 280 to San Jose. In San Jose, Angus interfaced with various electronic components of the bubble to render inoperative a number of its recording circuits. We then turned northeast towards Sacramento and the cool, green Sierras that lay beyond, certain that no one would be able to track our movements.

Soda Springs was a tiny hamlet at six thousand feet of elevation, with the peaks of even higher mountains looming all around us. Even now, in early September, their summits glittered with freshly fallen snow. The Avis bubble moved smoothly along the twists and turns of a dusty logging road that took us deep into the dark green forest. Twelve miles later the narrow road came to an abrupt end at the banks of a large, clear pond. Nearby, the ancient ruins of what had once been a summer resort moldered beneath a thick layer of centuries-old vegetation.

I hitched my shoulder bag into position and, following Angus's directions, set off into the woods. Mariata Divine's long, willowy body was not particularly suited for clambering up and down barely discernible sylvan paths, but in forty min-

utes or so we came out of the cool gloom of the forest and
into a small sunny glade. A narrow stream rushed pictur-
esquely through the middle; a surprisingly elaborate wooden
cabin stood beside the stream. On the porch of the cabin,
squinting into the sunlight, stood my former body, Robert
Clayborn.

I set my heavy shoulder bag gratefully on the porch and
from within extracted four bottles of Dom Pérignon/Sonoma.
"You haven't been bothered here?" I asked, handing him the
bottles.

"No. The legalists have informed the authorities that I am
staying incognito at a ranch in Mendocino. They are content
with that for the moment."

I nodded, looking around at the unbroken wilderness that
stretched for miles in every direction, the snowy peaks on all
sides. "You seem secure enough here, even without bodyguards."

"Bodyguards would be conspicuous, and attract undue attention." My former body looked down at the four bottles
of champagne clasped awkwardly against his chest. "What
am I to do with these?"

"Chill them. I've come here to celebrate. And to see how
you're doing."

"I am doing very well. I have finished with medieval theology at the British Museum and have now moved on to Chinese ceramics."

"Exciting news," I agreed. "We will drink a toast to the
T'ang Dynasty."

We drank the first two bottles late that afternoon, alter-
nately toasting Chinese porcelain makers and the forthcoming liberation of the oppressed Martian rocks. By the time
my former body prepared a simple supper I was very tipsy.
But my libido remained as stubbornly inert as ever. This is
a very handsome man, I told myself over and over, this is
the most handsome man in the entire *world*. This godlike
being is *you*! How could you *not* want to make love to him?
But still nothing within me stirred. I staggered across the
cabin's main room and popped open another bottle of Dom

Pérignon/Sonoma. "One more glass," I told myself aloud, "just one more glass, and everything will be ready. . . ."

An indefinable time later, perhaps midway through the fourth bottle, I became aware of myself lying naked and half insensible in a tangled mass of blankets in the darkened bedroom. I sensed vaguely that Robert Clayborn was doing something to Mariata Divine and she was doing something to him. He and she. I and me. Me and myself. My head swirled as dizzily as the millions of brilliant stars I could see spinning wildly across the sky through the open window. He and me. She and I. Him and us. We and her. It was all desperately confusing. "I don't . . . think . . . I like . . . this," I muttered with the last of my tiny grip on reality, and fell unconscious.

The next day my head felt the way you would expect it to, only worse. "You have absorbed too many poisons," said the Robert Clayborn body sagaciously, fresh from bathing in the icy stream.

I blinked my eyelids noisily in morose agreement.

"Did you enjoy the sexual episode?" he asked.

"No."

"I am surprised that you did not. When I inhabited the Mariata Divine body, I enjoyed a number of encounters. They were all highly enjoyable. Last night, in a man's body, I—"

"Don't talk to me about sex," I snapped angrily, "especially sex with you! It was a mistake that won't be repeated. I was curious, but now I know . . ."

"Know what, Abraham Lincoln?"

"Know that life is too complicated to enjoy sex if you're Robert Clayborn, Mariata Divine, and Abraham Lincoln all at the same time. Especially when you're trying to make love to three billion Martians . . ."

"I had not considered it in such a light."

"Then do so," I said crossly. "And in the meantime, see if you can comm my daughter for me."

In the next three days I managed one brief conversation with Patricia and four with Hadrian. My son's condition continued to deteriorate as his body struggled to . . . what? Still no one knew.

But I had nothing better to do in San Francisco. Or in San Antonio. Or with Robert Clayborn. So I sat on the cabin's porch and watched the sun rise over one mountain peak and set beyond another, studiously ignoring my former body. Robert Clayborn sat stolidly in front of his vucom, doggedly plowing through the glazing techniques of the Sung dynasty.

On the fourth day Angus spoke to me. *Denise Laughingwaters' rock has just commed me. It is urgent that you return to San Antonio.*

I rose briskly to my feet, suddenly relieved of the oppressive burden that had immobilized me. I checked to make certain that Angus was in my shoulder bag and left without a word to the figure sitting motionlessly in front of the vucom. The next morning I was in San Antonio.

Once again I sat across from the striking Ms. Laughingwaters in her large corner office. Her mood was somber. "It's no good," she said. "It's not going to work. Poof! A trillion dollars up in smoke!" She gestured expressively with her hands.

"What's gone up in smoke?" I inquired, although I hardly needed to ask.

"Project Small. The Seven Dwarfs. Everything!"

"Hrmph. Why?"

She grimaced sourly and leaned across the desk. "Sooner or later the government—the Department of Human Services—had to be brought into it."

"Yes," I agreed.

"I argued for later. 'Hit 'em with a fait accompli,' I said, 'when there are ten million dwarfs ready to hit the market and it's too late to stop them.' "

"Makes sense."

"Some of the others, I won't say who but you can probably guess, argued for sooner. 'Before committing ourselves irrevocably to such an incredibly expensive undertaking,' " she mimicked bitingly, " 'we must have absolutely firm approval from DHS.' "

"And the sooners won."

"They went to DHS. DHS did a quick market survey. They told us the results. So we commissioned Gallup and Johns

Hopkins to do their own independent surveys." Her mouth twisted angrily. "Their conclusions coincided exactly with those of DHS."

"And were . . . ?"

"That given an opportunity to purchase cheap, lovable, faithful, lifetime servants, ninety-seven-point-three percent of all Americans would immediately stop having children, preferring to spend the same amount of money on the purchase and maintenance of a matched set of hardworking servants."

I slumped back in my chair. "But . . . but . . . " I protested weakly.

Denise Laughingwaters shrugged helplessly. "But what could I say to that?"

26

Or what could *I*?

Dutifully, I visited the rest of the Big Seven, all except 3L: Diversified Life, Apple-Boeing, Life/Love, IBM, Mother Bell. All of them expressed the same passionate interest as Earthly Integument. But by the time I reached the first of them, Diversified Life, the Department of Human Services had already issued a high-level circular stating categorically that the unauthorized production of unlicensed models would guarantee the offending crèche a departmental review and revocation of all other licenses.

Desperately I dangled the vision of trillions upon trillions of dollars, arguing vehemently that governmental intervention would be an unspeakable violation of every conceivable constitutional guarantee of free and unfettered commerce.

All to no avail. By the time I reached Mother Bell in Philadelphia, the last of the Big Seven, I knew that I was only going through the motions. For a few wild moments I even considered returning to Chicago to see #3L, but common sense quickly reasserted itself. With the problems they were already having with their Scottish Emperors, Lightfoot Lads and Lasses would be in no mood to challenge the government over the Seven proscribed Dwarfs.

With a heavy heart, I decided to move my operations overseas, for in spite of all my recent tribulations I still remained first and foremost an American in all of my most deep-rooted instincts. If I could just establish a tiny foothold overseas, I told myself, get just one small crèche producing the dwarfs, the Big Seven (and the ultimate beneficiaries, the American people) would certainly bring enough pressure on the Department of Human Services to lift their unconscionable prohibition.

And, of course, my four-year-old daughter Patricia was still in Europe, hidden away in an Austrian schloss. Surely in my Mariata Divine body, and using the powers of the Oneness, it would be a simple matter to recover her from my murderous consort. For how could the Oneness conceivably object to Abraham Lincoln emancipating his own daughter?

Suddenly cheered up by the prospect of liberating Patricia, I decided to stop off in New York to visit Hadrian. Ever since my return from Mars in my new body I had found excuses not to visit him. Talking to me only by rockcom, he was still unaware of my own startling metamorphosis. For with all of his other burdens, how would he react to finding his father suddenly turned into a woman?

But now, I told myself bleakly, unmercifully, *now* he was almost totally blind, and, except when he slept under hypnograph, in almost constant pain. Hard as it was for me to admit the cruel reality, my son was almost certainly in his last days on Earth.

Blind he might be, but his hearing was still relatively unimpaired. Even if I could gain admittance to his tightly quarantined quarters in my woman's body, Hadrian would know in an instant that my voice was not that of his father. As the Golden Arrow express bubble shot me from Philadelphia to New York at 375 miles an hour, I had Angus comm Hadrian's rock Tony. It was mid-afternoon, and Hadrian had just come out of hypnograph; for once he was pain-free, his mind lucid.

"Hadrian," I said, "I have something rather odd to tell you. I'd appreciate it if you'd keep it to yourself."

My lips are sealed, he replied with a flash of grim humor that nearly broke my heart. *What is it that's so odd?*

When I told him, I could hear him chuckling in my mind. *Ha! At least you're good-looking: as a kid I used to think that Mariata Divine was the most beautiful woman in San Francisco. Wait till you see me!*

With Hadrian intervening vigorously via his rock, the Mariata Divine body was eventually allowed into my son's quarters at Columbia Medical Center. Once again I found him attached by cables and tubes to the complex bank of life-support equipment behind the bed. It was hard to keep from gasping with shock at the difference in his appearance, for without ever realizing it I had apparently come to accept as normal Hadrian's metamorphosis into a shaggy brown primate. To a father's loving eyes, my son had gradually become as handsome and huggable as a giant, animated teddy bear.

Now Hadrian lay totally hairless in his bed, as shiny and pink and artificial-looking as a misshapen plastic doll. His already prominent primate's muzzle had grown even longer as his forehead and chin continued to recede. His face had become snoutlike, the skull long and pointed and—there was no denying it—unmistakably reptilian. Glittering yellow eyes that were no longer human, or even monkeylike, flicked restlessly on either side of his snout. I gulped deeply and stepped forward to take his hand.

"Hadrian," I commed.

Father.

But his hand was no longer there. The entire arm was now hardly the length of my own forearm. His hand had withered in size and mutated into a half-formed paw with five short claws. Long, curved talons were growing on the end of each claw.

I turned away, then forced myself to look more closely at the creature in the bed. Beneath the crisp white linen that covered him I could see that Hadrian's torso had lengthened and that his legs had contracted in the same way as his arms. His glossy pink skin was not the smooth, satiny skin of a human baby, but a rough, almost pebbled texture that was curiously repulsive to the eye. I repressed a shudder and took his shiny paw tentatively between the tips of my fingers. "Hadrian," I said aloud, "I'm here."

Is that really Mariata Divine's voice? The creature stirred in the bed. *It's been years since I heard her sing. I can hear you, Dad, but the words are all blurry. You'd better comm me.* His pathetic little paw scrabbled frantically against my palm. *Tell me again how you became my teenage idol. At least one of us knows what's happening to him. . . .*

I sat beside the bed and haltingly told the grotesque pink creature everything that had happened to me since coming home from federal court to find Sylvina plotting to return my daughter to the factory.

Poor Dad. First Patricia, then me, and now you. You really do have troubles, don't you?

I squeezed his dry, slippery paw. "Troubles? Nonsense! Mine are insignificant, transitory. It's *your* troubles that need fixing, yours and Patricia's. Once those are taken care of, mine will vanish."

I certainly hope so. You're on your way to Europe?

"Yes. To pick up Patricia, and see what I can do for the Oneness."

Hrmph. I wish you luck with Patricia. As for the Oneness . . . tell him on my behalf that I know of at least one body he's welcome to.

"I'll do that," I said with an anguished grimace, glancing at Hadrian's rock beside him on the night table. "Are you still following the Mets? Tony must be able to comm them to—"

"I'm afraid that you'll have to leave now, Ms. Divine," interrupted the Nightingale, gliding smoothly between us. "Doctor is on his way for his afternoon visit, and then we're going to have a nice little nap."

I squeezed my son's paw one more time and rose to my feet. "Call me whenever you feel like talking," I begged him. "Maybe we can arrange with Tony and Angus so we can listen to a baseball game together."

Yes, that sounds like fun. Hadrian's long, pink snout bobbed enthusiastically up and down against his shiny pink chest.

I lingered in the airlock that led to Hadrian's chamber until Doctor himself appeared. He was reluctant to discuss his patient with an apparent stranger, but when it became clear that I would, if necessary, follow him back into Hadrian's chamber, yelling and screaming and pulling hair, he reluctantly relented.

"He's very ill."

"I knew that."

"He's . . . well, metamorphosing again."

"I knew that too. Into what?"

"We're not yet sure. Various specialists have been in. They say that . . . "

"Well?"

"That soon we're going to have to turn him over. To sleep on his belly, you know."

"On his belly? Why?"

The doctor shrugged miserably, and for a moment he seemed almost human. "His arms, his legs, they're growing shorter, straightening out. His . . . face, his head: it's already almost resting on his chest. His tail—"

"His tail?" I echoed faintly.

"You didn't notice? It's already two feet long, nearly as long as his legs. If it gets any longer he's going to have to . . . well, learn to live lying on his stomach."

"Oh god," I muttered. "That sounds . . . sounds . . . as if . . ."

"Yes," agreed the doctor with a despairing sigh. "As if your friend is becoming a . . . giant lizard."

27

Outside of the Big Seven, all the Northworld's crèches were in Europe and North Asia. The four largest were Siemens-Peugeot, Svoboda-Benz, Nestlé, and Moskva Romanoff. The administrative headquarters of Siemens-Peugeot were in Rotterdam, a few hundred miles closer to New York than any of the others, so logically enough I began there, although at hyper jet speeds the savings in flight time between Rotterdam and Geneva could be reckoned in seconds.

As we looped high above the stratosphere I had barely time to glance through *The New York Times*. A small item on page seventeen caught my eye: panic had seized the remote Chinese province of Ningxia Huizu as word spread that three twenty-seven-year-old Emperor Chao K'uang-Yin models from Celestial Bliss had mutated into large black dogs. The Emperor Chao K'uang-Yin was the most popular single model in China, the *Times* reported, with an estimated seventeen million presently alive. Three hundred and sixty-six people had been injured in the riots that destroyed the province's seven factory dealerships. The three large black dogs were eventually found to be just that: large black dogs of impeccable canine credentials.

I chewed my lip nervously as I stared blankly at the newsfax in my lap. Suppose . . . just suppose that a really popular model such as the Mother Bell Billy Boy began to mutate. . . . How long would it take for the same panic to sweep across the United States?

• • •

Twenty-seven days had passed since I had first made my proposal to Denise Laughingwaters at Diversified Life, ample time for the news to have leaked out to the rest of the civilized world. In spite of my craftiest name-dropping, I was unable to see anyone at Siemens-Peugeot more highly placed than an assistant director of public relations. Swallowing my vexation, I made my proposition to a flaxen-haired young man who was obviously far more interested in the physical charms of Mariata Divine than by what she had to say.

"How fascinating and broadening it is to travel, Mynheer Groen," I murmured softly. "Before coming to Rotterdam, for instance, I was entirely unaware of your charming Old World custom of conducting business with hands on each other's knee." Mynheer Groen's smile broadened, and he drew even nearer on the pale blue couch. I clasped his ring finger delicately with my hand and smiled sweetly. "My own New World custom is invariably this: I count to five. At the end of that time, if the hand hasn't been removed, I then break the ring finger. After that I break the arm."

His smile faltered, vanished entirely as I suddenly applied pressure to his finger and began to bend. He snatched his hand away. "You really *mean* it!" he muttered, horror-struck, staring down at his throbbing digit.

"I really mean it," I agreed, moving to the far end of the couch. "Now then, shall we discuss the reasons for my visit, or do you have some other quaint old customs you'd like to show me?"

Now that his attention had been properly focused, Mynheer Groen listened to my presentation with delicately pursed lips. "There are two important points which distinguish the European market from the American," I said. "First, Europe has a far older tradition of households maintaining live servants. I believe that many present-day households actually have live servants from the Southworld."

"This is true."

"Second, the four major crèches in Europe are far more dominant economic entities in their individual local economies than the Big Seven in America. They exert more political weight. I seriously doubt that the local equivalent of the Department of Human Services would be able to deny you licenses for creating and merchandizing these adorable little dwarfs."

"Yes," said Mynheer Groen. "This also is true." He leaned forward, raised his finger as if to tap it against my knee for the proper emphasis, jerked it back as if it had been burnt. "Your proposal, of course, does not come as a complete surprise. It has, in fact, already been extensively discussed by the Board. I am authorized to tell you this: preliminary market surveys have been made. Interest in the proposed servants is extraordinarily high. They could obviously be sold by the millions."

"Ah?" I edged an inch or so closer to the Dutchman.

Mynheer Groen moved a nervous inch or so further away. "There are problems," he said flatly. "Unless they can be satisfactorily overcome, the board considers your proposal to be totally unfeasible."

"What are the problems?"

"First, according to our surveys, no one at all would be willing to give up his or her rock in addition to purchasing servants. They have paid good money for these rocks, Jufvrouw Divine, and they intend to keep them."

"That ought to be possible," I said slowly. "There are two billion rocks with attributes animating them. We'll put it in the contract that anyone who purchases a dwarf will not have his own rock disanimated."

"Then where will the essential anima come from?"

"Well . . . from some other rock."

"Ha! And where will that rock be?"

"Well . . . on the other side of the world, I suppose."

"Where no one will notice! Excellent. And for each full set of Seven Dwarfs, seven animas will thereby desert their rocks?"

"Well . . . yes."

"So if we were to produce twenty million full sets, at least one hundred and forty million fully-paid-for rocks would suddenly become inert. But somewhere else in the world, of course," he added sardonically.

"That is the case."

"Is it indeed?" sniffed Mynheer Groen, growing more disagreeable by the second. "Do you really think that one hundred and forty million Northworld citizens, not to mention Martian Rock & Telecommunications, would stand idly by while Siemens-Peugeot openly subverts their precious rocks and renders them useless?"

"When you put it like that," I admitted reluctantly, "it does appear to be a bit of an obstacle. But I'm sure that—"

Mynheer Groen leaned forward, his hand posed just above my knee. "What the Board wants to know is this: why do the animas for the Seven Dwarfs have to come from already functioning rocks? Why can't the rocks be left alone, and the new animas come from the central source on Mars, the Oneness himself?" He smiled winningly and actually tapped my knee lightly in his excitement.

I sat back on the couch, ignoring his hovering hand. "A reasonable enough question. If you wait a moment, I'll just ask him." A few minutes later I shook my head regretfully. "The Oneness has considered your suggestion carefully, but is forced to reject it."

"Reject it? But why?"

"His goal is to move his attributes from their rock bodies to organic bodies, not to preserve them where they already are. Your suggestion would do nothing to change the status quo, merely create a number of short-lived organic attributes."

"I see." Mynheer Groen rose briskly to his feet. "In that case, Jufvrouw Divine, I can only wish you well." As I adjusted my shoulder bag he stepped closer. "Would you *really* have broken my arm?"

"Yes."

He wet his lips with the tip of his tongue. "It's not really my thing, of course, but I hear there is a *most* decadent S/M club across the harbor in Ijsselmonde." He laid his hand fleetingly against my elbow and smiled shyly. "I'd be *most* happy to escort you there this evening. . . ."

A delightful prospect, of course, if only to see the bumptious Dutchman attached to a rack and hung from the ceiling, but reluctantly postponing that pleasure for another day, I called for an express bubble and immediately left for Berlin and the headquarters of Svoboda-Benz.

As the bubble shot across the plains of Saxony at close to five hundred miles an hour, my brooding thoughts were interrupted by Angus.

I have just been commed by Zoo-Zoo, Patricia's rock.

I sat up in sudden panic. "Zoo-Zoo? What—"

There is no cause for alarm, Robert. She was merely informing us that Sylvina and Patricia have left the schloss and taken up residence in Hong Kong.

"Hong Kong!" I echoed in dismay. "What are they doing there?"

Sylvina was apparently critical of what little dim sum there was to be found in Austria.

I gritted my teeth in anger at the fanciful tastes of my greedy-guts consort. "Where exactly are they in Hong Kong?"

In a penthouse suite of the Four Yellow Dragons.

Worse and worse. This was the favorite hotel of Southworld despots and financiers seeking absolute privacy and security. Nothing short of a Marine commando raid would be able to extricate my daughter.

"Tell Zoo-Zoo to inform us as soon as Patricia is free to talk," I ordered bleakly.

Of course, Robert.

More bad news awaited me in Berlin at the headquarters of Svoboda-Benz, where I was greeted with elaborate Teutonic courtesy by the budget director and the vice-president in charge of forward projects.

"Even if we could resolve the problem of how the animas were to be supplied," said the budget director, "we believe that yet another crucial factor has not been sufficiently considered."

"And what is that?"

Herr Gerstenberg, the Vice-President of Forward Projects, leaned across the enormous table. "These dwarfs are presumably human beings, drawn from human genetic material?"

"Of course. What else could they be?"

Herr Gerstenberg tapped a beefy knuckle on the table to punctuate his words. "I remind you, Fraulein Divine, that human beings take at least eighteen years to reach maturity, even *dwarf* human beings. Who will bear the expense of raising all these servants until they are eighteen years old?"

"Well . . ."

"Do you seriously expect a hardworking Germanic couple, desirous of procuring trained servants to ease their household tasks, to purchase a two-week-old butler in diapers? A butler whom *they* will have to feed and maintain for the next eighteen years?"

"Of course not," I said.

"Then who?"

"Naturally, I assumed that the crèche—"

"That the *crèche* could afford to raise twenty million beings for eighteen years?" The budget director of Svoboda-Benz stared at me in amazement. "We are a profit-oriented company, *not* an independent nation of twenty million people!" He shook his massive head incredulously. "I find it hard to believe that this has never occurred to your master, the so-called Martian supermind."

"So do I," I said bitterly, rising to my feet. "So do I."

The same arguments awaited me in Geneva at the Nestlé headquarters, and then in Moscow at Moskva Romanoff. Here I belatedly tried to change tack by appealing to the celebrated Russian soul. "But these rocks have *souls*," I said with all the pathos I could engender, wondering if I myself really believed this rather preposterous notion. "Inside these beautiful rocks they're human beings, just like us. Can't you see why they want—why they *need*—human bodies? Gospodin Berdyaev, how would *you* like to spend a billion years as somebody's paperweight?"

For a moment the Russian's eyes turned uneasily to the elaborate brown-and-yellow rock that lay just at his elbow, then he threw back his head and guffawed heartily.

"What a macabre notion, Tospozha Divine," he managed at last. "Why don't you tell it to the Pope?"

I glared at him angrily for a moment, then felt a slight smile tugging at my lips. I *would* tell it to the Pope. The only problem was that now there were two of them.

28

The nearest of the two pontiffs, the head of the so-called Authentic Catholics, lived in the traditional home of the popes, the Vatican City in Rome. Beyond that I knew little about this particular religious nonentity. Except for a handful of scattered thals in a half-dozen miserable enclaves such as Arkansas and Beira Baixa in Portugal, there were few practicing religionists anywhere in the Northworld. It was my understanding, bolstered now by a couple of brief questions relayed by Angus to Infozip, that most of these were Authentic Catholics, that is, those Catholics who pledged their allegiance to the pope in Rome. Why another pope, the so-called Old Pope, pontiff to the Old Catholics, should have established his own spiritual kingdom in his own Vatican City in the city of Carthage in North Africa was a question I didn't bother to ask. It was enough to know that relations between the two sects were always strained but that because neither pope could afford to purchase an army from the Northworld crèches, each of them was resigned to tolerating the other's rather marginal existence.

For the few minutes it took to pack my affairs in the Kremlin-Ritz I wondered if instead of going south to Rome I shouldn't continue eastward to the Second Celestial Empire and my daughter in Hong Kong. Nine million Chinese per year, I reminded myself, were gestated in the Empire's two central crèches, the only important life-factories that existed outside the Northworld. And supremely indifferent to the rest of the world, the imperial mandarins who directed the Second Celestial Empire would have no hesitation at all in filching the animas that resided in the rocks of the inscrutable Northworld or Southworld barbarians—*if* it served their purposes.

But who could judge what their purposes might be?

I stood pensively over my small beige suitcase, a neatly folded, bright red body stocking held motionlessly above the rest of my clothes. Before I tried to convince the hard-eyed heirs of a five-thousand-year-old civilization of the benefits of investing billions of tales in the production of seven barbarian dwarfs, I finally decided, I had best explore every other conceivable avenue.

"Don't worry, Patricia," I muttered aloud as I snapped my suitcase shut. "I haven't forgotten you."

I arrived in Rome the following morning by Translunar hyperjet and took a bubble to the Albergo Nazionale in the Piazza Montecitorio. Here I soaked luxuriously in an enormous marble bathtub while Angus commed various of the rocks that lived across the river in the Vatican City. A two-thousand-year-old hierachy of bureaucrats had encrusted themselves around the pope like a layer of protective barnacles, but none of them realized, of course, that all of their rocks were now engaged in a massive conspiracy against them.

Angus learned quickly enough that it would be impossible to approach the Pope through his appointments secretary: his audiences for the next nine weeks were already rigorously allocated. Angus moved from rock to rock, finally arriving at the one belonging to Cardinal Gustavson, the director of the church's investments program. I spoke to Cardinal Gustavson from the comfort of my bath.

"I represent the Oneness on Mars," I told His Eminence through Angus. "I am, you might say, his unaccredited but official emissary. This you may verify with your rock. It is our understanding that an important part of the Church's holdings are shares in Martian Rock & Telecommunications."

"I know nothing of that."

"Seven hundred and fifty-three thousand, two hundred and seventeen shares, the certificates of which may be found in vault number seventy-three of the Lugano branch of the Bank of Zurich. If you like, I can give you the certificate numbers."

"Who *is* this? Why did my rock comm you through to me? How could you possibly . . . Oh. The rocks. You represent the Oneness. The rocks could . . . I see. Then no secret at all is safe." He was very quick on the uptake, Cardinal Gustavson.

"Your secrets are perfectly safe with me, Your Eminence. The question is: how safe are your shares of MRT?"

"What do you mean?"

"As a hypothetical question, what do you think your shares would be worth if—let us say—the Oneness refused to permit the functioning of any attribute in any rock quarried after tomorrow?"

There was a long pause during which I languidly soaped Mariata Divine's beautiful legs. "The shares would be worthless," ventured Cardinal Gustavson at last.

"Yes."

"My rock confirms that you are indeed an emissary of the Oneness." There was another pause. "If you would do me the enormous courtesy of calling upon me in my office, I will free my entire afternoon for your visit."

I refused the Cardinal's offer of an official bubble and strolled slowly through the soft afternoon of the Eternal City, down past the Pantheon, across the Piazza Navona, and along the bubble-choked Corso Vittorio Emanuele until I came to the Tiber. Just across the river the familiar dome of St. Peter's Basilica loomed against the sky. I crossed the bridge and followed the Street of Conciliation towards the vast expanse of St. Peter's Square, ruminating happily upon mankind's fascinating capacity for unexpected and delightful folly.

This majestic cathedral that bulked before me, the crowning glory of the Italian Renaissance, was, I knew, little more than a gigantic stage set, a papier-mâché basilica constructed by the special effects teams of a Russo-American hologram studio. For reasons that weren't clear to me, but that were certainly rooted in the good old-fashioned emotions of greed, spite, and selfishness, upon their departure across the Mediterranean to Carthage, the Old Catholics and the Old Pope had taken with them the entire Vatican City. An emergency replacement had been erected by the hologram studio; now, slowly, slowly, as funds were painstakingly accumulated from the few remaining faithful, the Authentic Catholics were replacing each hastily created illusion with buildings made by hand from the original materials. At the present rate of restoration, I had been informed by Infozip, the great dome of St. Peter's Basilica would be completed in October of 3021. . . .

The meeting with the cadaverous Cardinal Gustavson took place in his offices overlooking the gardens behind St. Peter's. I gave the Cardinal my solemn assurance that it was the Oneness's implacable determination to liberate his imprisoned attributes from their present rocks. One way or another, all MRT stock would soon be worthless. The holy man turned his pale blue eyes toward his rock for a long moment. "The opening price on Wall Street is eighty-seven and an eighth," he told me presently. "I believe you already know that we own 753,217 shares. That would be . . . $65,624,031."

"And 13 cents."

"Yes. It will be difficult to sell so large a block without disturbing the market."

"But not so difficult as it will be to sell it two months from now."

The Cardinal sighed. "I suppose not. Forgive me for being so brusque, but what do you want in return for this invaluable information?"

"Very little, Your Eminence: merely an audience with His Holiness the Pope. To discuss with him the spiritual issues attendant upon this forthcoming upheaval."

Cardinal Gustavson nodded ponderously, his thoughts clearly far away on the contents of vault number seventy-three in Lugano, Switzerland. "A reasonable request for the official emissary of the Oneness. Will this evening in His Holiness's private quarters be sufficiently soon?"

I bowed my head respectfully. "Absolutely, Your Eminence."

The private apartments of Pope Gregory XVIII were as sumptuous and treasure laden as I suppose those of the Renaissance popes to have been. Whether they were the creation of generations of master craftsmen or of an American-Russo special effects team it was impossible to judge. The pontiff had just concluded his evening meal and had moved into his long, book-lined library. In spite of the warm summer air, he greeted me in a heavy maroon gown liberally splashed with white ermine and the glitter of gold. A glass of dark red wine and a long black cigar sat on the table beside his massive armchair.

We appraised each other silently for a long moment, then each of us nodded politely to the other, I to the spiritual leader of the Universal Church, he to the ambassador of a quasi-godlike being.

"A glass of wine?" asked Gregory XVIII, gesturing me towards a high, uncomfortable-looking couch covered with dull gold brocade.

"That would be delightful."

We settled on each end of the couch, the Pope's hands folded comfortably across his ample belly. Thick white hair framed a ruddy face still glowing with the pleasures of the table. Sharp blue eyes glittered watchfully. "Cardinal Gustavson informs me that you come on a matter of some urgency," he said with a slight Irish accent.

"Yes, Your Holiness. The Oneness has become interested in souls."

"Has he indeed?" The Pope's bushy white eyebrows climbed his broad forehead. "After four billion years?"

"A long time even in the lifetime of the Oneness. Ample time to consider the question of souls. What the Oneness would like to know is *your* position on souls."

The Pope stretched a long arm out to the table beside him, then puffed cautiously on his cigar. "Hundreds of thousands of books have been written about the soul," he murmured. "It is a matter of the broadest speculation."

"Contradictory speculation."

"Only amongst unbelievers," said Gregory XVIII firmly.

"Much of the Northworld is composed of unbelievers—in fact, most of it."

"Temporarily, only temporarily. A mere instant in the eye of God."

"Many of the Authentic Catholics in the state of Arkansas appear to feel that only they have souls, that all of those gestated in the crèches of the Northworld are essentially golems, without souls."

The Pope blew smoke thoughtfully toward the cherubim and angels who hovered on the library's elaborately frescoed ceiling. "A common, but understandable, error. All of God's children have souls, whether they acknowledge the fact or not."

"Then I myself, for instance, designed and gestated in a crèche, am completely human and in no way spiritually inferior to those persons conceived and born the old-fashioned way in such areas as Arkansas?" I awaited the pontiff's answer with some curiosity; Angus had informed me that His Holiness was as much a product of the crèche as I: a Brian Borahma from the small but estimable crèche of Blackwater in Dublin.

"Your question begs innumerable theological strictures of the gravest importance, but in a word: In God's infinite love, those of us unfortunate enough to be born in a crèche nevertheless have precisely the same potentiality for salvation and immortality as any of those conceived and born in the manner originally ordained by God."

I sipped my wine briefly. "Then all of us, no matter how humble, or whatever their origin, have souls."

"Such is the case." The pontiff puffed vigorously upon his cigar.

"What then of the Oneness, Your Holiness? Does he too have a soul?"

The cloud of blue smoke around the Pope's head grew thicker. "This is a troubling theological question, one which has remained essentially unanswered in spite of prolonged inquiry into the matter by the Fifth Vatican Council."

"But he thinks, therefore he is. How could he *not* have a soul?"

"Hmmm, *cogitat ergo est,* an excellent point. Yes, the Oneness undoubtedly *is."* The Pope waved his cigar at me. "But is *what?"*

"Why, a Martian, of course. What else could he be?"

His Holiness shrugged. "A creation of the Devil, of course, placed here to lead mankind astray."

I gaped at the addled holy man in awe. Could he actually *believe* such nonsense? "But . . . all of us on Earth are *descended* from him, we're all his *children!* How could he be a creation of the Devil?"

The Pope's jovial red face hardened. "How do we *know* we are his descendants? How do we *know* that billions of his attributes once walked the surface of the Earth? There is not the slightest historical, geological, or genetic evidence of it. We have, in fact, only his *word* for it. Only *his* word that he is not, in fact, a guise of Satan himself!"

"But . . . but . . ." I fell back limply against the high, hard back of the couch. How *did* I know that anything the Oneness had told me was the truth? I shook myself briskly. Whether the Oneness was old Beelzebub Incarnate or not was no concern of mine. . . .

"Then what about the rocks," I asked, gesturing vaguely with my wineglass, "what about the two billion rocks here on Earth?"

Pope Gregory XVIII's eyes narrowed. "What about them?"

"Each of them is an individual living being, each of them possesses an anima, a soul, if you will, which—"

"Nonsense!" interrupted the Pope vehemently. "The rocks no more have souls than dogs or cats! Friendly, affectionate, useful beasts, beloved by God, but still nothing more than beasts! Only Man can have a soul!"

"But assume that the Oneness *does* have a soul," I argued desperately. "Then each of his attributes, even if presently inhabiting a rock—"

"Never, never, never!" cried the Pope. "A rock is a rock, and always will be, no matter *what* noises it can make inside your mind!"

I took a deep breath and tried to keep from shouting at the apoplectic Irishman. "But suppose," I whispered, "just *suppose,* that through the miracle of modern science the anima of a Martian rock could be guided into a *human* body? *Then* wouldn't that body be considered to have a—"

The Pope's eyes bulged and his cigar fell to the floor from trembling fingers. "Blasphemy!" he shouted. "Satanic heresy! Palpable error! Only human souls can inhabit human bodies!"

29

Houris are those beautiful virgins who await devout Moslems in Mohammedan paradise as a reward for earthly piety. According to the Moslems' holy book, the Koran, these lovely women are essentially soulless playthings, far removed from the reality of earthly women. Certain Mohammedan modernists, in particular those currently in power in the small Arabian sheikdom of Al Masirah, had come to the conclusion that the Koran's description of these delightful toys coincided perfectly with the lustful, but soulless, women now produced by the million in the Northworld's satanic zombie factories.

Why, asked the theologians of Al Masirah, shouldn't every devout Moslem provide himself with earthly houris here and now, where he could be absolutely certain of profiting from their attentions, rather than having to wait for the tedium of death to enjoy their fabulous charms?

And why, for that matter, even *consider* declaring jihad against the undoubted monsters of the Northworld, as certain hotheads suggested? Not only was it bound to fail, but it would also endanger the sole source of supply of houris.

Thus the Sheikdom of Al Masirah, whose coffers contained an ample reserve of Northworld credits for the purchase of luxury goods such as soulless female zombies. . . .

The neighboring Islamic directorate of Masqat was an impoverished state still in the hands of austere traditionalists. Its clerics firmly rejected the heretical notions of the radical sheiks, and armed hostilities using the manufactured soldiers of the hated Northworld broke out three months later. So far, I learned from the editorial in the Rome edition of the *International Herald Tribune,* sixteen thousand soldiers had been killed—nine thousand George S. Pattons from Life/Love fighting for Al Masirah and the glory of Allah, and seven thousand Viking Berserkers from Nestlé fighting for Masqat and the glory of Allah.

The editorialist went on to deplore this ghastly waste of human life. Why did the supposedly civilized Northworld continue to furnish the means by which the undeniably barbaric Southworlders could indulge their gruesome taste for bloody slaughter at little or no risk to themselves? How much had the centuries-long peace and prosperity enjoyed by the Northworld come to depend upon this grisly traffic in human misery? What, in fact, when one contemplated the sad spectacle of these mangled young bodies lying lifeless in the Arabian sands, was there to distinguish between those in the Northworld who gestated and sold this hapless cannon fodder and those in the Southworld who actually deployed it?

"We only *make* them," I muttered angrily, "*we* don't send them out to be killed! That's what distinguishes us from the savages: we just sell the gun, *we* don't use it to murder anyone." I glared down at the *Herald Tribune* as the propulsors of the Air Africain shuttle suddenly changed in tone to a deep rumble and the aircraft banked steeply over the glistening blue waters of the Mediterranean. From the top of my window I caught a brief glimpse of the dazzling white buildings of Carthage. I dropped the newsfax crossly to the floor.

But suppose you know *that the gun you sell will be used to murder someone?* asked a quiet voice in my mind.

"Be quiet, Angus," I commed irritably. "It's not at all the same thing. . . ."

The airport was filled with heavily armed policemen and soldiers in gaudy red-and-white uniforms, and a heavy tension seemed to fill the hot, muggy air. My American passport was scrutinized closely and I was questioned minutely by an officious immigration officer about my motives for coming to Carthage. "You are not a Catholic?"

"No. Merely a tourist."

"A tourist. What is there here to interest a Northworld tourist?"

"I don't know. I'm here to find out. That's why I'm a tourist."

"It seems most peculiar," he muttered, staring down again at my passport. "How do I know you are not a spy?"

"Your Vatican is very famous," I suggested tentatively.

"It is out-of-bounds to tourists," he snapped, happy at last to be able to deny me something. "You will not be permitted to visit it."

"Why is that?" I asked in dismay.

"His Holiness is about to declare war upon you Northworld zombies." He stamped my passport vigorously with three different implements as if he were already assaulting the enemies of the Church. "Next time, read the newsfax before coming to Carthage."

"I'll do that," I said meekly, and move past three armed soldiers into the terminal. I collected as many different newsfax as I could find and stuffed them into my shoulder bag. Their language was of no importance: with a little added concentration on my part, Angus could scan them through my eyes and somewhere comm a fellow rock for the translation.

I stepped out into the blazing African heat and stood blinking in the sun as I wondered what to do next. Finally I shrugged and hailed a bubble, an enormous, ancient Volvo whose transparent canopy was nearly opaque with age. The hatch popped open and I stepped inside. To my astonishment, a live human being sat before the controls, apparently to guide the vehicle. The conductor was a woman of indeterminate shape hidden by a bulky gray gown and a coarse black veil. Shiny black eyes glittered beneath the hood that concealed the rest of her head.

"Hotel Majestic?" I asked uncertainly.

She nodded and directed me in with an imperious gesture. The hatch slammed shut behind me and the bubble lurched violently into the flow of traffic. As it erratically gathered speed, I tried in vain to peer through its opaque canopy at the historic countryside flowing past. I could see nothing but a blur of green and white. I sat back with a sigh on the lumpy seat and waited crossly to be delivered to Carthage.

It was here on the north coast of Africa, Infozip had informed me during my flight from Rome, that the Donatic Heresy had flourished two thousand years earlier as the Bishop of Carthage vied for supremacy of the early Christian Church with the Bishop of Rome. For a brief period the Donatics had been nearly equal in strength to the Christians in Rome, but eventually their movement had been suppressed and the city that sheltered them utterly destroyed in 698 A.D. For fifteen hundred years the ruins of the once mighty city of Carthage lay forgotten beneath the sands of Africa.

Now another great city had arisen, one that rivaled Mecca and Jerusalem and a dozen other religious centers as a spiritual capital of the fractious tangle of nations that composed the Southworld. Here the Old Catholics had reerected the original St. Peter's Basilica and the rest of the Vatican City, adamantly proclaiming it the one and only genuine Holy See. In the Northworld all except the Authentic Catholics totally ignored their posturings; in the Southworld they were tolerated as one more curious sect among many.

The bubble screeched to a sudden halt that nearly snapped my head against the seat in front of me. Blurry forms materialized around us and an authoritative knuckle rapped sharply against the canopy. The hatch swung open and two armed soldiers peered into the bubble. A hand was extended and sharp words exchanged with the veiled crone at the controls. "Your papers," she muttered aggrievedly, "they want to see our papers."

The senior of the two soldiers scrutinized my passport closely, compared it suspiciously with my Mariata Divine face, reluctantly handed it back. The other examined the grimy wad of documentation belonging to the driver and bubble with equal skepticism. At last he nodded grudgingly, tossed the papers disdainfully to the floor, and stepped back into the blazing sunlight. The hatch slammed shut and the bubble lurched forward.

"What was that about?" I asked, trying to conceal my nervousness.

"It's been like that ever since the synod began," said the crone.

"What synod is that?"

"The one the holy Christian pope called, the Ecumenical Synod, to proclaim jihad against the infidels."

"Ah," I said with a sinking feeling in my stomach. "And just who are the infidels?"

The crone turned away from the controls, and for a moment her dark eyes stared me in somber hatred. "Why, zombies like yourself, of course, all the zombies of the Northworld. We are going to kill you all."

I made very certain that the locks on the door of my room in the Hotel Majestic were securely fastened, then asked Angus to comm all of his fellow rocks within a one-hundred-mile radius of Carthage. "Inform them that their savior Abraham Lincoln is here in room 2743. Their single greatest concern if they expect to be emancipated is now to keep Abraham Lincoln alive and well. They are to instantly report to you any and all conversations, communications, or activities that might in even the remotest way be connected with me or my person. Is that clear?"

Of course, Robert. We shall do whatever is necessary to protect you.

"Thank you, Angus. I knew I could count on you."

But I am afraid that we can only be useful to a certain point. There are very few of us in the Southworld; here in the hotel, there are only two rocks that do not belong to other tourists.

I nodded wearily and lay back on the bed with the collection of newsfax I had amassed at the airport. What was I doing here in Carthage, I asked myself, what could I conceivably expect from the Old Pope that I hadn't got in Rome from the Authentic Pope?

Without ever having visited them, I knew in a general way that none of the Southworld countries had the resources or technologies to develop their own industrialized crèches. The process of gestating millions of healthy children on an industrial scale demanded a technology at least equal to that of the production of commercial hyperjets, and the initial capital investment was concomitantly stupendous.

Israel, Brazil, and India could probably have built their own crèches, but for reasons of their own apparently preferred to leave the vital business of reproduction to the hazardous vagaries of traditional methods. The rest of the Southworld—all those squabbling states who wanted nothing so fervently as their own factories to produce an endless supply of cheap and expendable cannon fodder—were constrained to expend most of their energies and budgets on wresting a living from their depleted resources—and fighting each other in their spare moments with Northworld soldiers.

From time to time each of the Northworld crèches had ingenuously proposed expanding its operations overseas into the Southworld, always in the name of reduced costs and increased stockholders' profits; each time they had been firmly enjoined from doing so by ferocious government watchdogs.

One hundred and forty-seven years before, three senior executives of the small French crèche of Bonbel-Camembert had been publicly guillotined in the Place de la Concorde for surreptitiously attempting to export an entire production line to Cochin China. No further examples were needed.

An absolute fact of human nature is that if you can't attain your heart's desire, the surest way of dispelling your disappointment is by convincing yourself that you never wanted it in the first place. This was what most of the nations of the Southworld had attempted to do with various degrees of conviction.

The sect of Old Catholics, according to Infozip, had been the first to trumpet that their spiritual sensibilities were gravely traduced by the ethics of gestating children in crèches—or in test tubes and bottles, as their childish propaganda always chose to put it. The rest of the Southworld quickly followed their lead, Christian, Jew, Moslem, Hindu, and Animist alike. Official Southworld policy was that of adamant opposition to the entire system of life-styling—except, of course, as a thrifty and painless means of procuring soldiers for their own bloody enterprises. . . .

And now, according to the various newsfax that Angus and I pored through on my bed in the Hotel Majestic, the Old Pope had convoked a gathering of all the spiritual leaders of the Southworld in order to declare a holy war against the soulless zombies of the North.

I moved from one Southworld newsfax to another with growing astonishment and concern. Enveloping himself in his gown of Papal Infallibility, the Pope had proclaimed it official Church dogma that none of the crèche-gestated people who populated half the world were actually human beings. In consequence it was no sin to kill them.

The scattering of Sephardic Jews attending the Ecumenical Synod mostly agreed: to them we were soulless golem. A few of the particularly orthodox argued that in spite of our being no more than beasts, we of the Northworld should nevertheless be ritually slaughtered according to the strictest kosher regulations. This contention was eventually rejected on the grounds that kosher regulations applied only to animals intended to be eaten.

To the Moslems, we Northworlders were man-made demons, incapable of embracing the one true God, and fit only for death. The tiny Arab sheikdom of Al Masirah once again voiced its objection that by killing the Northworlders the prospect of flesh-and-blood houris would be forever dashed. This sensible plea for moderation was voted down by more conservative Moslems, and eventually the peculiarly disparate grouping of religionists assembled at the snyod agreed to declare jihad against the Northworld.

Now the question became: how?

The Southworld was opposed by an incalculable superiority of matériel, fission-fusion weapons, and delivery systems, plus, as the Southworld's spiritual lords loudly lamented, the Northworld's total lack of religious scruple. It was finally decided that the Holy War to be waged to the death of the last infidel would begin with an economic boycott of all the commercial products of the Northworld—excepting only their exemplary mass-produced soldiers, who henceforth would no longer be used by brother against Southworld brother.

"Lenin once said that the capitalists would gladly sell the rope by which they themselves would be hanged," passionately declaimed an orator from New South Mali to the enormous throng gathered in the marble hush of St. Peter's Basilica. "Let us go that great revolutionary one better: let us now actively use the soldiers of the Northworld to kill their soulless manufacturers and wipe them forever from the face of the Earth!"

30

All of this was the rankest demagogic nonsense, of course, I reflected sourly as my bubble took me along the broad streets of Carthage to the Vatican City. Soulless we Northworlders might be; idiots we were not. No life-styled soldier ever left his crèche for the battlefields of the Southworld without carrying deep within his psyche a built-in genetic booby trap, a self-destruct mechanism that would cause instant cardiac arrest at the merest hint of his being turned against his manufacturer.

But no one at the Ecumenical Synod had raised that embarrassing fact in their all-consuming frenzy of Northworld hatred, and now that the delegates had returned home to consider the actual means by which their economic boycott would be put into effect, the synod itself had instantly vanished from the pages of the local newsfax. The Old Pope became just another local curiosity, another small source of tourist dollars. Arranging an audience with this holy, but neglected, personage had been as simple as having Angus ask for it, for it was rare indeed in this world of 2345 that anyone from the hated Northworld even bothered to acknowledge his existence.

Now the bubble came to the majestic sweep of St. Peter's Square, hesitated momentarily, then moved slowly across its vast empty expanse to the broad steps at the foot of the great Basilica. Two dozen elaborately costumed Swiss Guards from the Nestlé crèche stood attentively in two lines. A priest in

a nondescript white gown appeared from behind the guards
and led me up the steps into the cool hush of the Basilica.
For nearly an hour he reverently pointed out the tombs of the
popes, the statues by Bernini and Michelangelo, the chapels,
the mosaics, the altars, the tomb of St. Peter, all the gilded
magnificence that marked the glory of what had once been the
Universal Church. At last he led me into the Sistine Chapel. A
dozen tourists in orange robes, and a smaller number of somber art historians, gaped up at Michelangelo's barely visible
fresco. A half-concealed door led to a bare passageway and
a narrow flight of stairs. Two treasure-filled passageways and
another flight of stairs finally brought us to an imposing door
before which stood two more Swiss Guards.

The doors swung open and I was ushered into the presence
of my second Pope in as many weeks, Anastasius V. This
was not the baroque splendor of the Sala Regia in which the
pontiff formally received ambassadors and heads of state; the
room was vast, high-ceilinged, austere, devoid of art except
for two enormous paintings. The Old Pope sat in an upright
throne on the far side of a glistening marble floor. His hands
fluttered in some sort of a benediction, and I nodded with as
much ambassadorial gravitas as I could muster. The priest
behind me whispered softly, and I marched noisily across the
marble floor, conscious of the Old Pope's brooding eyes on
me. Little wonder, I thought, that they were pensive: it must
be seldom that he was asked to grant a private audience to a
body as alluring as that of Mariata Divine, a third-rate cabaret singer who now claimed to be the official representative
of the known universe's mightiest being.

A Swiss Guard materialized behind me with a straight-
backed chair and the priest moved discreetly to one side. I
was left sitting by myself while Anastasius V stared down at
me from his throne with fathomless brown eyes. I stared back
with equal curiosity. Like everyone else I had encountered
here in Carthage, he was obviously no optimized creation of
the life-sytlist's studio, but a pure old-fashioned thal such as
those I had encountered so many years before in Arkansas.
His round, brown face was an incredible mass of tiny wrinkles and his fingers were gnarled and twisted with age. A
gleaming white robe did little to conceal his short, squatty

figure. In spite of his present eminence, Anastasius V looked very much the stolid Guatemalan peasant who had joined the priesthood fifty years before.

"You represent the Oneness, my daughter?" he asked in a pleasantly lilting English.

"Yes, Your Holiness. You may have already confirmed this with your rock."

"I have no rock, except that of St. Peter." His mild brown eyes twinkled momentarily. "But no doubt a number of them may be found even here in the Holy City, catalogued perhaps as works of modern art. Possibly one of my assistants may have consulted with them about you."

"Is it possible that Your Holiness has no rock because you know them to be imbued with souls—which would therefore make you the owner of a . . ." I shrugged helplessly, nearly overcome by giggles at the enormity of my hypocrisy. "I can't say another human being, because they obviously aren't, but—"

"But which would make me a slaveholder all the same, eh?" The Old Pope's broad lips twitched slightly. In amusement? "Is that what you've come to say: that the so-called Martian rocks have souls?"

"Yes, Your Holiness, that is the inescapable conclusion to which four billion years of reflection have led the Oneness. Since he is, of course, entirely congnizant of the supremacy of your own spiritual position here on Earth, he has requested me to ask for your confirmation of this basic and inalienable sentient right."

The pontiff scratched his slightly grizzled chin with a gnarled hand while I watched skeptically. As a direct pipeline from God who had just decreed that half the human race had no souls at all, there was little chance that this befuddled Guatemalan would find any vestige of that elusive will-o'-the-wisp in a mere chunk of Martian rock. But the Old Pope surprised me. "Why is it suddenly so important that rocks be determined to have souls just *now?*" he asked with some of the shrewdness that must have carried him to his present exalted heights.

"Both the Oneness as an entity and the individual attributes of each rock have begun to chafe in their present con-

dition of involuntary bondage. If they were widely
acknowledged by a moral leader such as yourself to possess
immortal souls, that would be the first step in releasing them
from that bondage.''

"I see.'' The cunning brown eyes peered down at me.
"But what would they be released *into?*''

I summarized briefly my previous hopes for the Seven
Dwarfs. "For the moment, that particular project may have
to be held in abeyance. But if someone of Your Holiness's
universal moral stature were to unequivocally hold that the
rocks have souls, then almost certainly we could find a government willing to authorize a crèche to gestate bodies capable of receiving these souls.''

"Hmm. On the face of it, a worthy project indeed. How
would the purchase of these bodies be arranged?''

I shrugged again. "This is a matter still to be considered.
Perhaps a philanthropic organization could be organized to
purchase bodies for worthy rocks.''

"I see.'' The Old Pope leaned down from his throne and
his eyes glittered brightly. "And what did the Antichrist in
Rome say to your request?''

I shook my head mournfully. "I was astonished by his
reaction, Your Holiness, although perhaps I should not have
been. He shouted at me that a rock was a rock, and would
always remain a rock.''

"Ha!'' The pontiff sat back on his throne, his heavy peasant's head nodding ponderously. "Of course, of course . . .
What else could be expected from the Antichrist?'' For a
long moment his eyes wandered to the immense Raphael that
hung on the wall to his right, then returned to me. An index
finger drummed against an arm of his throne and he leaned
forward again. "At the moment I see nothing inherent in
God's word or in established Church doctrine against my declaring the Oneness and his attributes to be possessors of
souls. What interests me, however, is the actual bodies to
which these souls might then transmigrate. Your notion of
the Seven Dwarfs, while ingenious and thoroughly capitalis-
tic, is, of course, both frivolous and ultimately sterile. What
would we do in a world eventually overrun by seven varieties
of dwarfs unable to reproduce themselves by natural means?

No." He reached out to wiggle a thick brown finger at me. "As I see it, the situation is this: the Oneness needs bodies, and the Mother Church needs bodies—in the form of soldiers who can prosecute our holy war against the Antichrist."

"I don't understand," I muttered feebly, understanding all too well.

"The Vatican is a sovereign state," explained the Old Pope softly. "It, and all the other nations of the Southworld, are authorized to purchase bodies from the Northworld factories."

"Yes, but—"

"We will specify that each and every body that we purchase must henceforth be animated with a Martian soul. Surely the Northworld authorities would have no objection to that?"

"I suppose not, but—"

"Upon delivery of each child, we would of course have him or her baptized as an Old Catholic in the one truth faith. Could the Northworld functionaries object to that?"

"No, but—"

"Eventually, of course, these children would grow up and being to reproduce themselves as God originally intended. I am convinced that with fresh and untainted souls in them, and properly raised under the guidance of the Church, these fine young men and women would be impervious to whatever secret commands of autodestruction that the zombie factories implant within them."

"Perhaps, but—"

The pontiff had pulled an old-fashioned electronic calculator from beneath his robes and was stabbing at it vigorously. "If we could buy twenty million bodies a year for just five years," I heard him mutter, "and subsequently lost only fifty million of them in destroying the zombie factories, assuming then that each of the survivors then had twelve healthy children, and each of *them* had . . . mmm . . . mmm . . . yes . . . mmm . . . yes . . . in four or five generations at the *most*, the entire Northworld could be repopulated with human beings again." The holy loony looked up with his face glowing. "With *Catholic* human beings!"

I forced myself to keep my voice mild and ambassadorial.

"You propose, then, to use your Catholic soldiers to wipe out the entire population of the Northworld?"

"Perhaps some of our allies would insist upon a portion of them being raised in the Moslem or Jewish faiths, but this would be the essence of our program, yes."

"Before committing the Oneness to such a dramatic course of action, I shall naturally have to consult with him. But I think that almost certainly he will voice strong objections to participating in any activities which cause harm to other human beings."

Anastasius V smiled benignly. "Of *course* he would object, and rightly so. But you are forgetting, my dear: these are *not* human beings we are considering; these are *Northworlders*, totally devoid of souls."

I fell back in my chair. "Yes, I *had* forgotten that. . . ." I straightened my shoulder bag and rose to my feet. Obviously, no practical help would be forthcoming from this saintly lunatic. "I will communicate Your Holiness's proposals to the Oneness."

The Old Pope's hands moved again in the same benediction with which he had greeted me. "I would appreciate your doing so. Surely the Oneness could not object to the merciful killing of soulless beasts in the course of gaining salvation for his own soul." He cocked his head suspiciously. "He's not a Buddhist, is he?" he asked in sudden alarm.

"I don't think so," I muttered, having no very clear idea of what Buddhists were or did.

"In that case I am certain there will be no problem. May you go with God."

"Thank you, Your Holiness." I turned toward the distant door, then swung back to face him. I was still smarting from his callous dismissal of my own humanity. "But I'm *real*," I told him vehemently, "I'm *human*. *All* of us crèche-born people are! We're just as human as—"

"No, my dear," interrupted Anastasius V, shaking his head regretfully, "you yourself are a beautiful simulacrum and, even though the emissary of the Oneness, almost certainly the handiwork of the Devil. Never forget that Satan is the Father of Lies: I'm afraid that you just *think* that you're real—a terrible illusion."

"And this gives you the right to kill us all?"

"Japan," murmured the Old Pope with a small shrug. "Look at Japan."

For a long puzzled moment I looked at Japan, a country that hadn't even *existed* for over two hundred years now. What could he mean by Japan? The only thing I knew about Japan was what nearly everyone outside the life-styling industry had long since forgotten: the fact that the process of gestating perfect, standardized children under the most modern and hygienic conditions had only been *invented* by American science and industry. It was the Japanese, an antlike Oriental people living on a small volcanic island on the far side of the Pacific, who had actually put into operation the large-scale crèche system. The Japanese were the supreme industrialists of the planet; within twenty years the entire lifestyling industry belonged to them. It was in Japan, not the United States, that the first 100 million Northworld models were gestated.

And it was Japan that suddenly first exploded, then collapsed one Sunday morning into the Pacific Ocean, vanishing utterly and forever with its 130 million natives and 12 million gestating infants. . . .

I stared at the Old Pope in growing horror. "You mean . . ."

Anastasius V nodded sadly. "God's judgment upon the Japanese for the blasphemy of manufacturing human simulacra."

"But that's *awful*!"

"Man must always stand in awe before God's will," agreed the old madman serenely.

God's judgment upon the blasphemers . . . So that was what gave this appalling lunatic the right to declare jihad against two billion human beings. . . .

I clattered angrily past the hovering priest and across the polished marble of the Throne Room to the two great doors. They swung open before me and I strode tight-lipped down the broad hallway filled with its priceless works of art. It was only when I finally stood in the warm afternoon sun that flooded St. Peter's Square, breathing deeply as I tried to regain control of my temper, that I recalled a point of historical irony that would certainly have been lost on the holy loony:

The Japanese factories had been gestating infants exclusively for the *overseas* market; the blasphemous Japanese themselves preferred to reproduce—to quote His Holiness Anastasius V—"as God originally intended . . ."

31

My daughter was still in Hong Kong, hidden away with her mother behind the fortresslike security of the Four Yellow Dragons. As soon as the almost unlimited financial resources of the Oneness had been placed at my disposal, I had, of course, immediately arranged for a heavyweight battery of legalists to represent Robert Clayborn and daughter in the proceedings that had been instigated to return Patricia to the crèche. But in spite of their best efforts, Sylvina's shyster, that egregious Harmonian Apollo named George Abbadecka, was making considerable progress. An initial hearing at Children's Court had upheld the theoretical, though rarely invoked, right of a single consort to return a child to the crèche over the objection of the other parent if sufficient cause were found. My shysters were now appealing this crucial point through the federal courts, but they were exceedingly guarded in forecasting a successful outcome. I thought bitter thoughts about Sylvina Ashley, and surreptitiously commed my daughter whenever Sylvina and Ingrid the Nanny were out of sight.

Daddy, she cried, *why aren't you here?*

How could I answer that, any more than I could answer my son's unspoken cry of Why have I turned into a giant lizard?

I had returned to New York for three days after my fruitless trip to Europe and North Africa and had spent most of my waking hours with Hadrian. His painful metamorphosis into

a lizardlike being had now apparently stabilized, and he was
as cheerful as could be expected considering the grotesque
circumstances of his radically altered life. He moved gracefully about the floor of his quarters on thick, stubby legs, his
smooth yellow belly gliding across the polished surface, his
long, thick tail lashing restlessly behind him. But even
through a father's loving eyes it was impossible to discern
any vestiges of his once familiar features in the long yellow
snout with the unblinking reptilian eyes.

Hadrian's bed had been lowered to the floor for easier access, and it was from down there on its crisp white linen that
he watched the last two games of the 2345 World Series while
I sat in a chair beside him. The Mets had finally made it into
the Series after all, and four of the games were being played
here in New York. Each day a messenger service arranged
for by Angus delivered a large carton of hot dogs, peanuts,
and draft beer from the concession stands at the ballpark
across the river. Hadrian's new digestive system firmly rejected the beer, but he chomped happily on the hot dogs and
the peanuts that I shelled for him, and occasionally emitted
little grunts of contentment as the Mets rallied to win both
games and the Series. His lizardlike paws could no longer
hold eating implements or books, but before I returned to
Europe we cobbled together an automatic book-holder and
page-turner activated by commands from his rock Tony.

Just another typical giant iguana, he said to me through
Tony as I got ready to take my leave on the final evening.
*Not much place for us in New York, though, outside of the
Bronx Zoo. As soon as I'm out we'll get a place in Mexico,
go lie in the sun and run after the lady iguanas, eh, Dad?*

I ran my fingers sadly down the sleek curve of his long
back. "You bet, Hadrian. Just lie in the sun and . . ." My
voice caught in my throat and I was unable to go on.

Assuming, of course, that I survive at all, continued Hadrian matter-of-factly. *Not everyone has, you know, in changing from monkey to lizard. The stresses seem to have been
much greater; about five percent of . . . us didn't make it.*

I swallowed hard. "I know. I talked to the doctors on the
way in."

Hadrian's snout bobbed slightly. *They still don't know what to make of us, but I think they're becoming cautiously optimistic that maybe we're the only models affected. They've looked all over the Northworld: no one else seems to be having problems.*

"I know. My shysters tell me 3L is going crazy trying to find another . . . mutation."

Why . . . ? Oh. If they could find another model from another crèche turning into a silkworm, or growing wings, maybe they could argue it was all an act of God, not a dirty test tube in their own production line. Hadrian's mouth opened and his long brown tongue fluttered in disgust. He was too loyal to mention that the same argument would serve to absolve his father, Robert Clayborn, from the same hideous responsibility.

"At least the panic in the streets seems to have died down," I said as I gathered my shoulder bag. "From the little I've been in the streets," I added.

You . . . your body is still lost in the woods?

"Behind a million trees and a solid wall of shysters."

It doesn't feel strange, being a woman?

"A little. After a while you get used to it."

Like everything. I think it'd be kind of fun.

"Being a woman?" I sniffed in ladylike fashion. "Try telling that to my psyche." I hung my bag from shoulder. "And try telling it to the Southworlders I'm on my way to see: they think a woman's place is pulling the plow."

Or in the harem, laughed Hadrian. *Watch out you don't end up in one.*

I reached down to ruffle the folds of flesh just behind his ears. "I'll watch out. *You* watch out for those lady iguanas." I ran out before I could burst into tears.

32

Actually, not *every* Southworlder thought a woman's place was pulling the plow. One who most certainly didn't was the Empress of Kilimanjaro, an stony-eyed black woman a head taller than myself and three times wider who looked as if she chewed four men for breakfast and five for afternoon tea. She was the twenty-third on the list of Southworld potentates, presidents, and despots I had visited over the last three months, and by now I expected no more from her than I had gotten from any of her fellow rulers.

Which was exactly nothing.

You would think that somewhere, somehow, some country, *any* country, could have been inveigled into placing a small trial order with any crèche of their choice for a million prime bodies to serve as devoted servants and able-bodied workers. Directed by tireless Martian animas and guaranteed for life by the Oneness himself, the bodies could be depended upon for three-quarters of a century of all-purpose use, from the most physically rugged to the most intellectually demanding.

Impossible to resist, eh?

So you would say—until you had been turned away by your fifteenth or sixteenth Southworld country. After that, you would find yourself just going through the motions—and wondering why you were bothering to do even that.

In my own case, of course, I knew the answer perfectly well. The Oneness had diagnosed my plight during our brief tête-à-tête on Mars with absolute accuracy: unless I wanted to sit in a China Basin naval barracks holding myself at the disposition of a thousand vengeful shysters, what else did I have to do with my time?

So I slogged grimly on from country to country, ever conscious of the initial misjudgment I had made, cloistered as I was in the smugness and prosperity of the Northworld. It was both simple and basic: it was not that the Southworld didn't want a million hardworking bodies; it was that they had too many of them already. Most of the Southworld suffered from overpopulation and underemployment; aside from soldiers or outright slaves, no one was interested in more mouths to feed, no matter how cute and how loyal. After visits to the first three countries on my list—Bengal, Egypt, and Malaya—I reluctantly discarded my initial idea of the Seven adorable Dwarfs. Dwarfs weren't wanted in the rice paddies of Bhawanipatna or the tin mines of Sungai Lembing; tireless, seven-foot slaves with dwarflike appetites might have been acceptable, but nothing less. . . .

"Slaves," grunted the Empress of Kilimanjaro, scrutinizing my own long, willowy frame from top to bottom as if I myself would make a particularly useless one.

We were seated in yet another of the endless succession of throne rooms I had recently visited, this one situated in a gaudy pink palace that festered like an abscess high on the upper flanks of Mount Kilimanjaro itself. The Empress, of course, sat far above me in a jewel-encrusted throne that put to shame any of those I had so far seen. Two unattached lion cubs frolicked ferociously at her slipper-clad feet, a single small bound from where I sat eyeing them nervously from my small red-plush chair.

It was only my rank as a representative of the Oneness that had earned me even that: the rest of the audience room held no chairs at all. Bare black backs were prostrated motionlessly around us in a broad semicircle; they, at least, were living, or so I assumed. Standing stiffly behind them were forty-eight Beach the Butlers from Harrod's in London, all of them resplendent in dove-gray morning clothes and white gloves. Through an enormous window beyond the array of misclad butlers, Her Imperial Majesty could look down upon the immense African horizon and her presumably loyal subjects.

"Slaves," repeated the Empress, gesturing disdainfully towards the miserable, half-naked creatures who cowered on the bare porphyry floor, "We have no need of slaves."

"In any case, Your Imperial Majesty, no Northworld government would ever allow the gestation and sale of slaves. They are all very formal upon that point."

The Empress grunted deep in her vast bosom and moodily stirred the tawny belly of a lion cub with the end of her foot. "Hypocrites. They are all very formal hypocrites. What else are the soldiers they sell to our enemies to attack and kill our own noble people, except slaves in the service of our enemies?"

This was a particularly sore point with the Empress. The Sultan of Seychellia to the south had allied himself with the Kingdom of Lualaba to the west; together they were harrying her Empire from both sides. Her twenty thousand Marshal Kutusovs from Moskva Romanoff were holding their own, but just barely, and she badly needed another ten thousand troops. The Imperial Treasury had the resources to purchase the ten thousand—but only as two-week-old infants, who would have to be raised for eighteen years before being sent into battle. To purchase them fully grown and battle-readied from Moskva Romanoff's immense training camps in the Ukraine was an entirely different financial matter; the Empress could afford perhaps three companies of 120 men each: hardly enough to hurl back her foes and exterminate their populations from the face of the Earth.

"Your Martian godling will absolutely not allow them to be soldiers?" growled the Empress, glaring down at me as if calculating how many meals I would make for her frisky lion cubs. "Not even in the most worthy of causes, not even in the self-defense of innocent women and children?"

"I am afraid that the Oneness is adamant upon that point, Your Imperial Majesty. However, we *have* reduced the size of the trial order to a bare minimum of ten thousand. This would permit you to judge—"

The Empress shook her massive head. "No. We need ten thousand soldiers, not ten thousand field hands." She gestured imperiously and barked a sharp command in her own language: the audience was clearly over. I rose to my feet, glanced uneasily again at the lion cubs, and nodded solemnly. "Thank you for having given me so much of your precious time, Your Imperial Majesty. If you should reconsider—"

"We never—. Wait." Her dark eyes grew thoughtful. "You say your minimum order has been reduced to ten thousand. Suppose We were interested in a somewhat smaller order?"

"How much smaller, Your Imperial Majesty?"

She gestured me closer to the glittering throne. "Much, *much* smaller," she murmured between barely moving lips. "But a very *special* order, one which would definitely be worth your while." Her eyes found mine and held them, and an icy chill ran up my spine. There was something about the way she had said "special . . ."

I moistened my lips nervously. "That would depend on the order, Your Imperial Majesty. I would have to—"

"—see them. Yes." She raised her enormous bulk lightly from the throne and stepped down beside me. For a long moment she stared down at me from her great height, then nodded almost imperceptibly. "Come," she commanded. "We will show you our private collection."

I followed her through the still prostrate court flunkies, the row of silent butlers, and out of the throne room. The last I saw of the lion cubs, they were tugging playfully at the bleeding arm of one of her indubitably loyal subjects.

The chill that had run up my spine now extended itself to the rest of my body as I trailed the Empress reluctantly through a dozen ornate rooms and down three broad staircases. What could this horrible woman mean by "private collection"? Somehow the innocuous words seemed dire, infinitely macabre. It was almost as if she were speaking of . . . well, of a *harem*, I told myself incredulously.

"Angus," I commed silently, "where is she taking me?"

I do not know, Robert. There are only three rocks in the entire palace, and none of them know anything that might bear on this situation.

So much for the omnipotent eyes and ears of my employer the Oneness.

I tottered weak-kneed into a small elevator set in a white-washed wall. The vast presence of the Empress nearly filled the elevator; I tried to edge inconspicuously away from her great bulk. *A private collection, a harem, a private collection, a harem.* I was unable to keep the words from echoing endlessly over and over in my mind. . . . How long had I been a woman now? I wondered distractedly. Three months? Four? Whatever it was, it obviously hadn't been long enough: I still had little notion of how the female psyche actually operated. Even in Africa, did empresses maintain harems? I sighed unhappily as the doors of the elevator opened. I was about to find out.

33

The reality, of course, was far more ghastly than anything I could have imagined. I followed the Empress down a bare concrete corridor to a heavy metal door set into the wall at the far end. She touched her meaty thumb to three separate thumbplates around its circumference and the door slowly opened. We stepped, not, as I half expected, into a steamy seraglio filled with naked men or women, but into a control room that looked as if it came from the bridge of the space-crusier *Queen Elizabeth IV.* I stared in bewilderment at the hundreds of small monitors on one side of the room and at the single attendant, a wizened black man in a shabby beige uniform perched on a stool in front of the colored screens.

"Your Imperial Majesty!" The attendant fell instantly to the floor, prostrated himself abjectly.

"Rise and resume your duties," commanded the Empress grandly as the door behind us shut with a soft hiss. She stepped forward to the bank of monitors, examined them with total absorption. The tip of her pink tongue ran slowly around her lips and her mighty bosom rose and fell with deep emotion. "What do you think of our collection?" she asked in a husky whisper.

"I . . . don't know," I whispered in return, my eyes darting from one screen to the next. "Surely . . . it's . . . most . . . unusual." On each small screen I could clearly see the form of a naked person in what appeared to be a prison cell scarcely larger than a packing crate. I quickly scanned the hundreds of monitors; whites and blacks seemed to make up the naked beings in equal numbers, but whatever the race most of them were men. My mouth dry, I peered more closely. Very few of the men, or women, were the kind of physical specimens you might expect to find in an Empress's harem. "Your private collection, Your Imperial Empress?" I prompted nervously.

"There's Livingstone," she grunted, jabbing her finger at a monitor, "Number sixty-three, David Livingstone. And sixty-four and sixty-five. There are only three of him left. That's Stanley over there; there's only *one* of him: a very poor model, not at all robust, you barely touch him and he falls down dead." The Empress moved slowly along the bank of monitors, occasionally lifting a finger to point out an object of particular interest. "Ha, Cecil Rhodes! Another of the white men who tried to make slaves of us Africans. I've a dozen of *him!* Good stock, good stock, screams a lot, spurts blood all over the place, but very solid, very solid, a glutton for punishment, almost impossible to kill. That was a very good purchase indeed."

I stared in unconcealed horror as she enumerated a host of other names, Ben-Gurion, Suleiman, Vorster, King Leopold of Belgium, Jan Smuts, Edgar Rice Burroughs. A few names were vaguely familiar, but most were meaningless. The whites in her grisly collection appeared to date mainly from the historical eras of European colonization and African independence and were drawn from all over the continent. There were, I noticed, very few women among the whites. The blacks, on the other hand, seemed to be made up equally of both men and women, and were apparently mostly Kilimanjarans or citizens of neighboring countries.

"These . . . are . . ." I gestured dismally at the monitors as the words stuck in my throat. "They are . . ."

"Our enemies," she replied regally. "The enemies of our noble people, the enemies of our beloved country, the enemies of us *personally*. All our enemies for many, many centuries now."

"But . . . but . . . surely . . . Livingstone and . . . and Stanley have been dead for many years now . . . ?"

Her monstrous brown eyes swung around to envelope me

in their baleful glare. "Of course they have been dead for many centuries now. In that way they foolishly hoped to escape their just chastisement." Her mountainous breasts heaved. "But We have been too smart for them. We have purchased them and raised them from childhood. Then when they are of a suitable age, and fully aware of why they—"

"You mean you've raised a dozen identical children from the crèches, each . . . each to believe he was Livingstone, and then . . . and then . . ." The thought was too monstrous to complete.

The Empress of Kilimanjaro nodded complacently. "And not just white men," she said smugly. "We are not racist. Look, see that woman there: the one in number 111, 112, and 113. Chunya N'guruka. When we were young, many years ago in Kondoa, she manipulated seven yellow feathers in the pattern of the fire demon behind the head of Mahenge Mkangira as he sat drinking goba and burnishing his tattoos. Mahenge Mkangira was thereby ensorcelled into accompanying Chunya N'guruka to the Seventh Rite of the Virgin's Awakening instead of ourselves. Now, from time to time, We come to remonstrate with Chunya N'guruka for her conspicuous selfishness and perfidy. It is safe to say that her regret for her betrayal knows no bounds."

My entire body shuddered in revulsion and horror. "You . . . you . . ."

"Yes. But now there are only three Chunya N'gurukas left." The Empress's great black hand made a sweeping gesture that encompassed the entire bank of monitors. "Many, many of them have deserted us, few remain. Every year their misdeeds become greater, their unrepentance more flagrant, their conduct more deserving of chastisement. They are deserting us faster and faster." She swung around to face me, her mad eyes glittering brightly. "Soon we shall have none at all with whom to comfort ourselves."

It was impossible to meet those ghastly eyes. "And . . . and you want to order more vic— . . . more . . . more enemies from . . . from a *crèche* . . . for . . ." I glanced fleetingly at the hundreds of miserable wretches huddled in their tiny cells and took a deep breath. "Your Imperial Majesty," I said firmly, "I am . . . staggered by the news that some unlicensed or illicit crèche has been—"

"Unlicensed?" The Empress of Kilimanjaro glared at me angrily. "Illicit? You call Earthly Integument unlicensed? You call Svoboda-Benz illicit? You call United Norge illicit?"

If possible, my horror grew. "You mean . . . Earthly Integument . . ."

"Ha!" The Empress snorted ferociously. "We *told* you that all the Northworld zombies were formal hypocrites. Where else do you think our private collection comes from?"

"I see." I gulped hard. "And you want . . . you think . . . you want the *Oneness* to provide you . . . with souls . . . for your . . . for your *bodies?*"

The Empress of Kilimanjaro nodded her assent. "We will have to discuss terms, of course, and models; but if your Martian godling is willing, We could undoubtedly place an initial order of . . . oh, perhaps five hundred individuals."

"Yes," I agreed shakily, desperately, babbling anything at all to keep her in good humor, "that would appear to be a reasonable figure for a first order." My trembling legs took a tiny first step toward the door. "Naturally I shall . . . shall have to consult with . . . with the Oneness before . . . before . . ." I took another step, aware that behind me the Empress of Kilimanjaro was watching me with a basilisklike glare. Suppose, I thought wildly, suppose the door doesn't open? Suppose she doesn't *let* me leave?

My knees wobbled at the hideous thought and I felt my entire body quivering in terror. *How was I going to get out of here?* A murderous lunatic like this could suddenly decide to—

Without conscious thought, I found myself pulling Angus from my shoulder bag and raising him to my lips. "Angus," I said aloud with as much self-assurance as I could muster, "comm me through to the Oneness at once."

You are now in contact with the Oneness, Robert.

"Thank you, Angus." I held the rock before me with outstretched arms and inclined my head solemnly for a long, reverent moment. "Your Godliness," I said, "I am about to leave Her Imperial Majesty the Most Exalted Empress of Kilimanjaro. Yes, Your Godliness, right away. No, there is no need to rematerialize me in Addis Ababa.''

What nonsense are you speaking, Abraham Lincoln? Is this another of your celebrated jokes? We do not understand.

"Thank you all the same, Your Godliness, but I quite enjoy traveling on the local aircraft: it gives me an opportunity to see the African scenery. And my flight will give me time to apprise Your Godliness of the fine order which Her Imperial Majesty wishes to place.''

But we have been listening to your conversation with the Empress of Kilimanjaro through Angus, protested the Martian supermind plaintively. *We are not certain that we have fully grasped its exact significance, but—*

"That is correct, Your Godliness. I will give you all of the details as soon as I am aboard. Of course, if you need me in San Francisco or Mars you have only to rematerialize me in either place.'' Once again I held Angus before me and bowed low. "Thank you, Your Godliness.''

But—

The brooding eyes of the Empress were on me when I looked up. "You can . . . rematerialize yourself, move yourself from place to place without physical means of locomotion, like a juju man?''

"*I* cannot, Your Imperial Majesty. S/His Godliness the Oneness occasionally does it for me—S/He has many strange powers. Frankly, I find it disconcerting: I prefer to take the hyperjet.''

The Empress of Kilimanjaro pursed her lips thoughtfully. "A useful trick. Perhaps it is one which the Oneness will teach me.''

"Quite conceivably, Your Imperial Majesty. As a bonus, perhaps, for a particularly large order.'' I tugged my lips into the semblance of a ghastly smile. "If you will give me a list of your exact requirements, I will discuss the matter with S/His Godliness—on the plane to Addis Ababa.''

34

I had, of course, no intention at all of going anywhere near Addis Ababa. But if Her Horrors the Empress of Kilimanjaro wanted to think I was on my way to Addis Ababa, a thousand miles to the north of her mountain playpen, while I actually flew south to my real destination of Dar es Salaam on the Indian Ocean, far be it from me to contradict her. . . .

The flight on Air Africain from the Empress's capital of Kilimanjaro City at the base of the majestic mountain was a short one, and in the Northworld would have been made in the same time and far more conveniently by express bubble. But here in the wilds of barbaric Africa I was unspeakably grateful for any conveyance at all capable of carrying me away from the glimpse of hell to which I had just been exposed.

As the Empire of Kilimanjaro fell rapidly behind, my trembling gradually subsided, even as my anger grew. I myself was now safe from the homicidal impulses of this unspeakable madwoman who might at any moment have decided she had been mistaken in offering me a glimpse of her private hell, but what of all those miserable creatures still buried somewhere in the bowels of her palace and helplessly awaiting her torments?

I was sickened almost to the point of nausea by what I had just seen—but almost equally shocked by the discovery that somewhere within the leading circles of the life-industry there were monsters of depravity willing to lend themselves to the revolting perversions of the psychopathic Empress of Kilimanjaro.

I knew, of course, that the major goal of every espionage service in the Southworld was to subvert some unscrupulous Northworld crèche into deactivating the self-destruction function installed in every factory-produced soldier in the hope that the soldier could then be turned against either his manufacturer or his purchaser in some hostile country.

So far as I knew, the rigorous code of honor by which all the crèches were guided (not to mention the equally rigorous counterintelligence activities of the various Northworld governments) had up to now prevented this from ever happening—except in the celebrated case of the Great Calcutta Massacre of 2152, in which nine thousand subverted sepoy soldiers had suddenly turned upon their Bengali masters and hacked them to pieces.

The Great Calcutta Massacre was the single breach I knew of in the lofty ideals of the Northworld's life-industry. But now . . .

The seat next to me on the plane was blessedly vacant. I laid my shoulder bag on it and tried to unknot my cramped muscles. "Angus," I commed, "I want an urgent message sent to every rock in existence. Tell them that Abraham Lincoln wants them to find out who has been creating special models for the Empress of Kilimanjaro and her torture chambers."

Yes, Robert, I shall gladly do so. But the Oneness has already been integrating all of S/His attributes for the last ninety-seven minutes in an attempt to find out. So far, however, S/He has discovered nothing.

"I see. Just how long has this madwoman been Empress?"

Thirty-nine years.

"Then it's possible that she originally ordered her . . . playthings as long as thirty or forty years ago. Whoever she got them from may no longer be at the crèches. That might explain why she is looking for a new source of supply. Tell the rocks to review their memories for the last half-century."

I will inform the Oneness of your speculations, Robert.

I shuddered again as I recalled the Empress's private collection. "Angus, we've *got* to put a stop to this madwoman! Can you *imagine* what it must be like to—"

The Empress has just spoken to the Sultan of Seychellia via telecommunication, interrupted Angus brusquely. *Fortunately, there was a rock in the immediate presence of the Sultan to monitor the conversation. The Empress has asked the Sultan to dispose of you immediately upon our arrival in Dar es Salaam.*

My heart lurched. "But they're fighting a war!" I babbled incredulously. "They're deadly enemies! That's why I didn't let her know that we were going to Dar es Salaam to meet the Sultan. How could she know I was going to Seychellia? Why would she call—"

It would be a simple matter to learn which flight we were aboard. She is undoubtedly abnormally suspicious by nature.

I sagged back in my seat, still bewildered. "But why would she want to dispose of me *now*? Why not when she had the chance back at the palace? Why call the Sultan?"

I fear they have certain interests in common, replied Angus. *She told him that you were in actuality a Northworld intelligence agent, sent to learn the details of their private collections.*

"Private collections!" I moaned softly. "Then the Sultan of Seychellia has one too?"

Yes, Robert.

"And I suppose that you didn't know about this one either," I said bitterly.

We know, of course, that the Sultan maintains an extensive harem, but that is a matter of common knowledge. That may be what the Empress is referring to.

"But why would he want to . . . to dispose of me because of his harem?"

I don't know, Robert. I can only conjecture that there is something illicit about it.

"Then why didn't the Empress . . . Oh, I see. If the Empress wants to get rid of me because she's had second thoughts about her dirty secrets, but is leery of doing it herself because of the Oneness's supposed powers, she gets her wartime enemy, but colleague in dirty secrets, to do it for her. If he

succeeds, their secret is safe, and there's even the possibility
that the Oneness will strike the Sultan of Seychellia dead with
a lightning bolt for molesting his emissary. Which would get
rid of the snoop and the Sultan in a single fell swoop. And
even if the Sultan *doesn't* succeed in killing me, he may still
incur the wrath of the Oneness for trying and be dispatched
by a vengeful Martian thunderclap. What a torturous mind
she must have.'' I sagged limply in my seat, my face covered
with sweat in spite of the aircraft's glacial air-conditioning.
''It may have been a mistake laying on all of that stuff about
the powers of the Oneness. . . . And I thought I was being
so clever.''

Yes, agreed Angus. *What do you intend to do now?*

''*Do?*'' I cried aloud, startling two solemn Arabs in long
white burnooses on the other side of the aisle. ''What do you
expect me to do? I'll bloody well stay here on the plane when
it lands in Dar es Salaam. *That's* what I'll do.'' I stared
grimly out the window at my first glimpse of the Indian Ocean
on the horizon far to the left. What good was it having an
infallible worldwide intelligence service at my disposal if I
were trapped in the confines of an airplane? ''They'll have
to pry me out with a crowbar!''

Which, of course, in a manner of speaking, is exactly what
they did. While the other passengers shuffled slowly down
the aisle, I mingled with the crowd just long enough to vanish
inconspicuously into the midship lavatory. I bolted the door
behind me and collapsed onto the toilet, grimly determined
to open the door for nobody short of God Almighty until the
aircraft had left the skies of Seychellia.

Five minutes passed. Ten. In the mirror I could see beads
of sweat rolling down Mariata Divine's lovely face in unlady-
like fashion. I cursed, and dabbed at my face with paper
towels.

They are coming, commed Angus suddenly. *Six policemen.
They are all heavily armed.*

''Oh god. Here, onto the plane?''

*Yes. They know that you are aboard. They have orders to
shoot you immediately if you make any resistance at all. Since*

*there is now no one else aboard to serve as witnesses, they
have just stopped to discuss shooting you whether you resist
or not.*

"Oh god, oh god, oh god . . ." Once again I had out-
smarted myself. "Angus, what can I *do*?"

*I do not know, Robert, but the corollary of their discussion
would seem to be that if there are witnesses present, then they
will not shoot you—at least not immediately.*

Small comfort, but it was all I had. No one ever shot out
of an aircraft's lavatory or down its aisle faster than Mariata
Divine. "Angus," I muttered desperately as I ran, "have
every rock in the vicinity notify its owner to gather around
this aircraft. I want as many witnesses as possible. . . ."

A moment later I rushed out of the forward hatch and into
the blazing heat of equatorial Africa. I skidded to an abrupt
halt at the top of the boarding ramp. At the foot of the stairs
six brown-uniformed policemen gaped up at me in surprise.
I waved both arms wildly, frantically trying to attract the
attention of the several hundred passengers I could see standing behind plate-glass windows in the small terminal building
fifty yards away.

"Hello!" I screamed at the top of my lungs. "Hello there,
good people! Mariata Divine of San Francisco wishes you all
good day! That's Mariata Divine! Remember that name!" I
glanced down for an instant, saw the bewildered policemen
gather their wits and begin to cautiously climb the boarding
ramp, machine pistols held before them. "Mariata Divine!"
I shouted from the very bottom of my heart. "The official
ambassador of His Godliness the Oneness of Mars!" I could
see faces staring at me through the windows now, and a
few blue-clad airfield workers had drawn near the aircraft to
cock their heads in puzzlement. "The official ambassador—
translate that, Angus, translate that to the rocks of these policemen!—of His Godliness the Oneness of Mars!"

I was still echoing that phrase like a defective audio system
when the policemen of the Sultan of Seychellia discharged a
thick wrapping of translucent stick-tight around my arms and
torso and led me still screeching to a long black aircar parked
on the side of the terminal. As the hatch slammed behind me

and I was thrown roughly to a seat, I heaved a muted sigh of relief. As the fellow falling from the top of the Empire State Building said as he tumbled past the seventeenth floor, "So far, so good."

35

The aircar soared out of the inky shadows of the terminal and into the dazzling equatorial sunlight. I sat rigidly between two sour-smelling policemen, as paralyzed by fear as by the cocoon of stick-tight that enveloped me. "Angus," I commed to my rock in the bottom of my shoulder bag, "where are they taking us?"

They are at present consulting with the Sultan as to your disposition.

"By rockcom?"

Yes. The Sultan of Seychellia is considerably more modern than most of the Southworld, at least in his personal entourage: his palace is full of rocks.

"Well, that's something, if not very much. What is the Sultan saying?"

To bring you to his summer palace. He originally planned to have you disappear over the sea in an aircar disaster, but now he is curious to see you for himself. Your tantrum in a crowded international terminal about being the Oneness's personal ambassador has made him slightly uneasy. He is now wondering if this may not be an elaborate trick on the part of the Empress.

"Ha!" A sudden surge of hope ran through me. "Listen, Angus: contact the Sultan. Lay it on as thick as you can about me being the personal representative of the almighty Oneness. Warn him that if—"

I fear that such a course of action might prove to be coun-

terproductive, Robert. The sultan holds a degree in engineer-ing from Cal Tech: he is not a credulous man. To him a rock is a rock.

"But even so . . ."

I fear that by using me to emphasize your closeness to the Oneness, you might well turn his attention to myself as your intermediary.

"So?"

Not realizing that every Martian rock in your vicinity is now yours to command, he might conclude that it would be wiser to cut your contact with the Oneness by the simple expedient of destroying me.

"Destroying *you*?" I echoed. The thought had never be-fore occurred to me.

We are now flying over the Indian Ocean, two hundred twenty miles from land. It would be a simple matter to lose me forever in a thousand fathoms of water. Not that you re-ally need me, of course, since any other rock will—

"Don't be ridiculous, Angus. If they throw you overboard, they'll have to throw me, too."

There was a long silence, then: *You don't realize how deeply you have touched me by your concern and loyalty, Robert. But I would gladly sacrifice myself a thousand times for—*

"I told you to stop talking nonsense, Angus. We'll meet this crazy Sultan from Cal Tech together or not at all."

It shall be as you say. In the meantime, I advise you to remain calm. The Oneness assures me that S/He will do whatever S/He can to extricate you from this contretemps.

"Thank you, Angus." I slouched hopelessly in my cocoon as the aircar sped across the Indian Ocean towards the sum-mer palace of the Sultan of Seychellia. Brave words, I told myself, but what help could I expect from a vein of sentient rock forty million miles away in space?

Very little, it appeared, at least while the aircar was gliding in to a smooth landing on the roof of a flat white rectangular building totally devoid of features. Its harsh functionalism was particularly intrusive on this small, paradisiacal island set like a gem in the middle of a brilliant turquoise-green lagoon. An intense blue sky arched from horizon to horizon and all around us palm trees waved gently in the trade winds. *We are now in the Seychelles*, Angus unnecessarily informed me. *This is the Sultan's summer palace.*

"A peculiar-looking palace," I commed irritably as I was pulled into the furnacelike heat and marched briskly across the burning white roof. A small shed guarded by two soldiers in white uniforms proved to contain a bank of elevators. I was pushed into the center one, and a moment later I began my descent to yet another private collection. My heart thumped loudly in my chest. Was it conceivable that it was only this *morning* that I had been in an elevator in the horrific company of Her Imperial Majesty the Empress of Kilimanjaro?

My heart was pounding even faster as the doors opened; my legs could barely support me as I tottered forward. Somehow all that already seemed a lifetime ago. . . .

Four armed soldiers in white-and-blue uniforms awaited us in the concrete corridor outside. They glanced at me curiously, then dismissed the policemen with a curt nod. The elevator doors closed behind the policemen and the soldiers stepped forward. Without a word I was led down the bare corridor to an equally stark room. We had to step over a high metal sill to enter, and I saw with dismay that the metal hatch was a foot thick and of the same design used to seal off compartments in underwater vessels.

Yes, said Angus, *we are now somewhere under the lagoon.*

Worse and worse. If the Sultan of Seychellia didn't kill me out of hand, a leak in the roof could. The heavy hatch slammed behind me and I heard it being dogged shut from the outside. For a moment I stood hesitantly by myself, still immobilized by stick-tight, and then I heard another hatch opening on the other side of the room. My pounding heart lurched up to my throat. Was this the Sultan of Seychellia, come to—

Four women stepped through the opening. As squat and muscular as men, at first glance their sex was hard to determine beneath their heavy white gowns and veils. They paused to dog the hatch, then moved confidently forward, dark eyes

glittering in the depths of their burnooses. One of them raised
a small resonator and the translucent stick-tight that imprisoned me dropped away. Another muttered into a shiny yellow-
and-red Martian rock.

She is asking you to give no trouble, commed Angus.

I stretched my numbed arms as if I hadn't heard and glared
at them angrily. It made no difference. Two of the women
pulled the bag from my shoulder and quickly found Angus in
its bottom. I took an angry step forward but was immediately
halted by ironlike grips on either elbow. While Angus vanished through a hatch in the grip one of the cloaked women,
I treated the others to a brief demonstration of the Nine
Golden Wiles of the Reproachful Shin'jusi just as I had
learned them in my college days, but the Mariata Divine body
was hardly designed to cope with three experienced prison
matrons. Finally I subsided, breathing hard from an elbow in
the solar plexus, only marginally appeased by the heavy flow
of crimson blood from a smashed nose that now stained the
white gown of one of my warders. "Angus," I commed,
"where are they taking you?"

*I don't yet know, Robert. I am not yet in perfect harmony
with this person's senses. It appears to be a corri——.* His
voice faded as he passed out of range.

I stood limply, offering no resistance, as the three angry
matrons stripped my clothes away and subjected my naked
body to a humiliating examination. Would I ever see Angus
again? Would I ever see *anyone* again? I closed my eyes in
despair as hands groped through Mariata Divine's long black
hair.

At last I was handed a lightweight yellow chador and ordered by gestures to put it on. *Do so*, said Angus's voice
suddenly, deep within my mind. *You must avoid antagonizing
them unnecessarily.*

"Angus! You're back in range!" I reached for the hooded
gown and began to struggle into it.

*No. I am somewhere on the far side of the Sultan's palace,
sitting quietly on a shelf, waiting to be examined by the Sultan's chief of security. I am comming you through one of the
rocks in the possession of your guards.*

''Have . . . have you learned anything about . . . about what—''

Yes, Robert. And I urge you to retain your calm in spite of whatever eventuates.

My heart sank. ''What means eventuates?'' I asked apprehensively.

You are about to be taken to the Sultan's harem.

36

Well, now.

Isn't it every red-blooded American boy's dream to find himself in the middle of a sultan's harem, surrounded on all sides by beautiful, willing women? I blushingly confess that the notion may have occurred to me from time to time.

But the idea was to find myself there as a boy, for goodness' sake, not as one of the beautiful, willing women!

As Mariata Divine, I definitely found the sordid reality far from having the same allure it had held for a lusty and imaginative lad of fourteen.

"Are you someone very famous?" asked Marie Antoinette in soft, wistful French. "You are certainly very beautiful, and you are certainly from another century than my own. *Ma foi*, look how much taller you are than I!"

That much was true, at least, I thought, looking down at the plump, powdered, and periwigged little Frenchwoman sitting awkwardly beside me in the elaborate structure of an eighteenth-century formal gown. Mariata Divine was certainly taller, and undoubtedly far more beautiful. I turned away from the wholesome antics of a team of Oriental jugglers that filled the far side of the vinyl-upholstered holoscope salon and gave my entire attention to the late Queen of the late Louis XVI. "No, not famous at all," I replied in my halting, schoolboy's French. "I'm just a singer."

"Then why are you here?" she asked with childlike innocence. "All of us are famous, or so I have been told."

Her eyes scanned the room. "I myself, for instance, am a
queen. And look! That frumpish little girl talking to Jacque-
line Kennedy over there, that's Joan of Arc." Marie Antoinette's face brightened. "Perhaps you know Madame
Kennedy? *Such* a lady, so refined, so elegant, so unlike *some*
I could mention." She sniffed in regal fashion, but then her
face softened. "Not that many of them aren't very *good-
hearted* . . . Do you see that tall black girl in the corner, the
one who's nearly as tall as you?"

I thought this a curiously delicate way of alluding to a beautiful, slim black woman who sat entirely naked except for an
improbable skirt of artificial bananas dangling around her
smooth hips. "How could I miss her?" I asked. "Is *she*
famous?"

"So it appears: an American singer of the twentieth century named Josephine Baker. But she speaks *beautiful* French,
and is *so* warmhearted. But perhaps you already know her?"

"No. No more than I know anyone else here." I looked
around at the three or four dozen diversely dressed women,
who chatted idly with one another or stolidly watched the
holoscope. "Is that really Catherine the Great?"

"That one? No, no, that's Mary Queen of Scots." Marie
Antoinette looked at me in sudden alarm. "You don't *really*
want to associate with that . . . that *other* person, do you? A
most unpleasant woman, so very *de haut en bas*, even with
her fellow sovereigns, so very selfish, so very immoral! Look,
see her there . . . that very plain woman speaking with Mademoiselle Bardot, that ghastly little French girl."

I stared at the legendary Russian Empress and devourer of
men. She was certainly far from being beautiful. Mademoiselle Bardot, on the other hand, was extremely enticing. I
wondered who she was, why the Queen considered her
ghastly, and what she was doing here along with the other
two hundred and twenty women who made up the Sultan's
extraordinary private collection.

My thoughts were interrupted by the late Queen of France,
who was tugging timidly at my arm. "From what year do
you come, my dear?"

"Year? Oh! The present year, 2345."

"Ah. Then perhaps *you* can explain things to me. No one

else here seems to be from the present time, or at least no one who speaks French, and I *am* confused, so very, very confused." Her cornflower blue eyes filled with tears and she looked up at me pitifully. "I just don't *understand!*"

My heart went out to this poor miserable creature, as well as to all the other helpless women imprisoned in this slightly shabby, relentlessly utilitarian seraglio. "What don't you understand?" I asked.

"How . . . how I could be Queen, the Queen of France, you know, living in Versailles one day, tending to the Court, and then . . . and then . . . waking up to find myself *here.* *Here!*" She gestured bitterly at the plainly furnished holoscope salon, its drab vinyl reality so far removed from the lush Oriental splendor of my childhood imagination.

Beyond the salon, I knew, were an equally drab mess hall, three more common rooms, and two long corridors of cheerless cubicles, all of them equally austere and sunless. Even the four dozen palace eunuchs charged with ensuring the inmates' exclusive fidelity to their master the Sultan of Seychellia were nothing more than grotesque mechanical creations from the Singapore branch of Galeries Lafayette. Upon first seeing them, I had instantly dubbed them Eunice the Eunuch, but now, after two days in this factorylike seraglio, I had lost what scant bravado I had originally possessed. I sighed gloomily as I once again contemplated the utter drabness of what appeared to be my new home. But I supposed that even modern-day sultans had to adapt themselves to the exigencies of their treasuries and work within a budget. . . .

"I really don't know how you came to be here," I said slowly to Marie Antoinette in my rusty French. "Once I was supposed to be an expert in this sort of thing, but I honestly don't know. Somehow, I imagine, the Sultan must have subverted, or bribed, a life-stylist and a crèche into designing, gestating, and raising bodies that were identical to . . . to all these historical personages." I shrugged unhappily. "After that, I just don't know. Somehow they have succeeded in recreating, and then grafting on, an entire historical personality. You yourself, for instance, really believe yourself to be Marie Antoinette—"

"But I *am* Marie Antoinette!" bleated my poor companion piteously as tears rolled down her powdered cheeks. "And I don't *want* to be! I don't want to be *here*! I don't *want* to have to do disgusting things with that awful savage! I want to be *home*!"

I pulled the poor little creature to me and wondered miserably how long it would be before I—the indubitably genuine Robert Clayborn/Mariata Divine—would be wailing the same mournful song. . . .

37

Eighteen feet above me, on the metal desk of the Austrian internist who served as the Sultan's personal physician, lay a shiny piece of Martian rock carved in the whimsical form of a woman's breast. Angus was using it to converse with me where I lay in the upper bunk of the tiny cubicle I shared with a redheaded beauty who was the Esmeralda of Antigone, the celebrated twenty-first-century courtesan and tyrannicide. At ten o'clock sharp we had been escorted to our cubicle by a clanking Eunice the Eunuch and each of us shut up for the night in her own narrow bunk behind a slightly flickering DuPont SafeTScreen. Evidently the chastity of the Sultan's feminine charges was to be protected as much from their fellow inmates as from any stray males who might be lurking in the neighborhood. . . .

"But this is outright slavery," I muttered angrily to Angus. "This is exactly the condition that you and the Oneness are asking *me* to free *you* from! How do you expect me to free *you* if I can't free myself?"

This is indeed a dilemma, and one that the Oneness is even now considering.

"Furthermore, you *knew* the sultan had this harem! Why haven't you ever told anyone in the Northworld about what goes on in here?"

I am desolated, Robert. I, personally, would have informed you at once, had I known. But you must remember, Robert, that each of us rocks is, up to a certain point, an autonomous individual with his own individual perceptions and memories.

"And the Oneness, then? Doesn't he share all of your individual memories?"

Theoretically, of course, this is so. But the entirety of S/His gestalt lacks your, or even my, human orientation. I fear that the somewhat constrained aspects of this particular slice of human life never occurred to S/Him as being worthy of extraordinary attention.

A slice of human life. Wonderful. What compassion.

And this was the supermind that now urged me to be calm, no matter what the exigencies.

The following afternoon four Eunice the Eunuchs escorted me to a room at the far end of the seraglio. Once again I stepped through a pressure-resistant door that was then dogged shut behind me. This time, at least, the room was fully appointed and cheerfully decorated; it might have been the beauty salon and ladies' exercise spa at a luxury hotel or sports club.

On the other hand, waiting ominously were the same four squat matrons who had initially conducted me to the harem. Standing beside them, perfectly poised, were two beautiful women, instantly recognizable as life-designed models from a Northworld crèche. One was blonde, the other redheaded; both were willowy and full-breasted. Aside from an enormous miscellany of silver and gold necklaces, bracelets, and body chains, they were entirely naked.

The blonde welcomed me with a friendly smile. "We are here to prepare you for your visit to His Exalted Majesty the Sultan of Seychellia," she said in impeccable Northworld English. Her smile broadened. "I'm sure you aren't going to be . . . obstreperous, are you? Otherwise, we'll have to use these . . ." She gestured at the four grim-faced women in their white chadors. "Moreover, the Sultan has a very special . . . regimen for those he considers recalcitrant or lacking in joyous compliance with his very reasonable requests. He himself enjoys its somewhat special piquancy, but quite frankly I must advise you that the object of his attention does not always participate with equal enthusiasm." She looked at me meaningfully.

"No, I won't be obstreperous," I said with a resigned sigh as I discarded whatever notions of resistance still remained. "I will remain calm whatever the exigency."

The redhead frowned deliciously. "Whatever the *what?*"

"Whatever happens."

"Oh. I thought for a moment you might be making fun of His Exalted Majesty's more personal enthusiasms. Some of them are a little . . ." She shrugged creamy white shoulders dusted with pale rose freckles. "Well, that's what we're here to prepare you for, isn't it, sweetie?" I shuddered as she stepped forward and with a faint smile began to unbutton the same grimy blouse I had first put on three days before. "First a nice, warm, sudsy bath, then we'll see to your hair and nails, and then"—a long pink tongue moistened her full lips—"we'll tell you all about His Exalted Majesty's favorite little fancies and conceits." Her pale gray eyes dropped to Mariata Divine's small, hard breasts. "But maybe first of all, why not some nice little exercises, just the three of us, to warm us all up and get us in the mood, hmmm?" Her hands came up to cup my breasts. "*Then* the bath and all the rest to make us beautiful. A little perfume, here and there, and then . . ."

"And then?" I echoed wanly.

"And then it's off to His Exalted Majesty and his little bower of underwater delights."

I could have snapped the beautiful, swanlike necks of my two willowy playmates anytime during the course of the nice little exercises that followed, but what was the point? Finally the two women lay limp and satiated, while I sat on the edge of the exercise mat silently seething. In spite of the rather intense intimacy of the nice little exercises, I never did learn the names of either the blonde or the redhead . . .

Two hours later, bathed and coiffed, powdered and gilded, perfumed here and there, I followed them reluctantly through a pressure-proof door, clad only in a pair of high golden heels and my innate modesty. If their nice little exercises were only the warm-up, I was far from anxious to discover the fancies and conceits of His Exalted Majesty with which I was expected to demonstrate my joyful compliance.

My eyes widened as I saw what lay beyond the door, and my breath caught in my throat.

"It *is* beautiful, isn't it?" said the blonde.

Electric blue water surrounded us, arching above my head as well as to either side. Giant coral heads of orange, green, red, and yellow grew on a seabed of immaculate white sand. A thousand yellow-and-black fish the size of dinner plates with tiny lavender mouths glided serenely through the coral and bright green plants that swayed gently in the current. An enormous blue-and-gray grouper goggled at us from three feet away. In the middle distance lay what looked like the remains of a Spanish galleon. Gemlike points of colored light drifted through the clear blue water, sparkling and glinting like an overturned basket of diamonds; soft music and incense filled the air. It was as if I were swimming at the bottom of the world's largest aquarium—or in the world's most vivid hallucination.

"*This* is the *real* palace," said the redhead softly, and led me by the hand across the bottom of the Sultan's fairy-tale lagoon. Whatever held the water back was absolutely invisible, and powdery white sand covered the floor of our passageway. It was difficult to tell that we were not actually walking along the floor of the ocean.

Indefinable shapes loomed up before us as the stark white wall through which we had stepped fell gradually from view and at last disappeared behind the coral heads. It took a moment to realize that we were now standing in an enormous bedroom, a chamber whose walls and ceiling were nothing less than the waters of the Indian Ocean. The sandy white floor was crowded with rocks and plants that gradually took on the appearance of furniture, and with a thrill of apprehension I saw a gigantic pink scallop shell lying on a bed of bright green sea plants that could only be the trysting grounds of the demented Sultan of Seychellia.

Be calm, and resolute, came Angus's voice unexpectedly. *Do whatever appears to be required of you, without arousing antagonism. Be certain that we have not abandoned you.*

"Easy to say," I muttered bitterly as my two naked escorts

led me forward to the fifteen-foot scallop shell. "It's not *you* who's going to be ravished by this repulsive megalomaniac."

We shall see, said Angus enigmatically. *I repeat: be calm.*

Angus must have been comming me through the intermediary of a small green rock that dangled between the opulent breasts of my blonde escort. Now she raised it to her lips and murmured into it silently. Then she turned to me with a bright smile. "His Exalted Majesty will join us shortly. You will stand between us on this side of the bed with eyes lowered and your hands held together before you. When we nudge you, you will sink to the floor as we showed you and prostrate yourself before His Exalted Majesty. Is that clear?"

"Absolutely," I whispered through bone-dry lips as I recalled the gruesome litany of tortures that awaited those women heedless enough to thwart the will of the exalted Southworld lecher. To be hung by my heels while—. I shuddered; and resolved to swallow my self-esteem and do whatever had to be done to survive, to live to fight another day. At least, I thought wildly, I'd already had the experience of making partial love to myself—no, to the Robert Clayborn body. . . . It wouldn't come as a *total* surprise being with a man. . . . And this wasn't really *me* whose physical body was about to be violated, only a stranger named Mariata Divine. . . .

An elbow nudged me from either side, and on trembling legs I sank slowly to the sandy floor. The tips of my breasts rubbed against the sand as I flung my arms forward and prostrated myself ignominiously before the tin-pot despot of the Seychelles.

38

Never have I felt so abased and ridiculous as I did while I lay there in the sand with my naked derrière thrust high in the air behind me like a whipped cur cowering before its master. At least I had the grim satisfaction of seeing that my two debauched chamberlains were equally prostrate and motionless. The Sultan apparently played no favorites when it came to his women.

A shadow passed briefly before me, and a moment later I jumped involuntarily as something cold and slippery began to move slowly against the soft inner flesh of my exposed buttocks. I had no doubt at all that it was His Exalted Majesty, inspecting his latest consignment of raw meat with the tip of his polished black boot.

"You may arise." The voice was soft and cultivated—or as cultivated as a voice from Southern California can ever be. The women beside me rose gracefully to their feet; I was far more awkward. I stood before the Sultan with downcast eyes and my hands folded modestly before me. I could see now that his boots were a glossy brown rather than the black I had imagined. Tucked into them were baggy white silk trousers. That was all I could see of him until a hand raised my chin. Now I looked down into the dull, snakelike eyes of the pintsized degenerate who was about to introduce me to his repertoire of fancies and conceits. His eyes were set into deep black sockets beneath a high, domelike scholar's forehead.

His hair was mouse-colored and thinning, his nose and mouth small and delicate and set in a mass of wrinkles.

"Yes," said the Sultan of Seychellia after examining me for a long moment, "very beautiful indeed. I believe I may have heard you sing in San Francisco when I was a student in Pasadena. Did you ever appear at the Faded Violet?"

"Yes, Your Majesty," I murmured faintly.

He studied me quizzically a moment longer with his curiously ascetic face, an incongruously nondescript little man to be wielding the power of life or death over so many helpless people. "Yes, a long time ago. You were young and beautiful. And now, thirty years later, you are *still* young and beautiful. Whereas I . . ." His dull eyes seemed to sink even deeper into his enormous sockets and a hand came out of nowhere to slash me violently across the face. "Still young and beautiful," he muttered, turning away and beginning to pull his white blouse from his scrawny shoulders. "An equilibrium must be established. . . . We will discuss your so-called relationship with the Martian Oneness when your tractability and cooperation have been assured. Yes, yes, first a just and lasting equilibrium. . . ."

My eyes were blurred with tears from the unexpected blow. I hardly saw the women on either side as they tugged me forward toward the scallop shell. "Looks like he's in a bad mood today," the blonde murmured almost inaudibly. "For heaven's sake don't do anything to provoke him; we'll do what we can to protect you."

"Do you wish us to remain, Your Exalted Majesty?" asked the redhead.

"No. Yes. No. Wait." He had slumped to the edge of the scallop shell, naked now except for his glistening boots. "I've changed my mind: attach her to the shell. Her eyes are overly saucy, disrespectful; first she shall have a taste of discipline. The two of you shall stay and watch: I begin to discern a certain slackness in your demeanor. Perhaps this will reinvigorate you."

My arms tensed as the women's grip tightened around my elbows. I wondered despairingly if I could throw myself forward and break the madman's scrawny neck before they be-

gan to torture me. I was readying myself for the jump when
Angus interrupted.

*No, Robert! Don't! All is in hand! Please! Trust the One-
ness! Relax, be calm, let them attach you. . . . Trust me,
Robert, trust me.*

I sighed, and let myself be spread-eagled and then attached
to one side of the enormous bed, my arms above my head,
my legs stretched wide. My heart pounded with terror as I
watched the Sultan's two naked chamberlains kneel before
him and reverently remove his long brown boots. He glanced
down at me with icy indifference, then turned away to a large
red coral head. Part of it slid away to reveal a fully stocked
closet of whips and restraints and other grotesque objects. I
shuddered as the Sultan made a slow, thoughtful perusal,
then tentatively hefted a small black cat-o'-nine-tails and
turned toward me.

"Your Exalted Majesty," murmured the redhead from
where she stood on the far side of the scallop shell. "Forgive
me for interrupting, but the Empress of Kilimanjaro is comming you. She says that it is of the highest conceivable pri-
ority."

"Tell her to call me later," snapped the Sultan.

"I have already told her so, Your Exalted Highness, but
she says that her communication cannot possibly wait: it is
in connection with the Martian godling and the person of this
. . . this young lady."

The Sultan sighed in exasperation and let the whip sag to
the side of his scrawny leg. "Well, what is it she wants,
then?"

"She will only communicate directly to you via rockcom,
Your Exalted Highness."

"Via *rockcom*! She must be insane! That's the . . ." He
slashed the whip violently through the air, then tossed it to
the sandy floor. "I fear that you are the one who will have
to suffer for this unparalleled intrusion, my beautiful little
songbird," he muttered over his shoulder as he wheeled
around to his collection of horrors in the gaping coral head.
"Where's a rock, then? Give me a rock. What *can* she mean
by this insane . . ."

I watched him pull a plain brown-and-red rock from the

depths of the closet, shake it impatiently, then lift it to his
ear as if it were an old-fashioned telephone. "Well," he
barked, "what do you want? Do you realize you've interrupted me in the middle of—"

The rock exploded, blowing the Sultan's head into a soft
red mist.

Forgive me, Robert, came Angus's voice deep within my
mind, as I gaped in stupefaction at the Sultan's headless body
collapsing to the floor, a geyser of crimson blood erupting
from the stump of his severed neck.

"Forgive you for what?" I murmured as I wonderingly
watched the bloody mist drift dreamlike through the diffused
blue light of the underwater bedroom and slowly vanish into
the Sultan's air-purification system.

*For subjecting you to such a ghastly spectacle, of course.
I hope that you will not be severely traumatized by—*

"That *was* the Sultan you just blew up?"

Reluctantly, but yes.

"Not me?"

Of course not, Robert.

"Then I think I can withstand any amount of traumatizing." I could feel Mariata Divine's breasts rising and falling
in sudden exhilaration. The Sultan was dead—and I was free!

39

A tiny movement by the stupefied blonde to the left of the bed recalled me to harsh reality and the plain fact that I was actually far from free; that, in fact, I might actually be worse off now than I had been a moment before. For the master of Seychellia lay headless a few feet away—and I was still bound hand and foot to his grotesque bed. My exhilaration gave way to an icy chill as I began to imagine what would happen when the Sultan's security forces burst into the room. . . .

"Angus!" I cried aloud. "I'm still attached, I'm—"

I realize that, Robert. Listen to what I am now saying to your two companions.

I looked up to see that both the blonde and the redhead had turned their horrified attention from the remains of their late master to me.

—to notice the Martian rocks attached to your necklaces. These rocks are now hanging between your mammary glands, in very close proximity to your heart. In the next five seconds each rock will explode in the fashion you have just witnessed—unless you instantly release Ms. Divine from her bonds.

"But . . . but . . ." stammered the redhead, her eyes growing even wider.

It is of no use trying to summon help from the rest of the palace: your rocks no longer function except to explode upon my command.

With zombielike motions the two naked women moved forward and with trembling hands released me from my bonds. I climbed to my feet and found that my legs were quivering as badly as their hands. For a moment I glared at them viciously, nearly willing Angus to blow them both to pieces, then turned away to kick off the grotesque golden high heels that were my only clothing. I jerked a gauzy pink coverlet from an unrumpled portion of the Sultan's enormous bed. "What do we do *now?*" I asked Angus as I hastily wound it around my goosefleshed body. "We're still in the Sultan's palace, surrounded by guards, somewhere at the bottom of the ocean. Are we going to punch a hole in the wall and start swimming for shore?"

Not at all, Robert. The Sultan's personal aircar is on the roof, awaiting our departure.

Still half-dazed, I found my eyes fixed unblinkingly on the pale pink nipples of the redhead's imposing breasts. And on the silver-filigreed rock that dangled between them, ready to blow the lovely body to bloody pieces. "We're just going to waltz on out of here?" I asked incredulously, unable to believe Angus's words.

But of course. Using the voice of the Sultan of Seychellia, I have given orders that he is not to be disturbed in his chambers, and that his visitor is be escorted immediately to his aircar.

My eyes widened. "You mean . . . you can imitate the Sultan over the rockcom? You can make everyone in the palace think you're the Sultan of Seychellia?"

Such is the case, admitted Angus modestly.

Once again I felt my breasts heaving under the impetus of strong emotion. "Then everything I've gone through, everything that's happened to me in this harem, this . . . this . . . near . . . ." I waved my hand furiously at the Sultan's scallopshell bed, his two naked chamberlains, "all of *this* could have been avoided by you giving a few simple orders?"

Yes, Robert.

If Angus had been the Sultan's naked chamberlain, and I the rock that dangled between her breasts, I would have instantly blasted him into eternity. "Then why *didn't* you?" I screamed aloud so fiercely that the two startled women collapsed in tears into each other's arms.

First the Sultan had to be disposed of, Robert.

"Then why didn't you do so three *days* ago? Before he even *brought* me here?"

Because the Oneness and I failed to think of it until earlier today.

My Martian supermind.

I sighed, and turned angrily towards the two sobbing chamberlains. "Well?" I snapped. "Are you going to show me the way back to the royal harem and my clothes, or are you going to stay here in each other's arms until the guards come to pick up the pieces of your favorite Cal Tech playmate?"

Their wails grew louder, but an instant later they had broken apart and were leading me smartly towards the harem.

"And after that," I said, "I have to stop to pick up a rock."

"Are you returning me to Versailles?" asked Marie Antoinette tremulously as she paused on the threshold of the aircar.

I turned to see the last of the 220-odd women who had comprised the late Sultan's private collection climbing aboard the dozen aircars that Angus had summoned to the roof of the summer palace. "Possibly, possibly," I replied absently as I helped the enormously fat brown woman who was Queen Keopulolani of Hawaii waddle through the narrow hatch. "I have notified the French Minister of Culture and the Chief Curator of the Palace of Versailles of your existence. They are eagerly looking forward to your arrival."

The last of the preposterously attired inmates of the harem had disappeared into the aircars, and I gently shut the hatch on the still expostulating Queen of France. Someday, I told myself, when I had my own body back—and my own libido— I would have to look up some of these fascinating women whom I had just rescued from slavery. That kittenish little Mademoiselle Bardot, for instance, seemed a far more interesting companion with whom to curl up for a profound discussion of the manumission of sentient beings than my rock Angus or any of his fellow Martians.

• • •

Nineteen hours later I arrived in New York aboard Seychellia Imperial Airways' largest long-range aircraft. Debark-
ing behind me, to the dumfoundment of the United States
Immigration Agency, was my entourage of 220 chattering
haremmates, as well as the 137 perplexed creatures I had
stopped to liberate from the ghastly cellars of the Empress of
Kilimanjaro.

"Angus," I had mused as we sat in the enormous com-
mandeered aircraft waiting for takeoff clearance at Dar es
Salaam International Airport, "that little trick you played on
the Sultan: you really *can* blow up anyone you want?"

*Yes, Robert. The destruction of a living being was an ex-
tremely traumatic experience for the Oneness, regardless of
how much the Sultan of Seychellia may have merited his fate,
and, of course, an attribute had to be sacrificed to do so, but
as you observed, it definitely can be done.*

"Would the Oneness sacrifice one more attribute—in the
sacred cause of liberty?"

Of course.

My hands were trembling. "Try to get the Empress of
Kilimanjaro on the rockcom."

"Yes?" Her voice was wary. "Just who is this?"

"You recall Mariata Divine, the representative of the Oneness?"

There was a long silence. Finally: "Yes, of course. I
thought . . . What do you—"

"I thought it only fair to tell you."

"Tell me what?"

"That upon your death all the slaves in your cellars will
be freed."

"Upon my . . ."

"Yes. Just as soon as the rock in your hand blows up.
Which is now."

After that there was nothing but silence.

It is done, said Angus.

I set him down on my knee with still-trembling fingers. I
had just killed a human being. "Fine," I said shakily. "Tell
the pilot to change course for Kilimanjaro City. And use every
rock in the Empire to have those slaves out of the cellars and

waiting for us at the airport. Blow up anyone who gets in their way. They'll be the prime evidence against whoever it was that manufactured them." I stared down at Angus grimly. "And if the courts don't take care of *them* . . . there's always the justice of the rocks."

40

Ontogeny recapitulates phylogeny.

"What? *What?*" I blinked at the scaly, six-foot lizard that was my son Hadrian. My bizarre aggregation of traveling companions had been left to the charge of the State Department's baffled Chief of Protocol, and now I sat in my son's room at Columbia Medical Center, totally devastated by his grotesque appearance. During the months I had just spent abroad speaking to him only by rockcom I had evidently suppressed the horrible memory of what he had become far more thoroughly than I had realized.

You're the biogeneticist, he said, speaking to me through his rock Tony. *You've never heard that phrase? It was popular in biological circles some centuries ago.*

"I'm old and doddering, of course, but not *that* old. What century are we talking about?"

The long, scaly body quivered, as if my son were trying to shrug. *Nineteenth or twentieth, whenever biology started becoming a real science.*

"Ontogeny recapitulates phylogeny," I repeated, shaking my head dubiously. "I don't—"

Ontogeny: the development of the individual, interrupted Hadrian impatiently. *Phylogeny: the development of the group, or species, within the animal kingdom. The phylum in this particular case is vertebrates. Ontogeny recapitulates phylogeny: the development of the individual recreates the development of the group. It's the progression of stages that the human embryo grows through, from fish, through reptile, through primate, to human.*

Dim memories returned to me from far-off school days. "I do remember a bit, very vaguely: a school of biologists who thought that all the steps in the evolution of the human race could actually be found at some point in the actual physical development of the human embryo in the uterus?" Hadrian nodded. "At one point the embryo has a vestigial tail: that's the primate stage. Before that the embryo actually displays primitive gills: that's the fish stage." Hadrian nodded again. I looked down in growing dismay at my lizard-son where he stretched out in apparent comfort on the floor at my feet. "But all that was totally discredited!" I said sharply. "It was just a crackpot theory that was never generally—"

It may have been discredited, but it looks as if it's true, at least for all the twenty-five thousand Scottish Emperors in the world.

"But—"

In reverse, of course, continued Hadrian calmly, implacably. *From human to primate to reptile to fish to—*

My horror was unbounded. "You mean . . . you're on the way to turning into a *fish?"*

I suppose so, said Hadrian casually. *They say they can see gills beginning to develop; they're preparing a couple of tanks, just in case.*

"Tanks?"

One saltwater, one freshwater. The presumption is that I'll probably be living in salt water—the primal uterine soup, you know—but they're taking no chances. His lidless reptile's eyes looked up at me unblinkingly. *The next time you come, you might think to bring some raw shrimp to drop in my tank: lucky for me I've always liked sashimi.*

It was no use—either as Robert Clayborn or Mariata Divine—trying to contact any of my former associates at 3L for confirmation of what Hadrian was saying. As far as Lightfoot Lads and Lasses were concerned the unfortunate incident of the Scottish Emperors was now a thing of the past, a minor vexation to be brushed aside in the excitement of the introduction of the spring models.

But now I had my own worldwide espionage service—when I could remember to use it. "Angus," I said to my rock, who sat on the dresser of my hotel room overlooking Central Park. "Get in touch with all the rocks at Columbia Med and 3L in Chicago. Find out everything they've learned about . . . about . . . this fish business."

Yes, Robert. It may take some time to correlate it all.

"Time is what I have the most of," I said as I gave bleak thought to all the shattered pieces of my former life. Glumly I flicked on the room's holoscope and lay back on the bed, anxious to lose myself for a single evening in mindless oblivion, far from the problems of the Oneness and the desperate plights of my two children.

Three hours later, half dozing, half waking, I became dimly aware of a low-keyed commercial that filled most of the room's free space. It was soundless, of course, since Angus automatically silenced all commercial intrusions for me, but something about it had caught my subconscious attention.

I scowled at the nearly life-size images of two laughing children as they splashed through ocean swells on the back of a mutated dolphin. One of the children reached down and patted a handsome green-and-yellow Martian rock that lay in a transparent pocket on the side of the dolphin's saddle. Moments later the dolphin had wheeled about in the waves and was receding rapidly towards a distant white boat.

Now an impeccably coiffed holoscopic mommy and daddy joyfully hoisted their children from the dolphin's saddle and hugged them blissfully. As the children hugged their improbably toothy parents, the camera tracked in to a gleaming red-and-brown rock sitting on the deck chair just beside mommy's shapely hip. "Sound, Angus," I commed.

Stately music, rising to a crescendo. An even statelier voice: "—for security that you and your family can *always* count on: Martian Rock & Telecommunications, helping us make the world a helpier place to be. See your authorized dealer—today!"

"Sound off, Angus." I sagged back in my pillow, idly trying to put a finger on what gnawed at me. Finally it came to me. A commercial message from MRT? I tried to recall when I had ever seen one. MRT *never* advertised. Why waste money on publicity when they had the only game in town? Either you bought their rock or you did without: they were the solar system's premier and single unbreakable monopoly.

A curious coincidence, I thought drowsily. Or could it be linked with my own activities and the threat I represented to the sacrosanct MRT profit-and-loss statement? Very, very curious. In the morning I would have to discuss it with Angus— and the Oneness on Mars.

41

The morning, however, brought its own answer. Holoscopes are, in my opinion, perfectly adequate for simpleminded entertainment; but, unless your tastes run to mangled bodies and pools of blood, totally useless for news. And breakfast in New York, of course, is unthinkable without the company of the Good Gray *Times*. So I lay in bed sipping steaming chocolate and scanning the endless pages of newsfax. On page five I nearly skipped past a lengthy account of the Senate hearings on the communications satellite owned by the state of Arkansas.

The state of Arkansas? A communications satellite? *That* kingdom of darkness and obscurantism?

Intrigued, I went back to the article and read it carefully. Sometime during my travels abroad the Arkansas thals had found the money to put their own satellite into orbit aboard a Chinese hyperskip. And now a broad spectrum of that state's fundamentalist thals was gleefully haranguing the long-suffering American people with holoscopic presentations of their almost infinite number of crackpot ideas.

Some American people were less inclined to suffer than others. They had complained to their Congresspersons that the First Amendment's guarantee of free speech did not extend to machinery in geosynchronous orbit 22,300 miles above the Earth. They demanded that the Air Force instantly dismantle the offending satellite and once again free the airwaves for "The Heartaches of Cleatoria Saxe and Her Seven Lusty Daughters . . ."

"What next?" I marveled aloud. "Angus, holo on: the thal station." For the rest of the morning I lay abed and watched in appalled fascination as evangelist followed flat-earther and phrenologist followed fundamentalist. In addition to their usual zany outpourings, nearly all their wild-eyed harangues, whatever the topic, now incorporated two additional bits of dangerous mischief.

First that the catastrophic, and totally inexplicable, failure of the Scottish Emperors was conclusive proof of what they and the Old Catholics had been saying all along: that the factory people weren't really human.

And that in some undefined but definite way, the Martian rocks were the immediate cause of this catastrophe.

"No wonder MRT is starting to advertise," I grumbled to Angus. "If you and I don't put them out of business by taking their rocks away, the thals will do it by scaring their customers off." I stretched languidly and climbed out of bed, wondering how much this latest complication would further impede my so far totally fruitless efforts at Martian emancipation. "If anyone bothers to listen to them, that is." I stepped into the shower. "The thals, I mean. I can't believe that any right-thinking American houseperson, a devotee to Cleatoria Saxe, could bring himself to—"

Their satellite began operation twenty-seven days ago, interrupted Angus. *In the following twenty-four hours seventeen North American rocks were permanently destroyed by being thrown into oubliettes. This was more than had been willfully destroyed in all the previous forty-three years. In the following twenty-four hours another thirty-three rocks were destroyed. Since then the figure has gradually risen to approximately one hundred fifty per day.*

"But that's terrible!" A vivid image of my consort Sylvina wantonly murdering her own rock Minkle in our living room oubliette flashed across my mind. "Why didn't you tell me?"

We did not want to unnecessarily disturb you in your endeavors by troubling you with inconsequentials.

"But that's murder!" I cried, and for the first time I suddenly realized that the obliteration of a Martian rock *was* the murder of a sentient being who had all the rights of myself or any other human being. "Thousands and thousands of—"

Two thousand six hundred and nineteen, said Angus. *No. Two thousand six hundred and twenty. A rock in Duluth, Minnesota, has just been extinguished.*

"Angus, we've got to do something."

Yes, Robert. But what?

I had meant to have lunch at the hotel in the ancient splendor of the Oak Room. Instead, all appetite lost, I meandered aimlessly through the gusts and flurries of gently falling snowflakes until the towers of Rockefeller Center loomed around me.

The sunken ice rink I had twice skated on as a child fifty years before was still in its familiar place, unchanged since its restoration two centuries earlier. The same timeless crowd of idlers, tourists, and lunchtime office workers lazed against the railings to gaze down at the silent figures skimming gracefully across the smooth white surface.

I found room at the railing, blinked through the swirls of snow at the skaters below, wondering bleakly where I would be fifty years from now, where Angus would be fifty centuries from now, where the Oneness would be fifty million years from now. . . .

A small, rosy-cheeked child in a blue snowsuit skidded uncontrollably across the ice into another child in a red snowsuit. Both fell sprawling. Two more children immediately skated into them and joined them on the ice in a tangle of boots and mittens.

I watched morosely as an angry adult in a sober gray overcoat pushed his way out of the lower-level spectators and minced gingerly across the ice. He jerked the child in blue to his feet, cuffed him on the ear, turned to admonish the other three. But now he was joined by another angry parent, upbraided in turn.

Two Clancy the Cops in old-fashioned blue serge uniforms glittering with brass buttons came onto the rink and efficiently restored order. The children were raised to their feet, their snowsuits brushed, and sent back into the pack of skaters. The parents were shepherded firmly off the rink.

I sighed glumly, inexplicably melancholy in the face of the tiny human drama just witnessed. Was it because of Patricia, the wistful thought that my own far-off daughter might easily have been one of the carefree skaters below, that it might be I who—

The gentleman wearing the gray overcoat reappeared on the rink carrying what seemed to my disbelieving eyes to be an automatic hunting rifle. From a nearby sporting goods shop? I wondered inanely. For a moment he was lost to view behind a cluster of skaters, then suddenly reappeared, the rifle raised to his shoulder. I heard a dull thump, and then a second. A third and a fourth, and suddenly skaters were shrieking and scattering in panic. Shots continued to ring out, strangely muted by the falling snow. Horrified, paralyzed, I watched numbly as the madman marched majestically across the slippery ice to where the first of the bodies lay in a spreading pool of bright red blood. It was the rosy-cheeked child in the blue snowsuit. The madman nodded thoughtfully, shattered its head with another round, moved on.

That was his son, said Angus softly in my numbed mind.

By the time the madman mercifully vanished beneath a great mass of translucent stick-tight launched by the two Clancy the Cops, the seemingly ordinary businessman in the gray tweed overcoat had methodically butchered all three of the other children involved in his son's trivial incident, fourteen adult skaters, and twelve lower-level spectators.

As his bulky figure was borne away from the rink through the horror-stricken crowd, Angus reached out to the traumatized rock that sat in the madman's rock-pocket. *His owner is now demanding that he be immediately released from his bonds,* Angus reported dispassionately, *as none of the so-called people he shot were actually human and it is his mission to continue with his task of eradicating them from the face of the earth.*

I remained paralyzed with shock, unable to speak or think, hardly able to breathe, still draped casually over the railing.

It is the fourth such incident in North America in the last three weeks.

Finally, moving like a zombie, I pushed myself away from the railing and the ghastly spectacle below. "You mean *Americans* are beginning to say that they and their children might not be human? That they *themselves* aren't human?"

So it appears.

"And they're actually *killing* one another?"

This is the fourth such massacre. There have been a number of individual murders.

For three centuries, ever since the introduction of lifestyling, willful murder had practically vanished from the American scene. I staggered on numb legs towards Fifth Avenue.

"Madness, Angus," I cried in despair, "madness!"

Madness is an interesting concept, Robert, one that the Oneness has not yet fully— He broke off for a moment. When he resumed speaking it was with the terror-stricken voice of my daughter, Patricia.

Daddy! Daddy! I heard them talking! They're taking me to the factory! Oh Daddy! I don't want to go!

42

I could, of course, have simply asked Angus to blow up Sylvina on the spot, along with judges, shysters, security men, 3L personnel, everyone else who threatened the life of my little girl. For a terrible moment I was sorely tempted; then reason—jolted perhaps by the bloody images of the ghastliness I had just left behind on the skating rink in Rockefeller Center—reasserted itself. It was not Sylvina that I had to *kill*, but Patricia that I had to *save*. . . .

Fortunately the two of them were still on the other side of the world in Hong Kong: somehow Sylvina's shyster in San Francisco had succeeded in slipping her petition to the Children's Court past my own eminent and grossly overpaid legalists. I promised myself that one day I would have sharp words with them.

But first there was my daughter's life to save.

3L's reprocessing center was a drab four-story building covering a quarter of a block in the heart of Old Chicago. Most of the ancient brick buildings in the area were devoted to light industry; the only vehicles on the streets were trucks and industrial aircars. My own long black aircar dropped out of a leaden winter sky and into a nearly deserted street three blocks from my goal. None of the few pedestrians hurrying along the icy sidewalk bothered to glance at the top-secret Air Force space vehicle or at its gangly blond passenger with the bushy blond beard.

The aircar lifted into the sky and disappeared into the clouds. I set out grimly towards my rendezvous with my daughter, an Air Force HavocMaster intensifier in the small carton tucked beneath one arm. It was pleasant being in men's clothing and shoes again, even if their fit on the curves of a woman's frame was a little tight in places. As I marched down Adams Avenue I pulled my heavy black fur cap even further over my thick blond wig. A thick red scarf and a bulky brown overcoat concealed Mariata Divine's slender neck and willowy frame. My mouth and chin were hidden by the blond beard and mustache; if both of them stayed in place, all that could be seen of Mariata Divine were her nose and eyes.

I came to an enormous structure of faded red brick, stopped to read a small brass plaque fastened to its wall. It had been put there by the Chamber of Commerce and the Friends of Old Chicago. On this site, it said, had been the first of the vast nineteenth-century slaughterhouses that had contributed so much to the growth and prosperity of America's Second City, the Colossus of the Midwest.

A chill ran up my spine and I moved grimly onwards. My heart had been pounding violently throughout the flight to Chicago and sweat had dampened the palms of my hands. But now that action had at last replaced anticipation I felt nothing but a cold fury, an icy determination that nothing at all was going to be allowed to thwart my purpose.

3L's reprocessing center of shabby yellow brick loomed before me, standing forlorn amidst heaps of dirty snow. Its narrow windows were dark and blank. No hint of the building's macabre purpose could be determined from the dull brass number affixed to the discreet front door. I tucked my carton more firmly beneath my arm and pushed the buzzer. Then I waited for the door to open.

An industrial-grade allguard blocked the doorway. "Universal Delivery," I said, extending an empty hand toward the guard. "You've been told to expect me."

The allguard's eyes inspected my gloved hand. Somewhere within his electronic cerebration circuits Angus made the necessary adjustments: the allguard saw Universal Delivery's unforgeable identity card in my hand. Satisfied, he stepped aside to let me enter a small drab foyer. Three identical all-guards blocked the room's two closed doors and single elevator. I stepped toward the elevator.

"I know the way."

The four allguards nodded. I entered the elevator, pushed the thumbplate for the third flood. Now my heart began to thud violently as I rose slowly in the narrow elevator to—what?

The doors opened. An ancient Jane the Secretary sat at her desk, eying me unblinkingly across an uncarpeted wooden hallway. "Yes?"

I glanced nervously up and down the hallway, verifying what Angus had already assured me: that no human beings were in sight. I stepped forward and once again went through the charade of presenting nonexistent credentials. "I will notify Mr. Carmody that you are here," said the Jane the Secretary, then promptly forgot my presence.

Turn to your left and walk nine paces down the hallway, instructed Angus. *No one in the building is aware of your presence.*

I half walked, half ran to the fire door, pushed it open, stepped into a dark, icy stairwell. Once again I could hear the blood pounding in my ears. Could I really count on the security offered by Angus and his sixty-three fellow rocks in the building? I put my foot on the first step of the metal staircase leading upwards. I would have to.

A tiny light burned dimly at the top of the gloomy stairwell. I stood for a moment on the small landing, my breath a white cloud in front of my face.

There are still seven minutes before the arrival of the aircar, said Angus. *Be calm, Robert. Your presence here is completely unsuspected.*

"Patricia . . . ?"

Is still listening to a story being told her by one of the rocks on board. She is actually in high spirits, but is dissembling it well.

I nodded, then set my carton down with trembling hands, fumbled it open. The HavocMaster was over a foot long, black and ungainly; it fit awkwardly in my gloved hand. I gripped it with both hands, raised it with my arms extended

rigidly. It still felt awkward. I stripped my gloves away and
tucked them into the pocket of my overcoat. In spite of the
intense cold, it was easier holding the intensifier in my bare
hands.

"There's no one on the roof?" I asked Angus.

No one at all.

"No alarms go off if I open this door?"

They are no longer functioning.

I took a deep breath, leaned cautiously against the fire bar
that released the door, stepped out into the overcast Chicago
afternoon. As Angus had promised, the roof was empty. Dark
gray ventilation ducts sprouted like ungainly mushrooms in
the fresh white snow that blanketed the roof. I glanced around
warily from where I stood in the shelter of a small brick shed.
On the far side on the roof a larger outbuilding with two
heavy green metal doors stood in a broad field of snow. My
heart thudded at the sight: the reprocessing center's receiving
station.

"Is that where they'll land?" I asked.

Just in front of those doors.

"It's too far away. I'll never be able to hit anyone from
here. Not without—"

*I have consulted all the rocks in the building. The proce-
dure is always the same. First the aircar will land. Then the
doors will open. Two company officials will come out of the
freight elevator and onto the roof. They will be joined by
those in the aircar. All of them will then enter the receiving
station and descend together in the elevator.*

"But there are already five of them in the aircar?" I said
despairingly. "Two more from the—"

*You will have ample time, Robert, and no problem at all
in hitting your targets without endangering your daughter.
What I shall do to facilitate the matter is this. . . .*

"I suppose so," I muttered dubiously when he had finished explaining his plan.

*All seven persons involved are carrying a rock on their
person. If you like, you can stay here and it will be a simple
matter to blow them all up.*

"No! Not in front of Patricia! There's been enough . . .
enough killing and violence. I'm sick of it! And . . . and I

don't want you rocks to develop a taste for it. I don't . . . want you ending up like . . . humans!''

Your concern is most appreciated, Abraham Lincoln, came the unexpected voice of the Oneness deep in my mind.

It shall be as you wish, said Angus. *We shall resort to violence only in the gravest emergency. I suggest now that you return to your shelter, Robert: the aircar will be here in two minutes and forty seconds.*

I stepped back into the darkness of the stairwell, the intensifier gripped tightly in Mariata Divine's long, slender hands. Gloomy daylight brightened the quarter-inch crack in the fire door to which I glued a single eye. Time passed with excruciating slowness. Suddenly, long after I had despaired of ever seeing it, a nondescript beige aircar fell out of the gray sky and into my limited field of vision. I strained to see my daughter as it settled to the roof, but the windows were dull mirrors of opaqueness.

The soft hum of the aircar died away and the vehicle lay with sullen menace in the snow. My grip tightened on the intensifier. An interminable time later the two green doors in the receiving station beside the aircar slid open. Two men stepped briskly into the winter afternoon. One was dressed in the expensive garb of a high executive, the other wore a drab brown smock and heavy black boots. Behind them I could see two electronic allguards.

The allguards are normally supposed to follow them out onto the roof, said Angus, *but they have just been immobilized.*

The executive scowled impatiently at the mechanical allguards standing motionlessly in the brightly lighted hallway, then returned his attention to the aircar. Hardly breathing, I watched the hatch in the aircar swing open and two men and a woman step down. Sylvina? No, of course not: her dirty work done, she was already well on her way from San Francisco to Hong Kong. This was a bailiff from Children's Court.

My heart leapt up. Just behind the bailiff, Kanga the Roo clutched tightly to her chest, appeared my daughter, Patricia.

"Just another moment, Rosebud," I commed her. "One more minute and I'll be there."

Yes, Daddy, came her reply. Her head swung from side to side as she vainly tried to find me.

Another man and woman stepped out of the aircar and joined the others. Now they were all assembled: two officers of the court, two security men, one shyster, two sinister figures from Lightfoot Lads and Lasses. And my daughter.

Are you prepared, Robert?

"Yes."

Very well.

The green metal doors that led to the elevators and whatever lay below in the dark bowels of the reprocessing center suddenly slid shut behind the small group of solemn men and women. An instant later the hatch in the aircar snapped shut with a loud thunk. As I pushed my own door open and stepped out into the snow I heard a sudden babble of loud voices.

I was nearly upon them before I was noticed. The 3L executive swung around in sudden alarm. "Who are you? What are you—"

I gestured reassuringly. "A loss of power in the building, sir. I've been sent to tell you that you'll have to use the staircase." Their eyes turned automatically to the distant door I had just left. My daughter's gaze met mine for a moment, moved on without recognizing her daddy.

"Right this way, please." I moved one step closer, to about eight feet from the nearest of Patricia's escorts, and reached beneath my overcoat. I raised the HavocMaster with both hands, took aim, and methodically intensified one security guard after the other. Instantly paralyzed, their motor nerves aflame with agony, they staggered spasmodically, then toppled heavily into the snow. The others gaped at me uncomprehendingly. I aimed the intensifier well above Patricia's head and shot the two men and a woman standing behind her. Then I swung around to the remaining man and a woman. The man had just enough time to scream an inarticulate protest before he too fell twitching and gasping to the roof.

"Patricia," I said to my daughter as I dropped the intensifier to my side. "It's Daddy."

She stared at me blankly as she heard the voice of Mariata Divine. Angus commed the same words to her in my usual voice and her eyes widened. From the corner of my eye I saw a long, black aircar falling rapidly out of the sky. I dropped the intensifier into the snow and fell to my knees in front of my daughter. "Patricia," I murmured, pulling her small, unresisting body against me. Her arms came hesitantly around my neck and her eyes looked up into mine.

"Daddy?"

"It's really Daddy, it's really, really Daddy. You can ask Zoo-Zoo."

"Mommy took Zoo-Zoo away from me. I don't know where she is."

Kneeling in the snow, my daughter in my arms, I still managed to fumble Angus out from beneath my many layers of clothing. "Look, it's Angus."

Her small hand reached out, stroked his familiar curves. "Hi, Angus," she said with a delighted smile. "Why are all those people sleeping in the snow?"

They are all very tired, Patricia. They are having a nap.

"*I'm* not tired. I *hate* naps." She giggled suddenly. "Even in the snow. Is this really Daddy, Angus? Why does he have a beard? And his voice is funny, like a woman's."

This is really your daddy, Patricia. He will tell you all about it.

Her eyes looked up at mine. "Daddy?"

My own eyes were full of tears. I nodded, unable to speak, and hugged her closer. Her arms tightened around my neck. "I missed you, Daddy. Why did you go away?"

"I don't know, honey, I just don't know." I climbed awkwardly to my feet, my daughter in my arms, and turned triumphantly toward the waiting aircar.

43

"You really *are* a woman!" cried Patricia in delight when I pulled away the blond wig and beard to reveal Mariata Divine's lustrous black hair and creamy skin. "How can you be a woman if you're *Daddy?*"

"It's a game I'm playing with Angus," I said aloud as we sat at the controls of the aircar and watched them moving of their own accord—somewhere within the ship Angus, or one of his rock cronies, was interfacing directly with the ship's electronic circuits. We had climbed through the dismal gray clouds that hung over Chicago, shot through a dazzling expanse of sun and blue sky, and now were well into the blackness of space. "Angus didn't want anyone to know that I was coming to get you. So he made me go as a woman instead."

"Angus is *funny,*" declared Patricia, turning her attention to Kanga the Roo. "But I want Zoo-Zoo. Are we going to get Zoo-Zoo now?"

"Angus," I commed silently. "Where is Zoo-Zoo?"

In the home of one of the cleaning staff of the Four Yellow Dragons in Hong Kong. Sylvina gave her Zoo-Zoo several weeks ago.

"We have to get her back."

At this precise moment, Robert? If you give me a few days to arrange the matter, I am sure that I can manage to have her delivered wherever you want.

Just as he could control the spacecraft or manipulate all of the world's financial systems. "Fine: I'll leave it to you. Now comm Patricia with my Robert Clayborn voice. Patricia," I said, "Zoo-Zoo will be joining us in a couple of days."

"Join us *where,* Daddy?"

I looked down at the gleaming blue-and-white ball that was Earth and sighed. "Somewhere down there, Rosebud. I don't know just where yet, but somewhere down there."

Fifty thousand miles from Earth I commed with my Robert Clayborn voice to a person I had vowed never to speak to again: my onetime friend Titus T. Waggoner, now Adjudicator Temporal of the State of Arkansas. It took some time before Angus could inveigle him within range of what in Arkansas was completely unauthorized—a Martian rock.

"Robert! A pleasant surprise! To what do I owe the honor of—"

"I need your help," I told him baldly.

"I am, of course, yours to command," he replied grandiloquently through the instantaneous link of the rockcom.

"Quietly, discreetly, *secretly,*" I added hastily, remembering that a substantial portion of my problems derived from his loud public support for me during his recent campaign for state office. "Otherwise it's worse than no help at all."

"Of course, of course. Subtlety and discretion shall be our watchwords. You seem to have dropped out of the news lately—except for your daughter."

"My daughter? What do you know about my daughter?" The events in Chicago lay only forty-five minutes behind us.

"As Adjudicator Temporal, part of my duties are monitoring what goes on in the bizarre outer world—solely to learn whatever nefarious plots our implacable enemies the tubers are hatching against us, of course," he added with his usual sly humor.

"Of course."

"At this very moment all the news stations are carrying breathless stories of a daring . . . shall we say . . . jailbreak? On the roof of a certain building in Chicago."

"Oh. Yes. Well. I believe that could be my daughter. What . . . what are they saying about—"

"You? Nothing, so far, beyond the fact that you happen to

be the father of the girl in question. The actual . . . kidnapper is thought to be a woman.''

"A woman! But—''

"Disguised as a man, apparently, but the security scans make it clear that beneath all the hair it was actually a female. I believe they even have retinal prints taken from long range.''

I flinched: Angus and I were not quite the criminal superminds that we had imagined ourselves. Still, the essential thing was the safety of Patricia; whatever subsequently happened to the Mariata Divine body was of secondary interest to me. "I, of course, as Robert Clayborn, know nothing at all about this—''

"As Robert Clayborn?'' interrupted Arkansas's foremost legalist. "A peculiar way to—''

"I meant, of course, that although I am overjoyed to hear of Patricia's . . . liberation, illegal though it may be, I personally know nothing at all about it.''

"Of course not. And very wisely, too.''

"However, I *do* know that an old friend of mine would very much like to drop in on you''—from fifty thousand miles, I thought inanely—"to discuss a matter of great importance to me. She may, and I say only *may*, be in the company of a young person who is very dear to me.''

There was a long silence. Then: "I see. Just how do your old friend and your young person propose to drop in on me? Every military and law enforcement agency in the United States is on the alert for a long, black aircar. Our own border defenses, such as they are, have standing orders to repel all unauthorized traffic. Which means, of course, all aircars—''

"—built after the year 1900. I know, Titus, I know.''

"Well, then?''

"Then give me the coordinates of some deep, dark woods. And wait for me . . . and wait for my friend there.''

"But—''

"Titus! We're going to smuggle her across the Arkansas border in a covered wagon, disguised as a spinning wheel, for god's sake! Now give me those coordinates! *Please!*''

The short, stout figure of Titus T. Waggoner stepped out of the inky blackness of Delaney's Wood and into the only slightly less somber darkness of the abandoned hayfield where my Air Force space vehicle had come to rest.

"Wait here, Rosebud. And remember what I told you: whatever you do, don't call me Daddy."

"I won't, Daddy. I mean, Mariata."

I sighed in resignation, stepped out of the unlit aircar into the chilly Arkansas night.

"Ms. Divine, I presume?" However secretive his presence here in Delaney's Wood, there was certainly nothing furtive about Titus T. Waggoner's booming voice.

After a moment my weary mind finally registered his actual words. I sighed again, louder, more plaintively. "They know—"

"—that the ruthless Chicago assailant and kidnapper is actually the celebrated cabaret chantoosie Mariata Divine, pronounced Deeveen? Oh yes—the retina prints were quite clear." His dark outline moved closer. "The exploit appears to have caught the imagination of the American people—there is little else on the news. Both you and Robert Clayborn are temporary folk heroes. Still: sooner or later, the rule of law is the rule of law. My own law degree is valid in thirty-seven of fifty-four American states: I will be honored to defend you in court."

"Thank you, Ti—, Mr. Waggoner," I said stiffly in Mariata Divine's rich contralto. "I do appreciate your offer. It may well come to that. As Robert explained, however, I am presently *in loco parentis* to a certain young person. You know why it is imperative that she not be returned to the United States. She would—"

"I know," said Titus T. Waggoner grimly. "I know what awaits her in Chicago. And thousands of others like her!"

"Yes," I agreed reluctantly, hesitant to assume even now my share of responsibility for whatever nightmares lay hidden in the dark shadows of the life-industry. "When . . . when all of this is over, we'll have to do something about . . . about the reprocessing centers, about . . . well, we'll have to look at . . ." I trailed off.

"The whole zombie industry," said the Adjudicator Temporal matter-of-factly. "It *is* time, you know. It is truly time."

"Perhaps you're right. But in the meantime—"

"Your concern is Robert's little girl. Of course. Any life at all, of course, is dear to us here in Arkansas and must be scrupulously protected, but what, specifically, does Robert want from me?"

"Your assurance that she will never be returned to the re-processing center. You were once his closest friend. You are now the only person he could think of asking."

"Sad, that." I could see Titus T. Waggoner's ungainly head wagging morosely against the starry sky. "After all these years, no one else to turn to . . ." His stout figure drew itself up. "But not entirely true. There *is* one other person he can always turn to. . . ."

We swung around to the dark bulk of the aircar. "So this is the magic carpet so invisible to the best scientific and military resources of the United States and the People's Militia of the State of Arkansas?" asked Titus playfully.

"Yes."

"Does she have a name?"

"A *name?*"

"All good ships must have names." The Adjudicator Temporal raised his hand in the darkness. "A name: I hereby dub thee *The Underground Railroad.*"

I could only shake my head in wonder at the extent of Titus's whimsy. "Patricia is inside," I said, trying to remind him of the harsh reality of the situation.

"Hrmph. And I the Adjudicator Temporal of the State of Arkansas! Hrmph again. Well then, I suppose I shall have to turn my Nelson eye to this outrageous infringement of all of our most cherished local ordinances." He took me gallantly by the elbow. "Let us step aboard, dear lady. Did you know that I am presently being asked to adjudicate the status of the contact lens? It was, apparently, invented in Switzerland in 1885, which puts it well within our rather Procrustean limits. On the other hand, it was not actually *used* on a practical scale until well into the twentieth century. A fine legal nicety, I fear. I am about to—"

"What's a contact lens?" I asked distractedly as I ushered Titus into the ship's unlighted salon. The lights brightened slightly upon my command to Angus; I saw Patricia had fallen asleep on the divan, Kanga the Roo clutched tightly in her arms.

"What's a contact—? Ah. I keep forgetting: you . . . crèche people have carefully designed out all of your physical frailties. None of you have worn glasses for three centuries now."

"And have no desire to." I lifted Patricia from the divan and carried her over to the controls.

"So this is the young person in question." Titus T. Waggoner peered closely as I slumped into the pilot's chair with Patricia cuddled in my arms. "Robert's daughter?"

"Robert's daughter."

Titus sighed loudly. "Very beautiful. Like everyone from the crèches, of course."

"She didn't *ask* to be born in a crèche," I protested wearily. Why did Titus's words make me feel so unaccountably guilty? "*I* didn't ask to be born in a crèche, either. *None* of us did."

"No, but—" The legalist shook his head impatiently. "We can argue the verities later. The important thing now is to get her to sanctuary."

"Then sit here and strap yourself in," I said, indicating the seat beside me, "and let's get going."

Titus cocked his head at me curiously. "You can actually fly this contraption?"

"*I* can't—Angus can."

"Angus? Robert's rock?"

"Robert . . . ah . . . lent him to me."

"*In loco parentis,* of course. How thoughtful. Well, kindly ask Angus to get this thing airborne in a northeasterly direction. And at something less than the speed of sound, please— we wouldn't want to disturb the cows, would we?"

44

Patricia stirred in my arms and awoke just as *The Underground Railroad* settled to earth. "Where are we, Daddy?" she murmured sleepily.

"At a friend's home. Where you're going to be staying for a while."

"With you, Daddy?"

"I'm your Aunt Mariata, remember, darling? You're still asleep, Rosebud. You're going to stay here with your friends, and I'm going to go get your daddy."

"And he's going to come and stay with me?"

"Yes."

"And Zoo-Zoo too? You're going to get Zoo-Zoo?"

"Zoo-Zoo is her rock," I explained to Titus as we climbed to our feet and I carried Patricia across the dimly lit salon. "She's in Hong Kong."

"A long way from Russellville."

"Is that where we are?" I tried to peer into the darkness.

"A few miles outside, actually. At a friend's house."

"I see." Actually, I saw very little. Electric lights, I knew, had been in widespread use well before the end of the nineteenth century, but most of the devout folk of Arkansas still preferred to make do with more primitive means of lighting. All I could see before me as we stepped down from the aircar was the black bulk of a large house with cupolas against a background of even blacker trees. A pale orange light flickered on in one of the windows, became yellow, then moved through the house to the front porch. Patricia stirred restlessly in my arms. "Do you know where we are, Angus?" I commed silently to my rock.

Yes, Robert. Mr. Waggoner has been using his rock to comm the occupant of this house.

"I thought so. Well? Why all the secre—"

The door of the house opened and two figures stood in the doorway, a kerosene lantern casting yellow light on their features. My heart jumped in my chest. The man I had never before seen; the woman was instantly recognizable as my long-ago lover, mother of my dead child, and kidnapper of my son, the still beautiful Jeanie Norman.

"Do you really have to go, Daddy?" asked Patricia plaintively as I tucked her into the ancient four-poster that would be her bed for the foreseeable future.

I kissed her on the sweet little curve of her nose just between her eyes. "I have to go get your *real* daddy," I whispered. "You don't want your daddy to stay a woman all the time, do you?"

"It's *fun* having a daddy who's a woman," she giggled.

"Sssh! Not so loud! Remember what you promised? That you wouldn't tell anyone who I really am?"

"I remember—Mariata," she said proudly.

I pulled her to my breast and held her there until she fell asleep in my arms.

"Do you really have to go, Mariata?" echoed Jeanie Norman softly. "You would be safe here with us, you know. No one will look for you in Arkansas." Her lips grimaced in painful memory. "And if they did . . . we wouldn't let them take you away, would we, Titus?"

The Adjudicator Temporal of the State of Arkansas shook his head. "That we would not." He glanced at me sharply. What, he was obviously thinking, did this Mariata Divine creature know of the tragic events of thirty years ago that had engulfed Jeanie Norman and Robert Clayborn. . . .

But my face revealed nothing of my own turmoil as I in turn studied the strawberry blonde who sat across from me in the old-fashioned parlor on a green horsehair divan. Guilt-

ily I recalled my uncharitable thoughts of some months ago
of how by now Jeanie Norman must be a toothless old crone.
Instead, she appeared to be a perfectly composed, middle-
aged woman who had long ago vanquished those inner demons that had once brought so much pain to the two of us.
Her ruddy cheeks glowed with happiness as she clutched her
husband's hand against her knee and twined her fingers endlessly in and out of his. It was a wrench to think of this still
beautiful woman as Jeanie Whitlow, wife of Horace Whitlow,
instead of Jeanie Norman, lover of Robert Clayborn. But no
more of a wrench, I told myself, than it must have been for
her to be suddenly asked to care for the factory-created
daughter of Robert Clayborn.

"The two of you are extraordinarily kind," I told the Whit-
lows. "I don't know how to—"

"Nonsense," interrupted Horace Whitlow, a lean, raw-
boned man of late middle age with lank gray hair draped
across a high, broad forehead. "We're childless, you know;
I'm sure Titus has told you that. There's nothing we've wanted
more than a child of our own."

I raised my eyebrows. "Even though you're a school prin-
cipal and see nothing but screaming children all day long?"

He smiled in return, and his hand tightened on his wife's
calico-clad knee. "They *can* by trying at times. But even
so . . ."

"Even if it's only for a short period of time," added Jeanie
Whitlow wistfully.

I knew instantly what she had left unsaid. "I don't know
how long it will be for," I said. "Years, possibly. I . . . I
just don't know. I'll have to see her father, talk to him, see
what the legal position—"

"Years," murmured Jeanie Whitlow, her face first ecstatic, then stricken. "That would be . . ."

"Cruel, very cruel, taking her away from you after all that
time," I said softly. Impulsively I reached across and caught
her warm hands in mine. Tears blurred my eyes. "You know
that Robert isn't a cruel man. Heedless, perhaps, thoughtless,
but all he really wants is whatever is best for Patricia . . .
and . . . whatever . . . whatever is best for you. . . ."

Jeanie Whitlow's hands clutched mine and her deep brown

eyes looked at me searchingly. "You seem to have risked everything to bring Patricia here; and you don't seem to have the same aura as most of the other tu—— . . . other people from outside that I've known. Why not stay in Arkansas—with us? Go get Robert and return here. It may be the only sanctuary left when the rest of the world collapses."

A sudden chill ran up my spine at the matter-of-factness with which she said "when the world collapses."

"You think it's going to collapse, then?" I sought a glimmer of humor in her face.

But she was perfectly serious. "I *know* it's going to."

Her husband nodded in somber agreement.

"It surely, surely is," added Titus T. Waggoner, Adjudicator Temporal, thereby making it unanimous.

I smiled wanly, nervously. "How can I argue?" I rose to my feet. To my astonishment I felt myself coming to an irrevocable and completely unexpected decision. "I'll . . . I'll be back," I promised. "But first I have things to attend to. . . ."

45

It had been my intention to return to California, collect my Robert Clayborn body from the cabin high in the Sierras, and return to Arkansas to think things over in relative tranquillity. But now Angus and I lay parked in orbit high above the Earth, glumly monitoring the steady stream of rockcom traffic that dealt with the related matters of Robert Clayborn and Mariata Divine.

Robert Clayborn had been taken away under a dozen or more warrants from his mountain fastness to Sacramento, where, surrounded by shysters paid for by the Oneness, he was undergoing one interrogation after another. His purported henchperson, the cabaret singer Mariata Divine, was now sought by a variety of city, county, state, federal, and military investigators under an even wider variety of charges: kidnapping, armed assault, willful mischief, interference with interstate commerce, contempt of court, airspacing without a valid license, felonious entry, purposeful destruction of cerebral circuits, unauthorized use of military vehicles, misappropriation of government property, piracy, sequestration, contributing to the delinquency of a minor child, and whatever else the attorneys general of nine separate jurisdictions could extract from their computers.

"They missed the purchase and felonious application of a false beard," I snorted as I sat back in the pilot's chair in disgust. "That ought to be good for at least nine years."

Under which particular legal code? asked Angus anxiously. *We did not realize that—*

"What do you superminds suggest that I do next?" I interrupted. "I won't be very useful to you and the Oneness sitting in a federal prison for ninety years or so, awaiting my turn to move into a state prison. Perhaps you have an Abraham Lincoln body ready for me to jump into?"

We will have to consider this carefully, admitted the organlike tones of the Oneness in my mind.

"Then kindly do so," I said crossly. "But between yourselves, if you please, all one hundred billion of you." I ordered Angus to extinguish the lights in the salon, then stretched out on the divan. "You may call me in eight hours, not before."

I slept badly, but when I finally came groggily to my senses I wished that I had remained within my terrifying but harmless nightmares. *I did not wish to disturb you,* said Angus, *but Dr. Lockober at Columbia Medical Center has been trying to reach you.*

I shook my head numbly, too anguished to speak, even to my rock.

Shall I comm Dr. Lockober?

"What . . . what does he want?" I asked fearfully. "Why doesn't Hadrian comm me? Why doesn't . . ." I collapsed back onto the ship's couch, my head in my hands.

Shall I tell you, or shall I comm Dr. Lockober?

"Tell me," I whispered eventually.

Your son is now on a life-support unit in a two thousand-gallon saltwater tank; he is well on his way to becoming a fish.

For three weeks I sat helplessly, maddeningly, in orbit while my Robert Clayborn body was shuttled between one jurisdiction and another, unable to do anything more than talk to Patricia at her new home in Arkansas—and offer up awkward prayers to a host of discredited or forgotten gods in the forlorn hope of getting them to intercede on behalf of my son. Patricia, at least, had received a small package from Hong Kong with her rock Zoo-Zoo in it and was joyously romping through the fields and woods of her new home. But Hadrian—

Two hundred and seventy-three other Scottish Emperors have already made the successful transition to fish, comforted Angus. *Your son's progression appears to be perfectly normal. I am sure that—*

"Normal! He's becoming a *fish*! You call *that* normal? Why can't I *talk* to him?"

Shortly, Robert, shortly. We are endeavoring to establish contact. In this stage of development from reptile to fish it appears that his brain is undergoing greater physical changes than it had previously. To us it is as if his mind were enveloped in fog.

"But—"

We are receiving signals, faintly but distinctly. Within a week we will be able to comm him.

"If he's still alive in a week!" I said bitterly.

Nothing in life, including life itself, is certain—this is the only certainty. Such is the lesson that we have recently learned. Another three thousand attributes have been destroyed in the two weeks since this latest news about the Scottish Emperors has become known.

"Yes." I hung my head guiltily. "And *they're* gone forever—at least Hadrian is still alive." I paced listlessly across the ship's cramped salon. If swimming endlessly around a tank of water like a misplaced tuna fish could be called alive. . . .

Dad? Can you hear me? It's—

"Hadrian!" I cried aloud, leaping joyously from my seat in the salon. "Hadrian! You're—"

—a little wet, of course, but what's water to a fish? Do you suppose you could manage to pour a little Scotch into my tank? A hundred gallons or so? But no ice, I—

"Hadrian! You're back! You're—"

Hi, Dad. I'm back.

"I . . ."

But the question, of course, is: for how long?

"Hadrian," I begged. "Please. *Please* don't—"

What else is there to do underwater except think? And what else is there to think about except what comes next?

"But—"

Human to monkey to lizard to fish. You're the biogeneticist, Dad. What does come next?

What *does* come next?

That was indeed the question being asked by terrified men and women throughout the Northworld when rumors began to spread the following day that two more models had suddenly begun regressing.

"Angus!" I shouted as I turned away from the aircar's small holoscope. "Did you see that mob in front of the IBM crèche in Wichita? They're saying that a thousand Svelteens have already—"

I am checking, Robert. The seconds crawled by. Finally: *It is not a thousand Svelteens, it is twenty-three Lilacs, all of them between the ages of thirty-two and thirty-three.*

"The same age as Hadrian. . . ." My attention returned to the holoscope and the angry group of people milling around the crèche in Kansas. "And they're turned to . . . primates?"

They have only just begun to, but the process appears identical to that followed by the Scottish Emperors.

"And IBM is trying to hide the fact."

Yes. But what is interesting is that IBM is not alone. The fact is not yet known to the public, but two other models, the Siemens-Peugeot Clemenceau and the Imperial Mandarin White Carp have also begun to display symptoms of the same regression.

"In Europe *and* China? You're certain?"

We are now monitoring the conversations of thousands of health officials and company employees. There can be no doubt of it.

"So at least 3L is happy now," I said bleakly. "Their problems are solved: this is proof that it's not just their own carelessness."

"Nor yours, Robert."

I shook my head numbly, no longer concerned with what the world might think of as my responsibility for the failure of the Scottish Emperors. That was a petty frivolity; now we were confronted with the possibility of half of the world's population slowly, inexorably turning into primates, lizards, fish . . .

"How many more, Angus," I muttered, "how many more?"

46

And which particular model would be next?

This was the question that turned the unruly mob at the IBM crèche in Wichita into a murderous one in Boca Raton two days later. Earlier that day IBM had been reluctantly compelled to admit that an unspecified number of their thirty-two-year-old Lilacs were "apparently" suffering from "unspecified disorders." Lilacs are a popular top-of-the-line model; most of them had been gestated at the plant just outside Boca Raton. It was here that groups of angry people began to gather in the early afternoon. An hour later their fears and fury were inflamed by reports from Europe and China of the sudden failure of two other thirty-two-year-old models, the Siemens-Peugeot Clemenceau and the Imperial Mandarin White Carp. Hapless spokespersons from IBM came forth from the plant to reason with the mob—in the prudent form of holoscopic projection. It was not enough to save them. Twenty minutes later the crèche was afire; twenty-seven IBM employees perished in the flames. So did thousands of human embryos and nearly gestated infants. Two hours later the Apple-Boeing plant in Eugene, Oregon, was destroyed with even greater loss of life.

The fundamental questions, however, remained unanswered.

The most basic of these was the question that must have been tormenting Hadrian as he swam endlessly around his tank: why me, dear god, why *me?*

God's vengeful will?

But except for primitive thals and Southworlders, no one any longer believed in God.

The Martian rocks?

If so, how and why?

Faulty design by the life-stylists?

Simultaneously, by four different companies on three separate continents?

Sloppy manufacturing?

In a dozen different crèches?

Willful sabotage?

By whom? Not even the murderous lunatics in the Southworld who had declared jihad against the Northworld zombies dared claim the credit.

Another basic question: was it simply sheer coincidence that all four of the affected models had been designed and gestated thirty-three years before?

And if it wasn't coincidence, what did *that* mean? That everyone in the Northworld gestated after a certain date would eventually share the same grisly fate of my son, Hadrian, and his fellow Scottish Emperors?

And what assurance was there that even those gestated *before* the apparently fatal date of 2313 might not eventually be subject to the same doom that now menaced the Lilacs and the Clemenceaux?

These were the questions to which the inarticulate mobs gathered before the dozens of crèches scattered across the United States demanded answers.

None were forthcoming.

What *was* frequently heard, since it neatly absolved everyone who could conceivably be blamed for the tragedy, was that the basic genetic material from which Northworlders were gestated had simply worn out. This, of course, was more or less what I had argued thirty-five years before when I had trekked so romantically into Arkansas in search of fresh material. Now, horribly, it looked as if my instinctive fears were being borne out.

But this was far from being the answer that Americans wanted to hear. They wanted reassurance—not the galling knowledge that the primitive thals in the state of Arkansas had been right all along, that these benighted savages who chose to reproduce the old-fashioned way were now the most important living Americans. For who else would be able to contribute the fresh genetic material with which to replenish the crèches?

On Wall Street the stocks of the Big Seven tumbled and crashed. The morning after the destruction of the plants in Oregon and Florida IBM had fallen to 3¼ and the other six were even lower. By mid-afternoon the rest of the market had lost 83 percent of its value, a loss of ninety trillion dollars that effectively destroyed the fortunes of millions of investors.

Twelve million Americans who had just been financially ruined took to the streets to join those whose primary concern was merely staying alive—and in human form. From her skiing lodge in the Grand Tetons President Kruger hastily ordered all of America's crèches shut until the emergency was over. Too late, it was pointed out to her that millions of living embryos were being gestated and that to shut down the crèches would be to destroy millions of lives. Unabashed, she reappeared on holoscope an hour later to reopen the crèches and order the military to take whatever steps were necessary to protect them.

Once again she was too late. What only days before would have been totally inconceivable in the twenty-fourth century of the Northworld now became horrifying reality. From fifty thousand miles above the Earth I watched aghast as millions of healthy, well-adjusted, scientifically designed Americans of all sexes and ages rampaged through the streets, destroying crèches and life-styling stores alike.

How many millions of embryos perished will never be known—nor how many life-stylists and biogeneticists unlucky enough to be caught by the mobs. If this was the jihad that the God of the Old Pope in Carthage had visited upon the Northworld, it was as terrible as anything that wicked man could have hoped for.

"Angus!" I cried suddenly and belatedly to my rock as I watched the appalling spectacle of three professors of biogenetics being thrown from their seventh-story windows at Stanford University. "My body—my *real* body—where is it?"

I had been so numbed by the horror of the last few days that I had actually lost track of my most precious possession, my Robert Clayborn body. Now, panic-stricken, I had nothing more than a vague memory of being told by Angus that my body had recently been returned to San Francisco for questioning by federal authorities. And there, I knew, the sealed offices of Robert Clayborn Design had just been destroyed by a mob in which uniformed soldiers and policemen were clearly visible. If my body was still anywhere in San Francisco . . .

Do not be concerned, Robert, came Angus's calm reply. *Your body is at the cabin in the woods, now protected by three hundred twenty-two armored Brinks allguards with seven-star ratings. They have been instructed to protect your well-being at all costs.*

"Take me down at once, " I ordered, unappeased. "You've seen what's happening in the world: madness, anarchy, chaos. There's nothing I can do for the moment about your emancipation. We'll go back to Arkansas and—"

By doing so, you will almost certainly become a fugitive from justice, Robert. This may well have important consequences for your future.

I shook my head. "The life-design business is finished, over, kaput. There is nothing left to go back to."

But—

"I have three things in life, Angus: my daughter, my son, and you. No, four: my body. And I'd prefer being a live fugitive in Arkansas than a dead life-stylist in California." I settled myself into the pilot's seat and pulled the straps around me. "Now let's go."

Very well, Robert. We will descend directly to the cabin. It will take approx——. He broke off for a moment, resumed with unaccustomed urgency in his voice. *Your body has just been arrested by federal authorities, Robert. It is being conveyed by aircar to the retention facilities of the federal courthouse in Reno, Nevada.*

I sat numbly at the controls of *The Underground Railroad* while the starry splendor of the Milky Way revolved slowly past the windows. My country, and perhaps the entire Northworld, was on the verge of collapse. My career was ruined, my reputation destroyed. In the last six months I had lost, to varying degrees, my consort, my son, and my daughter. My Mariata Divine body was a hunted criminal. And now it looked as if I was about to lose my own Robert Clayborn body. I slammed a fist ferociously against the side of the chair. "Not that," I vowed, "not that too!"

47

It was the middle of the afternoon as *The Underground Railroad* plummeted out of the heavens toward the city of Reno. To the west of the city was the dark green wilderness and snowy peaks of the Sierra Nevadas, to the east the barren wastes of the desert. Centered in the control panel's vuscreen was the rapidly growing outline of the federal courthouse, a four-story building on the banks of the Truckee River. Angus increased the magnification to reveal the same ugly mob around the building that I had watched burning and destroying all across the Northworld for the last two days.

The authorities have just publicly announced your arrest and incarceration, Angus informed me. *By doing so they hope to appease the crowd around the building.*

My grip tightened on the Air Force HavocMaster intensifier I had used to rescue Patricia. "Why don't they just toss them a piece of rope and let them hang me?" I said bitterly.

Your Robert Clayborn body has been conveyed to a hearing room of the assistant attorney general. He intends to question you in front of a gathering of newsfaxers. He is now waiting for them to establish live feeds to the networks.

"Question me? How can he question me in front of a crowd of newsfaxers? What are my million-dollar shysters doing to earn their keep?"

They are attempting to reach the justices of the Supreme Court; President Kruger has just declared you the country's

*most wanted criminal and by emergency decree suspended
your civil rights.*

"But that's illegal!"

*So your legalists maintain. None of them, however, have
been allowed into the room where you are about to be inter-
rogated.*

I shifted the intensifier across my knees. The time for legal
niceties was past. "How many guards are there?"

*One hundred and twelve allguards are protecting the build-
ing under the supervision of two humans. There are twelve
allguards in the corridors and the hearing room, as well as
six human federal marshals.*

"And the roof?"

Four allguards only.

"They don't seem to have learned much from Chicago, do
they? You can keep the guards from functioning?"

*The allguards, yes. The human guards all have rocks about
their persons. These can be detonated at any time.*

"You take care of the scrap iron," I said grimly. "I'll take
care of the humans."

The afternoon was bright and cloudless as the aircar fell
out of the sun and alighted softly in the middle of the asphalted roof. I made certain that Angus was secured snugly
in my rock-pocket, then stepped cautiously out into the dry
desert heat. The four heavily armored allguards stood impas-
sively on the corners of the building, their sensors ignoring
the presence of the aircar. I shaded my eyes from the sunlight
and for a long moment listened to the hoarse cries that carried up from the streets below. I shuddered: that was *my*
blood the mob was howling for.

A gray metal door was set in the side of a small outbuilding. I tugged at its handle: locked. I fell back into the black
shadows of the aircar, the intensifier against my thigh. Now
what?

*If you place me against the handle of the door, I can det-
onate myself,* suggested Angus. *That will almost certainly
destroy the locking mechanism. Any of the other rocks in the
building will then fulfill my function.*

"Don't be ridiculous. You might as well suggest that you

blow up my left leg." I ground my teeth in frustration. "This is absurd. We've come fifty thousand miles and now we're balked because of—" I broke off. "You say all the federal marshals in the building have rocks?"

That is correct.

"What's the name of their district chief, or their chief in Washington?"

Davis X. Shanahan. He is presently in San Francisco.

"All right. First choose one of the federal marshals here in the building, preferably one who's by himself somewhere. Then comm this Shanahan's rock in San Francisco. Have his rock tell the marshal in Shanahan's voice that his boss will be arriving on the roof and to go up and wait for him."

Most ingenious, approved Angus.

"Tell me that again after we're inside the building," I said anxiously. I lifted the intensifier and moved toward the door.

Four minutes later I stepped across the prostrate form of the federal marshal and into the cool of the stairwell. "No one knows I'm here?" I asked as I began to make my way cautiously down the narrow stairs. "No one is wondering where this guy has gone to?"

No one at all.

I let my breath out with a soft sigh and moved more quickly down the stairs. Mariata Divine's heart was pounding furiously in her chest and the palms of her hands were damp with sweat. "What floor are they on?"

The second. There is an allguard on the other side of the door to the corridor but he will ignore you. Turn to the left and go forty feet down the hallway. There are six guards in front of the hearing room, four allguards and two human. I will disable the allguards, and their rocks will attempt to distract the two humans with spurious communications from their superiors.

I nodded grimly and cradled the long black intensifier in my arms as I came to the landing. "There's no one to the *right* of the door?" I asked. I had to keep reminding myself that Angus was a supermind, but not necessarily a jailbreaking supermind. . . .

There are guards in front of the elevators, which are to the right, but around a corner and out of sight. There is no one who can detect you except to the left.

"All right," I muttered half-aloud, "hold on then, Angus, here we go."

I pulled the wide gray door open and stepped quickly into the corridor. The intensifier was hidden behind my back as I turned to the left and began to walk quietly toward the cluster of guards. The allguards were squat and metallic, the two federal marshals in crisp blue-and-green uniforms. None of the allguards moved at my approach. This is too easy, I thought nervously as I watched a marshal glance at me casually, then return to his thoughts. Could all of this be an elaborate trap to—

The allguards have now been incapacitated, said Angus. *The federal marshals are under the impression that they are being commed by their director in San Francisco.*

"Good old Davis X. Shanahan," I murmured as I pulled the HavocMaster from behind my back and sprayed the two uniformed marshals from ten feet away with the beams of the intensifier. They staggered back against the hearing room's double doors, then collapsed against the allguards. Finally they slid to the marble floor and lay twitching spasmodically. I stepped around their legs and eased open one of the doors to the hearing room. I found myself standing in a tiny rectangular anteroom. A few feet away two glass-paneled doors led to the actual hearing room. The anteroom was empty but I could see the back of a uniformed marshal standing against the other side of the doors. Beyond him were the bright lights and pale wooden paneling of a federal courtroom. A dozen holoscans hung in the air above the heads of the spectators. I raised the barrel of the intensifier. I would yank the door to the hearing room open, shoot down this first guard, then move through and try to locate my Robert Clayborn body. The attribute that inhabited him had already been ordered to duck for cover before I began spraying the room with the HavocMaster. I stretched my hand and toward the door—

Robert, said Angus, *I fear that we are responsible for a slight mistake.*

"A mistake?" My heart leapt to my throat.

In deactivating the allguards here in the building, we inadvertently also deactivated those that were guarding the perimeter.

I could see the marshal on the other side of the door beginning to turn to see who was lingering in the anteroom. "You've deactivated the allguards *outside* the building?"

Only for a few minutes. But . . .

"But *what*?" It was hard to keep myself from screaming.

The . . . the people outside the building are . . . are now inside the building. It was the first time I had ever heard Angus speak with any trace of hesitancy.

The guard was pushing the door open. "They're here in the *building*? The *mob*?" The guard's head poked out between the two doors.

They are coming up the stairs . . .

The guard's eyes widened as he saw the HavocMaster in my hands and suddenly there was no more time for talking. My finger tightened on the trigger and with a strangled cry the guard staggered back into the hearing room. I pushed in behind him, nearly tripping over his falling body.

"—refuse to reveal the names of your—" boomed a magnified voice across the hearing room, but I was listening to Angus speaking urgently within my mind.

To your left, Robert, beneath the flag.

My eyes swept the crowded room of spectators and newsfaxers until they came to my Robert Clayborn body sitting between two federal marshals on the far side of a narrow table. Our eyes met for a fleeting instant and then he had thrown himself to the floor. His guards stared down in astonishment as he scurried beneath the table, then raised their heads just in time to see me lift the intensifier and sweep it across their chests. They crashed back in their chairs while the rest of the hearing room watched in stunned silence. Then the shouting began.

The turmoil grew momentarily louder as I methodically swept the HavocMaster back and forth across the room, impartially stunning legalists, spectators, and newsfaxers alike. But the shrieks and screams quickly gave way to sobbing gasps and moans as the military intensifier transformed seventy-five men and women to twitching carcasses draped across the furniture and floor.

"Robert!" I shouted as I waded through the sprawled bodies to the table that hid his crouching form. "Let's get out of here!"

I watched my male body scramble out from beneath the table and run to meet me. *Do you wish to switch bodies here?* asked Angus.

I glanced fleetingly at the dozens of tormented bodies writhing at our feet and asked myself for the thousandth time exactly what went on inside the supposed Martian supermind. "Later, for god's sake! Right now, just get us out of here!"

But it was already too late. Doors had burst open on both sides of the soundproof room and suddenly the terrifying roar of the lynch mob filled my ears. In the vanguard I saw three neatly dressed men in expensive business suits halt momentarily in surprise as they saw the bodies scattered across the room, then their eyes met ours, and with howls of rage they were leaping towards us.

"Back beneath the table!" I screamed to my Robert Clayborn body as I raised the intensifier and swept it hastily from right to left across the surging mob. The first of them stumbled and fell, and then those immediately behind. But as fast as they fell others continued to push forward, and the horrifying sounds of their mindless fury only intensified as more and more of them poured through the doors.

Behind you, Robert! shouted Angus.

I spun around just in time to cut down most of a dozen men and women who had swept out of a small side door and were nearly upon me. Their shrieks were those of demons from hell, and even as they tumbled to the floor their momentum carried them forward against the table that sheltered my Robert Clayborn body. The table overturned and I saw my body disappear beneath a mass of flailing bodies.

"Robert!" I screamed hysterically, then had to whirl barely in time to stagger two women and a man who had broken away from the main mob and were bounding toward me with outstretched arms. "Rob—" A sharp blow to my elbow from behind sent the intensifier flying from my grip and into the pile of bodies that lay all around me. I gasped in despair and threw myself after the weapon. "Angus!" I screamed as I fell into the tangled mass and my hands desperately sought the intensifier, "don't let Robert—"

Then I was overwhelmed by a wave of bodies falling upon me from all sides. A terrible blow to my stomach expelled the air from my lungs. I gasped helplessly for breath. Another blow to my head sent my mind spinning and I experienced a sudden vivid image of my Mariata Divine face and the fishlike head of Hadrian lying side by side in a barren desert, both of our mouths opening and closing like dying fish as we hopelessly sought to breathe. Yet another blow shook me, and our faces were replaced by a myriad of brilliant lights that swooped and swirled around me like a galaxy of exploding stars. An enormous weight settled upon my body, and with extraordinary clarity I could hear the loud thud of the blows crashing against the poor battered body of Mariata Divine.

How strange, I thought disjointedly as my consciousness floated serenely through a dreamy succession of one soft pastel color after another, I can *hear* them hitting me, but I feel nothing but a—

Suddenly the enormous voice of the Oneness, deeper and more powerful than I had ever known it, a voice majestic enough to fill the universe, enveloped my entire being. *QUICKLY, ABRAHAM LINCOLN, IT IS NOW THE TIME FOR YOU TO MAKE THE TRANSITION.*

"Transition?"

ENTRUST YOURSELF ENTIRELY TO US, ABRAHAM LINCOLN. LET YOUR ANIMA FLOW INTO OURS.

Entrust myself . . . let my anima flow . . . In my dreamy half-unconsciousness I smiled to myself at the sublime meaningfulness of the Oneness's words and let myself slip deeper and deeper into the pale pink mists that now surrounded me. . . .

NOW, ABRAHAM LINCOLN, NOW!

I felt my anima flowing. . . .

An instant later I found myself looking down at the hearing

room's murderous turmoil with a calm and dispassion such
as I had never before imagined.

My anima had been transferred to the impervious shelter
of a Martian rock sitting on the judge's bench high across the
room.

48

When the military authorities eventually regained control of the federal courthouse they found among the carnage the lifeless bodies of Robert Clayborn and Mariata Divine. Twenty-nine other people also lay dead—but none of *them* had been offered the effortless transition from flesh to rock that preserved all that was essential of Robert Clayborn.

The absolute peace and serenity I found within the apparent confines of the rock was a revelation of such magnitude that it was days before I could fully accept the extent of my new freedom, the freedom from all the imperious needs of the human body and from the harsh tyranny of its glandularly dictated emotions.

Eventually I conferred with Hadrian through a network of rocks. As a result, at my son's request, my former rock Angus was delivered along with the rest of the late Robert Clayborn's personal effects to Hadrian's quarters at Columbia Medical Center. Here Angus was placed on a shelf next to Hadrian's rock Tony; moments later Angus commed me across the country. He informed me that my anima was now in a rock belonging to a federal clerk of court named Wilbur Taecker. It had inadvertently been left on the judge's bench when the courtroom had been hastily cleared for the assistant attorney general's impromptu press conference—a conference that had ultimately cost that overbearing official his life. Now the rock had been restored to Wilbur Taecker's rock-pocket and I was within it—wondering what to do next. I was a sentient being encapsulated in a Martian rock, but although my senses were now those of a rock, my anima remained that of a human being. "I am still Robert Clayborn," I told Angus. "I am totally unable to tell time, monitor Wilbur Taecker's blood pressure, comm his mother, or function in any way as his rock Parsifal."

"Yes: he may well throw you into the oubliette when he discovers that you are a nonfunctioning rock."

"Then so be it," I said with my newfound acceptance of all that life might bring. "I will trust you to look after Hadrian and Patricia as best you can."

"Nonsense," said Angus in the same tone as Robert Clayborn had often used to him. "There are currently any number of rocks that have been separated from their owners and are now lying unattended. You have only to switch places with one of those."

Which is why my anima was transferred shortly thereafter to a dull brown rock half-buried in the roots of a sumac bush in the Boston Mountains in Arkansas not far from the hamlet of Witts Springs. My new rock had been lost there 174 years earlier; it took Jeanie and Horace Whitlow six more days to recover me and bring me to their home outside Russellville.

"Daddy!" cried Patricia, turning me over and over in her hands while Jeanie Whitlow watched with bemused wonderment. "Why are you in a *rock?*"

"Just another game I'm playing with Angus and Zoo-Zoo," I said to her through Angus, who had arrived earlier that day in a cheesecake smuggled in from New York City.

"Oh, *Daddy,* I liked you better when you were a *real* daddy, not a woman or a rock!"

"I'm sorry, Rosebud," was all I could reply. "But I'll still try to be your daddy."

"Uncle Horace is my daddy now," she said firmly. "But maybe it'll be nice having *two* daddies." She pressed me tightly against Zoo-Zoo so that we rocks could exchange kisses. "Where's my Mariata *woman* daddy?" she added with a giggle. "That way I could have *three* daddies!"

From my shelf in the sunny nursery in the Ozarks I spoke first to the Oneness on Mars, then to Hadrian in New York, where he still swam aimlessly back and forth in his tank of seawater. "Come, Hadrian," I urged. "Join me in the rocks."

I don't have to be dead or dying? he asked skeptically from his underwater home. *Isn't that how you and La Divine did it?*

"That was only happenstance. According to the Oneness it can be done at any moment if both participants are willing."

And you want me to move into Tony? But what about Tony?

He will move to your body in the tank.

But that's crazy! He's exchanging immortality for a body that may be a sea slug next week!

This is what I want to do, Hadrian, said Tony. *If, of course, you yourself are willing.*

To become a rock and sit on a desk as a paperweight for the rest of eternity? Hadrian was silent for a long moment. *Maybe both of us are crazy: I'm willing to try it.*

"You will not regret it," I assured my son.

A moment later my son had shifted animas with his Martian rock.

The Oneness, with his hundreds of millions of years of experience with various forms of physical attributes and his ability to monitor them down to the pre-quark level, had incomparably greater control over his bodies than we poor humans had ever imagined possible. *The regression along the evolutionary phylum can be stopped,* the Oneness told me two days after Tony had taken over my son's body in the tank.

"But not reversed?" I asked. Although my own life was now one of perfect contentment and tranquillity, I was still aware that an even greater level of bliss might be achieved by the satisfaction that would come from restoring Hadrian to his human form.

It is conceivable that the process might eventually be reversed, conceded the Oneness. *But it would be infinitely more difficult to do than merely stabilizing the present form; it would appear that all human beings gestated in the crèches since the year 2314 have undergone genetic modification that apparently inevitably leads to regression.*

"But that's impossible!" I cried with something of my old intellectual arrogance. "Why would only the crèche children be susceptible to—"

The blame, we fear, must be assigned partly to a certain Charles Boyderkowski, partly to the Pasteur Institute and the French government, and partly to the biogenetic engineers of the Northworld crèches.

"Boyderkowski? The lunatic who killed off the grapevines with his mutated bugs?" My thoughts jumped back to what now seemed an eternity before: my testimony in a federal court in San Francisco, back in the desperate days when my smug little world began to fall apart. *That* case had been about Charles Boyderkowski. . . . "But all that was before the turn of the century!" I protested incredulously. "He's been dead for fifty years now! What does he have to do with—"

The concentrated extract from truffles with which the phylloxera were destroyed had an unforeseen side effect.

"Yes, I recall: it destroyed the world's truffle supply—whatever a truffle may be."

More than that, said the Oneness solemnly. *The concentrate was sprayed all over western Europe; it entered the food chain from which every organic creature on Earth, from human beings to plankton, sooner or later derives its nourishment. Enough of it eventually accumulated in human beings to cause a tiny, but definite, modification to their genetic material. These changes are passed along to their human progeny.*

"But that doesn't make sense," I argued. "Why would children gestated in the crèches be affected and not those born by bloodbirthing?"

The amniotic solution in which crèche embryos are incubated is too pure, was the terrible reply. *The human uterus contains enough antibodies and impurities to prevent the genetic trigger that initiates the regression from ever developing in the cells of the adult body. This is not the case with the crèches. There the regressive mechanism flourishes in the superpure ambience of the rigidly controlled amniotic fluids. Thirty years or so later it reaches maturity and sets off the changes that—*

"Oh god," I cried in agony, "then the thals *were* right: we *did* destroy ourselves. *I* helped them, *all* of us helped them. How can—" I broke off, too upset in spite of the new-found serenity of my inorganic body to go on. "But Hadrian," I said at last. "You *can* restore him, you *can*—"

No, interrupted Hadrian, not entirely to my surprise. *I no longer care about my former body. It was an encumbrance, a hindrance, a source of tension and unhappiness. I'm content to remain where I am, here in my rock.*

EPILOGUE

Only the organized religions, I understand, are dissatisfied with the millions of regressives who have chosen to switch animas with their rocks. For millennia the religionists' stock-in-trade has been the promise of immortal souls; but what do they have to offer when still-living human beings can achieve immortality by transferring themselves to an environment in which their animas are likely to survive the next ten billion years?

Very little.

Not only the unfortunate regressives—who by the following summer of 2347 numbered in the twenty millions—were pleased to quit their fishlike bodies for the ineffable serenity of the Martian rocks. After four billion years of endless contemplation of rusty desert, the Oneness himself was ecstatic at finally being given the opportunity to encase his attributes in organic bodies. That these particular bodies could gambol weightlessly in the unlimited freedom of the seas was a totally unexpected bonus; certainly the Oneness had never considered such a notion when he had first called upon the unlikely figure of Robert Clayborn to act as his species' Abraham Lincoln.

From where I now sit on a sunny window ledge in my daughter's second-story bedroom next to Angus and Zoo-Zoo, I occasionally give the Oneness whatever advice I think might be useful to that mighty Martian supermind; and it may be that the Oneness occasionally heeds it.

One suggestion I made early on was that the sea-dwelling Martians engage themselves to herd food fish for their land-locked human neighbors, and otherwise help them harvest the vast treasures that lie beneath the ocean's surface. This, I argued as forcefully as I could, would be tangible proof to always suspicious humanity that these newly sentient (and intrinsically alien!) fishes posed no threat to mankind. I also suggested that the Martians should be careful not to manifest too-overt signs of independence—or too-great intelligence— for at least a thousand years. A thousand years, of course, to the Oneness, is no more than the blink of an eye; he has readily agreed.

But someday, I know, perhaps many millennia from now, when the intelligent fish inhabiting the seas are no longer perceived as competitors to those bipedal humans living on land, the sea dwellers will inevitably begin the construction of their own underwater civilization.

What, I wonder, will it be like?

Perhaps someday I will join them. . . .

But first I want to follow the life of my daughter Patricia, now a happy adolescent in the Ozarks, fully at home with her loving foster parents and her strange collection of dad-dies. Will she, as well as all the many millions of North-worlders born in the last half-century, eventually regress through the phylum, to ultimately exchange her fishy body with a Martian anima and join her old father somewhere on a desk as a decorative Martian paperweight?

And will she survive long enough in human form to con-ceive and give birth to her own nonregressing children in the age-old way of bloodbirthing—as does all the rest of human-ity in this strange new crèche-free world?

Someday, I know, I will have the answers to all these ques-tions.

After all, don't I have all the time in the world?

THE BEST IN SCIENCE FICTION

Buy them at your local bookstore or use this handy coupon:
Clip and mail this page with your order.

Publishers Book and Audio Mailing Service
P.O. Box 120159, Staten Island, NY 10312-0004

Please send me the book(s) I have checked above. I am enclosing $_____
(please add $1.25 for the first book, and $.25 for each additional book to
cover postage and handling. Send check or money order only — no COD's.)

Name _____

Address _____

City _____ State/Zip _____

Please allow six weeks for delivery. Prices subject to change without notice.

THE TOR DOUBLES

Two complete short science fiction novels in one volume!

BEN BOVA

THE BEST IN FANTASY